ELEMENTAL DETECTIVES

PATRICE LAWRENCE

ILLUSTRATED BY PAUL KELLAM,
AMANDA QUARTEY AND LUKE ASHFORTH

■SCHOLASTIC

Published in the UK by Scholastic, 2022
1 London Bridge, London, SE1 9BG
Scholastic Ireland, 89E Lagan Road, Dublin Industrial Estate, Glasnevin,
Dublin, D11 HP5F

SCHOLASTIC and associated logos are trademarks and/or
registered trademarks of Scholastic Inc.

Text © Patrice Lawrence, 2022
Cover illustration by Paul Kellam © Scholastic, 2022
Map illustration by Luke Ashforth © Scholastic, 2022
Inside illustrations by Amanda Quartey © Scholastic, 2022

The right of Patrice Lawrence to be identified
as the author of this work has been asserted by her
under the Copyright, Designs and Patents Act 1988.

ISBN 978 0702 31562 6

A CIP catalogue record for this book is available from the British Library.

Printed by CPI Group (UK) Ltd, Croydon, CR0 4YY
Paper made from wood grown in sustainable forests and other controlled
sources.

3 5 7 9 10 8 6 4

www.scholastic.co.uk

Answer to the Dragons' riddle: FLEET

PRAISE FOR
THE ELEMENTAL DETECTIVES

"A beautifully written book, bristling with magic, set in an ancient London filled with dragons, ghosts, water spirits, and a mysterious, creeping sleeping-sickness that must be fought by the brave young heroes. I loved it"
Cressida Cowell, Children's Laureate & author of
How to Train Your Dragon

"*The Elemental Detectives* is a rip roaring magical adventure… Patrice Lawrence has done a marvellous job of building an imaginative and creative mythology which lurks just under the city streets"
Catherine Johnson, author of *Freedom*

"*The Elemental Detectives* is a richly imagined, inventive and immersive fantasy adventure"
E. L. Norry, author of *Son of the Circus*

"I loved reading about a re-imagining of London with so much invention and energy. The world-building is well, … out of this world. Patrice Lawrence is amongst the greatest voices for young people writing today. I'm honoured to be a peer of hers"
Alex Wheatle, author of *Cane Warriors*

"BRILLIANT … history and fantasy woven magnificently into a thrilling, magical adventure"
Sophie Anderson, author of *The House with Chicken Legs*

"A fantastic adventure, packed with rich world building and stunning elemental magic"

PATRICE LAWRENCE was born in Brighton and brought up in an Italian-Trinidadian household in Sussex. Her first novel *ORANGEBOY* was one of the most talked-about YA books of 2016 and won the Waterstones Children's Book Prize for Older Fiction and the *Bookseller* YA Book Prize that year. Ever since, her work has consistently featured on prestigious prize lists and her recent novel *EIGHT PIECES OF SILVA* has won a number of awards including the CrimeFest YA Prize, the inaugural Jhalak Children's and Young Adult's Prize for UK Writers of Colour and the Woman and Home Teen Drama Award. Patrice has been awarded the MBE for services to literature.

BOOKS BY PATRICE LAWRENCE
FOR OLDER READERS

Orangeboy
Indigo Donut
Rose, Interrupted
Eight Pieces of Silva
Splinters of Sunshine

Diver's Daughter: a Tudor Story
Needle
Rat

TO DREAMERS

BRITISH MUSEUM

FOUNDLING HOSPITAL

THE SERPENTINE

MADAM BLACKWELL'S
PUMP ROOM

TYBURN GALLOWS

CHICK LANE

HYDE PARK

LEICESTER FIELDS

BLACK MARY'S HOLE

SADLER'S WELLS

CRYPT ST. BARTHOLOMEW'S CHURCH

BAGNIGGE WELL

MANSION HOUSE

ST. STEPHEN'S CHURCH

FLEET BRIDGE

THE MITHRAEUM ON WALBROOK

ST. GEORGE'S, BLOOMSBURY

HIBBERTS'S MANSION

ST. PAUL'S

A ROCK DOVE FALLS

The rock dove fell from the sky on Sunday. Its slumbering body lay beneath a hedge, hidden from the carriages clattering by on their way to church. As the sun rose towards midday, a cat slunk past. She had failed to catch a single mouse in Mr Browbridge's grain store – she was too weak and clumsy. But here was food served up and waiting for her.

She nudged the plump bird with her paw. Its heart was beating. It was alive and fresh, even more tasty. The cat batted it again. It rocked sideways but didn't wake.

Enough. She needed to eat now. She bent towards the bird and—

Something was oozing from it: something she couldn't see until it was inside her head. It was a yellow mist, as thick as butter. All her thoughts of hunger disappeared. Instead, she remembered her mother and her brothers and sister. She had not seen them for so long. She closed her eyes and she was there again, curled up in a ball, her whiskers twitching against the comforting warmth of her mother's stomach. Her sister nipped her neck. It wasn't to hurt her, but just to remind her that she was here too. In a moment, they would peel away from safety and play.

A human yelled. A horse snorted. The metal rims of carriage wheels scraped against a stone close to her – too close!

Her eyes snapped open. She was not a kitten; she was old and alone and hungry. She leaped away from the bird. She would search for food elsewhere.

The rock dove slept on. So did many more. Robert Strong cleared two of the birds from the path of Lady Hibbert's carriage as they paraded around Hyde Park on Tuesday. He was quick before the horses' hooves smashed down on the bodies. He had seen the wings twitch and knew they weren't dead. Even as he scooped them up, they didn't wake. He hoped they'd be safe on the verge where he lay them.

Further north, in Clerkenwell, Marisee Blackwell noticed nothing. The sickness hadn't reached her – yet.

Up above, in the murky London skies, the Fumi air elementals were gathering and whispering. What was bringing this new heaviness to the dirty London air? It was more than just the Solid human folk blasting muck from their chimneys into the sky. This was more powerful. The Fumis could weave the air into a hurricane and blast it away, but they had signed the truce and would not be blamed if London was ruined again.

In the wells and hidden rivers, the Chad water elementals felt it too: a strange, joyful weariness seeping into the streams. They didn't like it. The Solids clogged up the waterways with filth from the abattoirs and manufactories, but this was new and wrong and also a little familiar. They would need to call a full court to discuss it.

The Dragon fire elementals patrolling the City of London took note of the dreaming rock doves, the anxious horses, the merchants complaining of their lazy servants. It would only take one fiery roar to burn this sickness away, but they were still not forgiven for the unfortunate incident of 1666. They would guard their Guilds and merchants and stay vigilant.

The last of the four elementals, the earthbound Magogs, slumbered in the layers of London earth beneath the Thames. Their agents knew what was at stake here, but they could be patient; everything returned to them in the end.

On Friday, the rock dove still lay under the hedge. Its heart had stopped beating three days before and soon its skin would pull away from its bones. Its last dreams had been happy ones.

MARY BLACKWELL'S WELL

Marisee Blackwell's grandmother looked like a goose. Of course, Marisee had never actually told Grandma that. And she didn't look like one all the time. But Grandma definitely looked goose-like in the grey Clerkenwell dawn. Perhaps it was her long, slim neck, or her delicate round head, or even the hat with a peak that she pulled low over her brow. In the morning shadows, it *could* be a beak. Grandma was wearing her cloak too. When she raised her arms, it became wings, and the candles made the black silk lining shine like deep water, because Grandma wouldn't be *any* goose. She'd be Queen Goose, majestic, proud and beautiful.

Marisee crouched on her bed and peeked out of the window. Grandma's arms were stretched over the well. For a moment, she was very still. So was everything else.

The village wasn't usually a quiet place. If it wasn't baby Joseph screaming in the room above the chandler's, it was an early-morning carriage risking a hold-up by highwaymen as it clattered from Hampstead down to London. At least twice a week, there was an argument outside the Fox Inn – often more than an argument. Clashing swords and shouting men would jolt Marisee out of her sleep, and she'd look out of this same window to see lanterns bobbing in the dawn mist hanging over the field beyond the well. Grandma always rushed out to break up the fighting. She wasn't having anyone bleeding over her land and ruining the water.

Grandma was getting to the bit that Marisee liked and the reason why she looked forward to Fridays. Of course, people came to take the special Blackwell water every day except Sunday, but Fridays were special.

Grandma let her hands fall slowly to her sides, then

stepped up on to the low ledge surrounding the well mouth. She raised her arms again, took one step forward and then – she dropped.

It wasn't a whoosh-bang drop like the time the bell fell out of St Chad's tower. Instead, a trickle of water rose up from the well, snuffed out the surrounding candles, settled in mists around Grandma and wafted her down into the shaft.

Marisee knew that not everybody's grandmother stepped into a well on a Friday morning. But hers did, and she'd been doing it for as long as Marisee could remember. Grandma, whose name was Mary-Ay; Mama, who was Mary-Bee; and she, Mari*see*, had all grown up on this land – and they were just the new Marys. Grandma said that Mama used to watch from the very same window where Marisee was now. Grandma herself had watched her own grandmother many years before that. Marisee tried to imagine her mother's hands pressed against the cool panes and her breath smearing mist across the glass. It was hard. She couldn't remember Mama at all.

Grandma said that Mama had always been restless. When Marisee was two, Mama had taken a boat to Europe to search for plants that would help water stay clean. She'd told Grandma that she'd be away for six months, but that was ten years ago. No one had heard from her since. Grandma still didn't talk about Mama much because it made her upset. Marisee still secretly hoped that her mother would return. It was different with her father. He'd been kidnapped into the Royal Navy before she was born. The boat he was sailing in was sunk by a storm on the way to Virginia.

So it was just Marisee and Grandma, for as long as she could remember. She knew other children who lived with their grandmas. But none of their grandmas were the Keeper of the Wells of London. It was a duty that Grandma said came with great responsibilities, but, even though Marisee was twelve, Grandma always wouldn't say exactly what they were. Marisee begged to go down the well with her, but Grandma always insisted that there was no need for Marisee to bother herself with all that tiresome elemental business just yet. All Marisee knew was that Grandma looked after the Chads, the water elementals that guarded the watercourses of London and made sure that the wells were full and the ancient hidden baths were brimming with sweet, clear water. Mostly, it seemed, she had to stop the Chads getting into trouble.

Most Chads were steady sorts, but some of the old rivers didn't like the modern world – or Solid humans – and kept sending Grandma off to the Lord Mayor to demand new laws to keep the rivers clean. And she seemed to spend a great deal of time sorting out arguments between the Chads and the other London elementals.

Marisee often wondered who else knew about Elemental London. If Grandma hadn't told her about it, would *she* know? Even though it was there all around her.

The Fumi air elementals were supposed to keep the air fresh but seemed to have given up long ago. London's chimneys belched dark, stinking smoke all day and night. Grandma complained that the Fumis just wafted between the belfries, ringing church bells and twisting weather vanes. They used to have a Keeper who lived in a windmill on the Isle of Dogs, but apparently he'd come to a bad end and nobody else wanted the job. Certainly, nobody else wanted to live in that windmill. Grandma said that it wasn't just wheat that it liked to grind.

The Dragon fire elementals stayed in the City of London, watching over all the gold and money that passed between the Guilds and the merchants. When Marisee was little, she had wondered if the merchants were annoyed at having to step over giant fiery lizards all the time. Dragons always looked as if they took up so much room. Not so, Grandma had said. All the pictures of dragons were out of date now, even the ones they used as boundary markers in the City. The Dragons had stopped using their old forms several hundred years ago. (They'd grown tired of knights trying to hunt them down all the time just to impress the Ladies.) Dragons were now much smaller. Much, much smaller. But they had big voices, or had done until the Great Fire of 1666. These days they kept themselves to themselves. They believed that they were the true rulers of London and hated the Fumis with a fiery fury. Dragons may have – accidentally – started the fire, but it was the Fumis who blew it down to a dock full of ships heavy with barrels of pitch and oil and made it tear through crowded streets of wooden houses. Did they ever get the blame? No, they didn't. Grandma reckoned that the Dragons would be sulking far into the next millennium about that.

While the Dragons declared that they only answered to the Guilds, the earth elementals, the Magogs, never answered to anyone. They never spoke to anyone. They were named after the giant wooden statues Gog and Magog that were kept in the Guildhall, and the rumour was that the real life giants slumbered in the green-grey clay at the bottom of the Thames, waiting to be woken when the time came. The time for what, Grandma didn't know, but a couple of years before Marisee was born, Fleet Street had trembled and cracked apart. The roads were jammed with Londoners fleeing to the countryside. Grandma once admitted that it was the Magogs who had done that, to remind the other elementals that they were still watching – and waiting. They had eyes all over London.

The Chads complained that the Magogs had deliberately silted up their streams, the Fumis had deliberately dropped soot in their ponds and the Dragons had deliberately instructed the Guilds to cover over rivers to build their new halls and warehouses. Grandma reckoned that she had the calves of a circus strongman from rushing backwards and forwards between the Guild Masters and the architects and the engineers. In her eyes, it was about time the Lord Mayor did some proper mayoring to sort out Elemental London instead of leaving it all to her. They hadn't built that shiny new Mansion House just for Lord Mayors to idle around enjoying the view. Still, she always sighed, if all that running around kept the truce in place, then she'd carry on doing it.

The last time there'd been an elemental battle was during Roman times. The Romans had had to abandon London and leave it in ruins. It was centuries before anyone would live inside those walls again. Elemental rage had burnt into the very stones of London and drawn something strange out from them.

Again, Grandma wouldn't – or couldn't – say what. It was another item on the long, long list of What Grandma Might Tell Marisee One Day. For the moment, though, the truce held. Elementals had agreed not to wage war against each other. They had also promised to leave the Solid folk of London well alone. Marisee tried to imagine what could happen if it was broken. It would be like the Great Fire but with a furious Fumi wind driving the flames even quicker. Roads would split apart and swallow the Londoners as they fled. Rivers would burst through their banks and sweep everything away. And if Gog and Magog really did sleep on the riverbed, well…

Marisee sighed. Today was Friday and she needed to forget all this and get ready. The best thing about being Keeper of the Wells was that Madam Blackwell's was the best well in London with healing water that actually healed. It didn't make Grand Claims about fixing broken ribs and draining stinking wounds of noxious liquids in double time so that they healed and left no scars. No, their water healed eyes. Sore eyes, itchy eyes, sticky eyes, eyes with cysts and carbuncles and cataracts. Fashionable women bought it to make their eyes brighter, though they didn't come to collect the water themselves. They sent footmen to queue outside the pump room.

Customers were probably on their way this very moment. Marisee yawned. She'd need to get up soon to organize the flasks and set out her little table. She'd need a pen, new ink and paper, and string for the labels. There'd been an outbreak of red eye at the Foundling Hospital. She and Grandma were going to be busy.

She stretched and slowly unwrapped the blanket. *Whoo!* It was cold. Her breath steamed out of her nose. Which reminded her – she had better get the fire going. Grandma was never wet when she returned, but she was always cold. She said that the clay down there hadn't seen the sunlight for thousands of years and the chill could really get into an old woman's bones.

Marisee eased herself off the bed and rummaged through the drawer. Today was a day for thick woollen socks and gloves to stop her fingers going stiff from filling the flasks and writing so many labels. What would they say today?

Madam Blackwell's
Exceedingly Effective Eye Cure
Or
Madam Mary Blackwell's,
The Site for Sore Eyes

When they were busy, of course, she'd just end up writing "Water" on the label and tell customers how many sips to take and how many drops to apply to the infected area.

Marisee took one last look out of the window. It was definitely getting lighter. Even the stupid cockerel up by the tollhouse had stopped crowing, probably because he'd realized that everyone already knew it was morning.

She headed down to the kitchen, her woolly feet sliding on the stones. Good! Grandma had already set the fire. All Marisee had to do was light it. Breakfast was easy too. There was a loaf from yesterday that could be sliced for toast, with butter and plum preserves. The kettle would be full of water for tea. It always was. Constant fresh water, wherever and whenever they needed it, was one of the benefits of being the Keeper.

Marisee unhooked two cloths from behind the door. The yellow one was for her face, folded into a triangle and wrapped round and tied at the back of her

14

head. The blue one was for her hand. She bound it carefully, tucking the corner in firmly. It must not fall off. She used her padded hand to pick up the polished red jar from the dresser in the alcove. How could this thing be so heavy? It was hardly bigger than her hand! Grandma said it was because it held a year's supply. *Even so, be careful, Marisee. I can tell you that getting a refill is a serious trial!* Marisee bent over the firewood and gave the jar a good shake. It went straight from stone cold to tingling hot beneath the cloth. She took a deep breath in and held it. The cloth filtered out most of the smell but not all. One. Two. Three. Now! Holding the flask tight with one hand, she popped out the cork with the other and flicked the jar backwards and forwards twice.

The Dragon fire streaked out and splashed on to the wood. The kindling sparked immediately and Marisee shoved the cork back in. She let her breath out slowly but made the mistake of taking another breath in too quickly. The stink of sulphur spiked up her nostrils and down her throat. She really must learn to hold her breath longer, especially if she was ever going down that well. (Grandma insisted that she didn't need to hold her breath in there, but Marisee planned on being careful – if Grandma ever did take her.)

She replaced the jar of Dragon fire and unwrapped the cloths from her hand and face. How *did* other people get their fires going? She wasn't allowed to ask "other people" in case she gave away their own secrets. People must surely know that Grandma was a bit – well – different, but Grandma said that it suited everyone to pretend otherwise.

The door opened. The flames swayed with the whoosh of air, then jumped higher.

"It's cold down there this morning!" Grandma shut the door behind her. "I suppose it's the bottom of a well. It's not going to be like a summer meadow, is it?"

Marisee ran over to help Grandma remove her cloak. As she hung it on the coat stand, it stopped shimmering. There was dirt streaked across the back. Hanging there, it could belong to any street vendor, not the Keeper of Wells. Grandma's hat followed. She ran her hands through her hair, loosening her curls from her plaits. The heavy old soldiers' boots she wore beneath her gown were crusty with clay.

"Do you need help taking them off?" Marisee asked.

Grandma slumped on to a chair. "Not yet, my darling. I am hungry, though."

Marisee headed to the pantry and took out the

butter dish. In spite of the cold, the butter was perfect for spreading. She lay it next to the bread and plum preserves on the table.

"How were the Chads today, Grandma?"

Grandma stared into the flames. "They were frightened."

"Frightened? Do they think more rivers will be covered over?"

"I'm certain that will happen, though some Chads will fight it all the way." Grandma picked up the bread knife. "Or make me fight it. They don't like change. But if they want to survive, they have to flow with the modern world."

Marisee spooned plum preserve into a dish. Grandma started sawing away at the loaf with much more force than she needed. A thick, uneven slice of bread thumped on to the plate. Her slices were usually thin and precise. Her hands must be cold from the morning visit. Marisee had tried to make Grandma wear gloves, but Grandma said she liked to feel the moss and the cracks between the bricks on her way down. It was how she knew her well was healthy.

"So why are they frightened, Grandma?"

The knife went backwards and forwards.

"Grandma?"

Grandma speared a hunk of bread with a toasting fork. "They think something in London has changed. Something very big and very wrong."

"Something?"

"Yes."

"They don't know what it is?"

"They say they don't." Grandma looked thoughtful. "But I think they may know more than they're telling me."

"It's not like… It's nothing like what happened before the truce, is it?"

Grandma held the fork over the fire. The crust immediately started to singe around the edges. She moved it away from the flames. "No, Marisee. They're not fighting the other elementals. I would certainly have heard about that. But they are right: something is wrong. I've known it in my heart but I've been ignoring it. I should have noticed the rock doves."

Marisee had no time for the fat bully birds that swooped down and seized the food from her hand. "What about them?"

"I'm sure they want to be human. They prefer to steal the food from our hands than the corn in the fields. They could fly anywhere, but linger on our streets and live in the ruins of our houses. If they are troubled, we should worry. Have you seen one recently, Marisee?"

She frowned. "I don't think so. Have they disappeared?"

"No. If you look carefully, they are everywhere, except in the air. On Monday, I saw three in the gutter by the map-maker behind St Paul's."

"Dead?" Would that be so wrong?

Grandma eased off the slice of bread, turned it over and jabbed the fork back through. "No, not dead. Just still. Even when a cleric dropped a husk of corn right next to them, they didn't stir."

"Were they sick? Or poisoned?"

"I don't know, Marisee. Later, I found a rag seller sprawled across Lincoln's Inn Fields. I thought it was drink or fever because his breath had turned yellow. But now I believe it was neither. I know a blacksmith near the square. We dragged the poor man to the forge and laid him on blankets in a corner, but still he didn't wake."

Grandma handed the toasting fork to Marisee and started hacking off another slice of bread.

"The strangest thing," Grandma said, "was his face. The man was so thin that I could see the blade of his bones beneath his skin, but he was smiling like his pockets held more coin than King George." Grandma shook her head. "I'm not sure if I'll forget that soon."

By now, Grandma was usually slathering her toast with butter and heaping on the jam. She was just sitting there, staring into the fire, one hand on the loaf, the knife discarded.

"You're sure it isn't one of the other elementals causing trouble, Grandma?"

A knot of worry was tugging at Marisee's stomach. She imagined the streets collapsing, rivers bursting their banks, walls of fire, wind-storms – everyone fleeing with nowhere to go.

"I don't think so," Grandma said. "But I can't know for sure. They don't like humans. They won't speak to me and they won't speak to each other." Grandma yawned and rubbed her temples. Then her eyes opened wide. "Can you hear that, Marisee?"

"Hear what?"

Grandma was as still as the stones beneath Marisee's feet. Even the firewood stopped crackling for a moment. Marisee didn't move, just listened. She could feel her heartbeat. Her head was thumping, too. It wasn't a headache, more like a tiny bass drum being beaten hard between her ears. A woman was singing far away, perhaps on the edge of the field nearest the village. It was too distant to hear the words.

There was a hard knock on the door. Marisee and Grandma looked at each other.

"Were you expecting a visitor, Grandma?"

"No…" Grandma didn't sound very sure about it.

"Perhaps it's one of the women from the workhouse," Marisee said.

The workhouse mothers were always welcome to free healing water, but they were often too shy to come to the pump room.

"I'll go and see who it is." Grandma's chair scraped as she stood up. She pulled her cloak off the hook and fastened it around her neck, then jammed her hat back on. "But do you know what I'm really hungry for, Marisee? Seville marmalade. Get the jar down, but wait before you open it."

Marisee grinned. "Of course, Grandma!"

Grandma bent over Marisee and kissed her on the forehead. "Take care, my gorgeous girl!"

Marisee laughed. "I always hold on tight. You know I do!"

Grandma opened her mouth as if she was going to say something else, then just gave Marisee a little smile and headed out. The flames whooshed again as the door opened and closed. Marisee made her way towards the pantry. It was always well stocked with preserves and pickles, many of them gifts from grateful customers. The Seville marmalade was kept on the top shelf to help Marisee and Grandma resist temptation. It was usually eaten on St Chad's Day.

Marisee grasped the ladder that ran from the floor to the marmalade shelf. Grandma had fixed perfect round wheels into the inside of the handles so it could easily roll along the shelf. Marisee stepped on to the lowest rung – well, the only rung – stamped down with her left foot and waited for the whoosh of air. The rung slowly rose, sliding through the long grooves on both sides of the ladder. It paused with a click at each shelf, then carried on until it reached the top. Why would Grandma worry about Marisee being careful? She'd been doing this since she was nine. Marisee grabbed the clay pot of Seville marmalade. It felt lighter than it should. They would need to buy some more soon. She shoved it in her apron pocket and tapped the rung with her right foot to descend. The Fumis might be airheads but you couldn't complain about their air tribute to Grandma. Who wouldn't want a ladder that was powered by air?

She ran back into the kitchen and placed the marmalade bang in the middle of the table. She wouldn't open it until Grandma came, because one quick taste led to a spoonful, then a bigger spoonful. Then that led to an even bigger spoonful and a slice of toasted bread spread with butter and a thick layer of marmalade.

"Come on, Grandma!"

Even untoasted bread was good with Seville marmalade. It was better when freshly baked, shiny with butter, then topped with bitter shreds of orange seeped in syrupy sweetness.

"Hurry up, Grandma!"

Would there be any harm if Marisee just lifted the lid? She didn't have to taste it. But could she stop herself? As soon as the lid was up, her spoon would be in there.

"Grandma! Where are you?" It wasn't fair to tempt Marisee with Seville marmalade and then disappear again.

She opened the back door and peered outside. She could see across the field and down to the village. No sign of Grandma, just the large clay boot print she had left on the step as she had headed out. But, of course, Grandma would have walked down to the pump room to fill a flask. She'd be asking after the health of every woman, girl and baby at the workhouse and probably filling up a few extra flasks to take back.

Marisee sighed and shut the door. She sat down at the kitchen table and slid the marmalade jar from side to side. The lid rattled gently like it was asking to be removed.

Just one spoonful, Marisee, it was saying. *One spoonful!*

She would do it! Just one. Marisee took a spoon from the pot on the cabinet. It wasn't the smallest spoon, because then she'd only have to return for a second spoonful. It was a good-sized spoon that would keep her happy until Grandma returned.

She waited and listened. No footsteps. No anything. It was the quietest Friday that she could remember. It felt like there was nothing else in the world except for her and the marmalade. She picked up the spoon and lifted the lid.

She stared into the jar. There was no marmalade. A folded sheet of paper was curled around inside. Had Grandma already eaten it all? Was this a joke? If it was, Marisee was not laughing. She tipped out the note, smoothing it on the table.

My beautiful girl, if you are reading this, I have had to leave urgently. I am so sorry that you must find out this way. I keep telling myself that I must teach you more about your full duties, but I didn't want to lay that weight on you yet. But if you are holding this note in your hand, I am too late. An emergency has befallen us.

Marisee, there is something I keep that is even more important than the wells. It is called the Freedom of London. If it falls into the wrong hands, the city will be lost again. I must protect it. Danger will follow me and I fear that it will follow you too. I need you to be brave. I need you to gather your strength and your wits. I will fight the danger that will hunt me. You must fight the danger that will hunt you. Together, we must stop this threat and keep London safe.

You will not be alone. If you need help, ask the well.

I love you.

Grandma

What … what was this? It was a joke, wasn't it? No. It was a test. That's what it was. Grandma must have written the note, ready for the day that she planned to test Marisee. And today was the day! If Marisee solved the puzzle, Grandma would let her help with more Well Keeper duties.

But what *was* the Freedom of London? Grandma had never mentioned anything like that before. Was it something real or did it just mean that Grandma could go anywhere in London that she wanted? Why did she need to keep that safe? Marisee felt so confused.

She read the note again. Perhaps there was a clue that she'd missed. She stopped at *If it falls into the wrong hands, the city will be lost again.*

That sounded much too serious to be a puzzle, especially after what Grandma had told her about the rock doves and the rag seller. Even worse, the Chads were frightened.

Marisee ran and flung open the door again.

"Grandma!" she yelled. "Grandma!"

There was no answer. Just like Mama, Grandma had left her.

DREAM PIE

Robert Strong was sitting on top of a giant pie. The pastry was sagging beneath him, but he knew it was thick enough to hold his weight, even though he'd never actually ridden a pie before. It was warm, like it had been taken out of the oven an hour ago, so perfect for eating without burning the roof of his mouth. He breathed in the rich meaty smell. It was chicken. And mutton. And beef. And potato.

His hands brushed against the slits in the pastry. They stopped the pie from exploding in the oven. He'd seen Mrs Wandle, the Hibberts's cook, stab the supper pie she made every Thursday. How many times had Robert wanted to dab his hand in the thick gravy and taste it? How many times had Mrs Wandle run her finger across the side of the heavy knife, gathering every drop of gravy and shoving it in her mouth? Then she'd grin at him so he could see the gravy between her teeth. If Robert tasted even the tiniest crumb without permission, Mrs Wandle was allowed to beat him. And, of course, she never gave permission.

Mrs Wandle kept a willow switch on the shelf above the flour barrel especially for beating purposes. Once, she'd threatened Robert with the poker, but Lady Hibbert had caught her. The Lady hadn't wanted Robert bruised as she'd arranged a supper party for that evening and Robert was to look his best as he stood behind her chair.

But who cared about Mrs Wandle and Lady Hibbert when this pie was Robert's? No one was going to take it away from him. He stretched out his leg. If he could jam his foot between the top and bottom crusts and lever them open… He just needed to shift closer to the edge, and then he would swivel himself upside down and dive right in.

The pie swerved. Was it trying to escape? No! He

hadn't even had a taste yet! This wasn't what should happen. Robert clung on, his nails scrabbling against the pastry. He was *so* hungry. He would not let go. This was the biggest pie so far. It was for *him*. He dug his nails in further, felt the pastry crust giving. Just a little bit harder and he could break through…

Another hard swerve. He squeezed his eyes shut and pushed his fingers down harder. The meat was there, just below the surface, waiting for him to scoop it up and – a jolt! Like a giant hand was trying to shake it free from its dish. Robert slipped and scrabbled for a hold as the pie bucked like a ship in a storm.

"Robert! Wake up!"

He landed.

The ground was hard and cold beneath him. He should be used to that by now. He'd been sleeping in this corner for more than a year and a half, but every morning he still woke up aching all over.

"You've got to get up, Robert! No one's lit the fire yet!"

It was Lizzie's voice. Maybe if he kept his eyes tight shut he could bring back the dream and this time she'd be there with him. There was definitely enough pie for two. Only last week, he'd dreamed that both of them were enjoying a very well stocked hamper of cakes in Bloomsbury Square.

She shoved him. "I haven't got the time for this, Robert!"

It was no good. He opened his eyes. It was darker in the real world than it was in his dream. Lizzie was holding a tallow candle close to him, already dressed in her scullery maid pinafore and bonnet. The stinking tallow blotted out the last memories of pie aromas. Robert made his unwilling body sit up.

"At last!" Lizzie muttered.

"It's not my job to light the fire."

"Doesn't matter. If Mrs Wandle finds it's not been done, who do you think she's going to blame?"

Robert arched his back. It was still sore from the whack Mrs Wandle had given him when he spilled coffee over Lady Harbinger's stole last week. It had only been a couple of drops and the stole was so furry it would have soaked it up easily, but Lady Hibbert had seen. And Lady Hibbert didn't forgive. He still didn't want to unroll himself from the blanket, though. This corner of the kitchen was always cold, even when it was sunny outside. At this time of the year, it was worse. No sunshine, and today no fire. He rubbed warmth into his bare toes.

"Where's Percy?" Usually the kitchen boy already had the kindling cracking and was feeding in the small logs.

"I don't know," Lizzie said. "But you must get up, Robert. Mrs Wandle left some pots out for you to scrub."

"I finished them last night!"

"Well, she found some more! I'll try and help you later, but there's some plates for you to clean too."

Robert gritted his teeth. The pewter dishes had to be scoured with sand, then rinsed over and over. It made his fingers sore.

"And the Duchess of Bedford is visiting this afternoon," Lizzie said. "So you need to trim the candles in Mistress's parlour. She'll want you to serve them tea, won't she?"

Robert pushed himself out of the blanket. It felt like he was pushing himself right out of the dream too. These dreams were always so real. It made the hard, hungry days better knowing he could dream food like that.

"It took ages to wake you up." Lizzie yawned so hard he thought her face would split. "It almost made me go back to sleep myself."

"I was having the best dream."

"So was I. I was falling down the chimney."

"A chimney?"

31

"Not *a* chimney. *The* chimney!" The cow-fat candle made Lizzie's eyes shine and the smoke blurred the air pale yellow. "If I'm cold when I go to sleep, I fall down the chimney and land in the fireplace. I'm not scared, though. There's no fire, but it's still warm. It's like the chimney's warming me up."

"Is it always the same fireplace?"

When Robert went to sleep hungry, his dreams rarely took him to the same place. He'd be strolling towards a pie shop or crawling out from beneath a soup stall or, once, he even found himself sitting on the shelf inside a giant pantry.

"You and your questions!" Lizzie grinned. "Yes, it's always the same fireplace and then I go somewhere else. Once I walked into a dressmaker's shop and started trying on jackets. Nobody stopped me! And the jackets fitted me perfectly, Robert! Every single one of them! There was a dark blue one with a matching long cloak." Her grin faded and she held up the edge of her frayed apron. "I could have had it if I wanted. Then I woke up and there was ice inside the window and I knew my nose was bright red and my fingers were so cold I thought they would snap off. But when I'm asleep, it's so real, like I could never be cold again."

Robert flexed his own fingers. They felt heavy and stubborn.

"Were you dreaming about jackets last night?"

"No." Lizzie was so quiet that even in the strangely empty kitchen he had to lean towards her to hear. "I was with my little sister, Nelly, and we were in the fields outside Hockley. We were making daisy chains. I'd tried to teach her before, but her fingers were too chubby. This time she made a chain so long we could wrap it around us."

"Maybe you could ask the Mistress for a Sunday to go and visit her?"

Lizzie took a deep breath. Suddenly, Robert knew what she was going to say and wished he could take his words back.

"She's in God's arms, Robert. Smallpox took her when she was just three. I used to dream about her all the time, and I loved those dreams, even though I knew deep in my soul that she'd gone away from me. Then I came to London and never dreamed of her once until last night. Only it wasn't like a dream. She was really with me." Lizzie cuffed Robert gently. "But *I* still woke up on time."

"I'm sorry about your sister," Robert said, even though he knew that words were never enough when someone you loved died. "What was Nelly like?"

Lizzie wiped her eyes. "There were two babies lost before me, but I didn't know them. I loved Nelly from the moment she was born, even though no one could call her a pretty baby." She took a deep breath in, then out, staining the air a deeper yellow. "I shan't be sad if I can have dreams like that again. I'm just going to open the shutters and wake the others."

"The others?"

"Kate and Margaret are like you were, dead to the world. Little Annie stirred and started tying her apron, but she didn't seem like she was in this world, neither. So I came to you as I knew you would be in the most trouble. I'll be back in a moment."

Lizzie took the candle, but by now Robert could find everything without light. He felt for his slippers hidden behind the pickle barrel. He never left them in the open after the first pair were stolen the same night Lady Hibbert had given them to him. He'd met Mrs Wandle's willow branch up close because of that. He'd taken worse beatings on the plantation, but new pain had bloomed where the willow sliced through old bruises. He hadn't cried, especially as he'd suspected that she'd stolen his slippers in the first place.

Luckily, there was already wood by the hearth. He

wasn't in the mood for going out in the cold and searching through the wood pile for logs light enough for him to carry. England had made him weak. No, all those months at sea, in that cold dark cabin had made him weak. Before that, he'd been strong. Even with the endless days of work on the plantation and the overseers yelling at him to work harder and faster, he'd been strong. His aunties had tried to feed him well and keep him healthy. But here… His stomach rumbled. He'd set the fire and then he'd find Lizzie and maybe they could eat together before the day really started. She still had some of that raspberry jam she'd stolen from the pantry.

And, after that – well, it was Friday, water day. After he'd finished his kitchen chores, he'd have to dress up in those stupid clothes just to ride on the footplate of Lady Hibbert's carriage. His finery was to make sure no one else stole him; the show-off clothes proved he already had an owner, and a rich one, too. He hated that red jacket and the velvet collar with the heavy beads that poked his neck. He hated the puffed-up red trousers even more. They made him look like a tomato and were so tight around his waist they left marks. Then he'd have to stand by the coach, as straight and tall as Hibberts's gatepost, while John the footman went into the pump room to refill the bottles. Robert had no idea why they had to travel to Clerkenwell for water when there were so many wells close by, but at least it made Lady Hibbert happy. A happy Lady made everyone's life easier.

Robert swept up yesterday's ashes and set the fire. He didn't light it as there was no one here yet. Mrs Wandle might get her willow switch down if she thought he was wasting wood. As he stood up, his stomach made a noise so loud he was surprised it didn't wake the Lady, all those stairs above him in her luxurious chamber.

"Lizzie," he called gently. "Did you hide any of that bread from supper last night?"

Hard bread wasn't the same as a thick, juicy slice of pie, but it wouldn't be too bad slathered with jam.

"Lizzie," he called louder.

He couldn't hear her moving. The shutters were still closed too. Maybe she'd gone outside to find Percy. He usually slept in the hayloft because the horses made the stables warmer. Or she could be in the attic trying to rouse the other two scullery maids.

As Robert crossed the hearth, his foot touched something soft. He jumped back.

"Lizzie?"

She was curled up on the cold stone. Her eyes were

closed and she wasn't moving. Was she…? His heart banged inside his chest. Lizzie couldn't be dead. Just a few moments ago, she'd been talking away, so full of life. He bent towards her. He knew what death looked like. He'd seen it enough times on the plantation and even on the boat over to England. He uncurled her hands from each other. They were warm. She *was* alive.

"Lizzie!" He didn't want to shout any louder. Mrs Wandle could hear the faintest whisper from across the kitchen. She hadn't beaten Lizzie yet, but she was eager for an excuse.

"Lizzie!" He shook her. Then harder.

The air around her was yellowish, even without the candle. Perhaps she was sick. What had the old physician said when he visited Lady Hibbert's cousin at Easter? Her fainting fits were due to an excess of yellow bile. Maybe this was the bile coming out through Lizzie's breath. She let out a little snore and her face broke into the widest smile Robert had ever seen.

"Nelly," she whispered, "we're going to make a cloak out of all those daisies. And a crown to go on top."

Robert lay her back down. How could he wake her when she was so happy dreaming about her sister? He would wait just a moment. The kitchen was so quiet he could hear a woman singing. It sounded like a lullaby, perhaps a nursemaid settling a baby as they crossed Bloomsbury Square. Now his own thoughts felt too thick to pass through his head. He closed his eyes. He was so tired. There was no one here. It wouldn't matter if he stole a few more minutes, sleep. Perhaps, if he was lucky, there would be someone waiting in his dreams for him too – someone he missed so much.

Suddenly, a shriek cut through the silence.

THE SILENT
KITCHEN

"Robert!" It was Lady Hibbert. "Get here right now or you will feel that whip on your back!"

Lady Hibbert's voice was like a furious dog snapping away at the edges of Robert's dream. Wherever he tried to hide, it would chase him. She must be standing at the top of the stairs that led down to the kitchen. He forced his eyes open. Next to him, Lizzie was still fast asleep.

"Robert! Mrs Wandle!" Lady Hibbert shrieked. "You lazy oafs! Get here now!"

"Just one moment, Mistress!" It was hard being

polite and loud at the same time. Actually, it was hard to be polite to her at all. Robert nudged Lizzie again. There was no sign of wakefulness. If Lady Hibbert found Lizzie sleeping, she'd take Mrs Wandle's switch and beat Lizzie herself. Robert had to move her. He grabbed Lizzie beneath each arm. She wasn't just sleep-heavy; she was like a rock.

"Lizzie!" he hissed into her ear. "Come back to me!"

She giggled and snorted, but her eyes stayed firmly closed.

"Robert! Mrs Wandle! If I have to take one step further, there will be trouble!"

Where could he hide a snoring scullery maid? Of course, he knew where! The scullery. Lizzie's feet scraped across the rough floor of the kitchen as he dragged her. When he rested her down to open the scullery door, her head knocked the ground with such a clunk Robert rubbed his own head at the sound of it. She still didn't wake. He picked her up again, struggled into the scullery and lay her down by the sink. Robert banged the scullery door shut and ran back into the kitchen court.

And then – he saw it.

Lady Hibbert's ghost was standing by the table.

Robert's throat closed up before a shriek could burst out. The ghost's face was a pale, solid mask. Red-rimmed eyes glowered out. There were no eyebrows. The lips were grey and crusted. Dark tails of hair drooped over its ears as if the creature's night-cap had brought rats from the grave.

Robert tried to take a step back towards the scullery, but his legs had forgotten what legs were for. The only thing moving was his heart, still banging like Mrs Wandle's mallet trying to soften tough beef.

Then the ghost spoke. No, it shouted. "Boy! Get in here!"

The ghost had kept Lady Hibbert's furious-dog voice. Robert had heard of spirits wandering from beyond the grave. They wailed or muttered. They didn't bark at you. The ghost glided over to the shelf where the willow switch lived, picked it up and ran it across its human-looking palm.

"If you think *this* hurts, boy, I have news for you. My husband is sending the horsewhip from the plantation. The special one. The one made from manatee skin. You know the one I mean, don't you?"

That whip... Robert's heartbeat was filling his whole head. His heart must be so soft it could pass straight through his ribs. Yes, of course he knew that horsewhip.

He hadn't felt its cut in his skin, but his mother had, and his brother Zeke and many of his aunties. How would a spirit know of this? He forced himself to look harder at the "ghost". Ghost? How could he be so stupid? It wasn't a ghost. It was the real Lady Hibbert, her face smothered in one of the beauty concoctions her apothecary had mixed up in the still room.

Robert instantly bowed his head. It was wrong to look a white person in the face; his mother had told him it was one of the most dangerous things he could do. It was considered deeply disrespectful. Then she'd whispered to him: *and they get frightened if they see the anger in your eyes.*

"Where is everyone?" Lady Hibbert's dog-voice bounced around the empty kitchen. "My bedroom fire isn't lit and my tea wasn't waiting for me when I woke. And where's Jane? I need her to help me dress! I must have the laziest, stupidest household in Bloomsbury!"

"I'm sorry, Mistress." The scullery door pushed into Robert's spine as he backed further away from her. The last thing he needed was the door flying open behind him and Lady Hibbert being presented with Lizzie, happily asleep. He straightened himself. "I was just going to search for them."

Lady Hibbert frowned. Or Robert thought she did. With her face caked in potion, it was hard to tell.

"You've done some sort of savage magic, haven't you, Robert?" She stepped closer to him. He leaned back. The door pressed into his skin. "My husband said I should be careful with you. If I feed you well, you'll get ungrateful. He knows how your people forsake good and do wicked things at any opportunity." She tapped her palm with the willow switch. "I'll have strong words with Mrs Wandle. You need less food."

"Madam? Madam?" Mrs Wandle ran out of the servant quarters on the other side of the kitchen court. Her feet were bare and her cap askew. She was clutching her apron to her gown, the ties swinging as she ran. Her face was crumpled like she had just woken up. She glared at Robert as if it was his fault that she was late and looked around. It may have been the gloom, but the air around Mrs Wandle's mouth looked pale yellow.

"Where is—"

"Exactly!" Lady Hibbert shrieked. "Where is everyone indeed? Get those fires lit and my tea brewing and a bowl of warm water on my dresser, right now!" The switch slapped hard against the table. "Or else."

Mrs Wandle gave a little bow and her cap almost fell

off. She grabbed it and straightened up. She turned to Robert. "You! Get the…"

"No, no, no!" Lady Hibbert's forehead cracked as her eyes narrowed. "You know full well what day it is. We have to collect my water. My eyes…" She rubbed her face and greasy white smeared across her hand. "My delicate eyes need their special medicine."

"Yes, Madam! Of course, Madam!" Mrs Wandle spun a full circle, still clutching her cap and apron. She looked as if she couldn't quite remember what she should be doing. Lady Hibbert didn't notice.

"So, what are you waiting for, boy?" She flicked the willow switch at Robert. It swished close to his leg. "Go and prepare yourself!"

She dropped the switch on to the table and walked back up the stairs.

Mrs Wandle looked at the switch, then at Robert. She yawned a cloud of yellowish mist. Did she have the same illness as Lizzie? "You heard her! Get going!"

Robert ran into the pantry and watched behind the half-open door. What if Mrs Wandle went into the scullery and found Lizzie? She liked to start her morning by shouting at the maids. She started walking towards the scullery door, stared at it for a few seconds, then stumbled away, out towards the stables.

Lizzie couldn't stay in the scullery. Anyone could walk in and see her legs sticking out from behind the crockery sink. Robert had to move her. He'd think about it while he dressed. The show-off clothes were in the box behind the salting barrel. And yes, it was going to be the tomato-red silk with the beaded collar. He'd never owned new things until Lady Hibbert's seamstress fashioned this costume for him. In the plantation, he'd worn clothes passed down from his brother, Zeke, and other boys. Mama had done her best to sew up the holes. Robert had worn Zeke's tattered shirts to bed until they had fallen apart. He'd managed to cling to one last shirt through the whole journey to England, but Lady Hibbert had made Mrs Wandle burn it as soon as he set foot in this house. The cook had grinned as she'd doused it with oil and made him watch as the flames tore through it. She'd said it was riddled with lice. It wasn't. He'd checked.

That was all he'd had left of his brother.

These breeches hurt if he tried to move quickly and even more if he sat down. Perhaps it was just as well that he was always expected to be on his feet. The jacket pulled across his chest and made it hard to breathe. A button had popped off last week and Lizzie had "borrowed" one of the Mistress's good needles and thread so he could replace it. He'd have to dodge the willow switch if he came back with any of the outfit speckled with street dirt.

Turban or not? He had never seen one in his life before that dressmaker wrapped it around his head to great admiration. But it was cold out there and it would keep his head warm. He'd just have to remember to duck when any of the street children threw a stone. He'd once heard a mackerel seller promise one of them a penny if they knocked it right off. He had to secure it with a massive cut glass brooch that made the front slide down over his eyes. He reckoned that was what the street children were aiming for. Maybe they thought it was a real jewel and they could steal it away. He'd be more than happy to give it to them if he could. Or, even better, tear it off and jump up and down on it. He closed his eyes for a second to imagine the coloured glass smashing beneath his slippers.

He struggled into the breeches. They'd definitely tightened, but it certainly wasn't from good food. In his first few months in England, he could barely eat or sleep. He'd hated the plantation and the brutal work tending the cocoa pods in the blistering sun, but that was where his family was: his mother and baby twin sisters – and

Zeke, his best friend in the world. He'd refused the hard bread and ham scraps Mrs Wandle gave to him. After a week or so, she'd taken him to the garden and the willow tree that grew next to the pond. Robert had watched as the gardener was instructed to saw off a bendy branch.

"Lady Hibbert is going to blame me if you die of starvation," she'd said. The branch had whipped through the air, just catching the tip of his ear. "So you'd better start eating."

He hadn't. He'd still carried out his chores for Lady Hibbert, growing weaker and clumsier. And the clumsier he'd been, the busier the willow switch. Lizzie had helped him when she could, smuggling him better food, a slice of beef or a fresh muffin. Once, she'd handed him a couple of segments of orange, but its scent had thrown him back to Zeke pulling apart juicy green oranges to quench their thirst. He'd started crying and Lizzie had hugged him until he stopped. Her kindness had kept him alive. He owed her. If she had caught some kind of sleeping sickness, he needed to keep her safe until she was well. Luckily, he was heading to Madam Blackwell's and her special well. What if the water really did heal? He'd find a way of taking a small draught for Lizzie in case she was still sleeping when he returned.

Robert finished tugging the buttons together on his silk jacket and wrapped the ridiculous turban round his head. The pantry door flew open. Mrs Wandle stood there, red-eyed and still crumpled.

"I can't find Mr Ropeton! He's not in the stables. There's no one to drive the Mistress's coach! And no footmen for her chair!"

She didn't seem to be looking at Robert, though. Her eyes were half-closed and red. She kept blinking, like there was something in her eye and she couldn't see the world properly around it. That pale yellowish tint still floated around her mouth. Suddenly, she stood very still.

"Oh, Jack," she sighed.

"Jack?" Mr Ropeton's Christian name was Robert. Robert was named after him as Sir Hibbert had wanted a reminder of his favourite servant back in England. He'd told Mama enough times that she should be grateful for such an honour to her son.

Mrs Wandle's eyes widened and then her forehead squeezed into a frown. "Jack? Who mentioned Jack?" Her face reddened. "Have you been prying into my business?"

Robert jumped back. "You said 'Jack', Mrs Wandle."

"I did?" Now she seemed to be looking over Robert's

shoulder. "It was like he'd come back to me, as young as the day we were married." She smiled.

Robert took a bigger step back. Mrs Wandle only ever smiled when something horrible was about to happen.

"You must collect the Mistress's water. Don't you dare linger or you'll be feeling..." She picked up the switch from the table. It dangled in her hand. "I'm just going to..." She let it drop on to the floor. "I'm just going to rest a little," she muttered.

She staggered back towards the servants' quarter. A door slammed shut.

Perhaps everyone was suffering from excess yellow bile except, of course, Lady Hibbert. She must be so filled with it, a little extra made no difference. Robert breathed out, his breath clouding into a mist in the cold, empty kitchen. He squinted. It was definitely not yellow. Imagine if Lady Hibbert was right and he *had* done magic in his sleep. It would be so much better to have magic available when he was awake and could use it exactly how he wanted. And he would never, ever do magic on Lizzie.

He padded back into the scullery. Lizzie was just as he'd left her. He bent down, took a deep breath, and then lifted her up and over his shoulder.

He whispered into her ear, "If you hadn't brought me food, I wouldn't be able to do this."

He couldn't risk taking her to her room in the attic even if he thought he could climb that far with her on his shoulder. He checked the kitchen court again – still empty – and carried her to the cupboard where the brooms were kept. There was just enough room. He laid her down inside and fetched his blanket from the kitchen. He tucked it around Lizzie's neck and under her feet.

"I'll be back soon," he said.

The healing-water flasks were kept in a special drawer in the scullery. He took out three, all polished blue glass that Lady Hibbert constantly reminded the footmen had cost a fortune. She'd also warned them in great detail what would happen if they as much as chipped one. He wrapped the flasks in cloth and nestled them in a basket. He looped it over his arm and opened the door out to the yard.

The noise from the stables ripped through the quiet. The grooms had complained that the horses had been anxious all week, but it was nothing like this. They were kicking at their doors and whinnying in a chorus that built like a Barbados thunderstorm. Where were the grooms and stableboys? They should be rushing from stall to stall with their buckets and brooms and polished tackle. Mrs Wandle was right. There was no one.

Perhaps the horses were hungry. It would be cruel if Robert just left them like that, but … he hated horses. So much. He'd tried to explain it to Lizzie, how Mr Soothing made his horse, Firebrand, rear up at the small children on the plantation. Once, Firebrand's hoof had knocked Robert's cousin, Moses, on the head. Mr Soothing had ridden off laughing, leaving the child lying bleeding under a bush.

Lizzie had said that it wasn't the horse to blame. It was the person riding it. But Robert wasn't convinced. Firebrand always looked like he was enjoying himself.

"Oi! You!" A groom called Benjamin was striding across the yard, a bucket of water swinging from each hand. His little brother, Daniel, was just behind him, wheeling a stack of hay bales. A puppy darted around Daniel's heels. At least the dog didn't seem any different from normal. Benjamin stopped in front of Robert and rested his buckets on the ground.

"This got anything to do with you?"

"What?"

"You're awake and everyone else is sleeping. Did you do something to them?"

Robert offered his sweetest smile. "Lady Hibbert is awake, Benjamin. I can fetch her for you, if you'd like. She's very angry that the horses aren't ready for her carriage yet."

Daniel rubbed his eyes. "Leave him alone, Ben. We need to get these horses fed and…" He was blinking, just like Mrs Wandle. "I want to see Mama again."

"No, you can't!" Benjamin shook Daniel by the shoulders. The puppy growled and the horses kicked harder at the stable doors. "She wasn't real! It was a dream!"

"How do you know? You weren't there!"

"Because you never knew what she looked like!"

"I do! I remember more than you think!"

Benjamin picked up the buckets, threw another furious look towards Robert, and then hurried off towards the nearest stall.

"I'm coming!" he called, opening the stall door.

Daniel followed him, his legs moving like they were being pulled by strings, his breath the colour of buttercups.

London streets were all noise. It had filled Robert with terror when he first arrived. The plantation was noisy too, but the sky seemed higher in Barbados and the air – well – wider, so sound had scattered. But in London, there were church bells tolling and river bells clanging, rag merchants and ballad sellers calling their wares, horses, hooves clattering over the cobbles, musicians with trumpets and drums blasting their tunes from the street corners. Robert had grown more used to it, but he always felt it seething around him.

He stepped into the street and waited for the noise to hit him. The bells in St George's tower rang half past the hour. They sounded dull. It was like the pie in his dream had left a thick coat of gravy inside his ears. He blinked. His eyes didn't want to open again. The thick, rich smell of the pie was stronger than ever. And…

He was walking into a pie shop near Fleet Market and the warmth of the oven made his cheeks tingle. A pair of giant tongs rested against the counter. That mutton and pastry and gravy would be his again and all Robert had to do was pick up those tongs, reach into the oven and he would pull out…

A horse whinnied. Wheels clattered. A man's voice shouted a warning. Robert fell out of the dream. He jumped back just in time as the hackney carriage swerved past him into the church courtyard. It shuddered to a stop, the two horses panting and tugging at their harness. The gentleman passenger flung the coach door open and stormed up to the driver's seat. It was pointless. The driver was slumped sideways, his horsewhip balanced across his knee. It fell from the driver's slack hand on to the cobbles and, for a moment, Robert expected it to rear up like a snake and lash out at him. The whip was still, but evil hands could make it sting.

The gentleman shook the driver so hard the driver's wig flapped like a bird. The mist around the driver's head churned like buttermilk. The gentleman leaned close to the driver's ear and shouted loudly; then he stood back, wiping his forehead. He shook his head at Robert, then walked away.

Robert ran over to the driver. The gentleman was as wide awake as Lady Hibbert, but the driver looked like he was in a dead faint. Or even really dead. Robert lifted the driver's hand. It was warm, but his body had the heaviness of a corpse, just like Lizzie's. His smile, though, was so wide it was like a skull's grin. As he snored yellow smoke curled from his lips. Robert dropped the hand quickly and it slapped against the side of the coach.

Was all of London heavy with this sickness? It must

have crept in overnight, settling across the streets and buildings, easing through the cracks in the windows and down the chimneys. It had slipped into Lizzie and tiny Daniel and even Mrs Wandle, filling them with a heavy death-like sleep. It could infect Robert himself. He could fall down on this street and never wake again. Six months ago, he wouldn't have minded that; he had been so lonely and sad. But Lizzie was his friend – his only friend – and if this was a true sickness, he must help her. If Madam Blackwell and her waters could heal Lizzie, Robert had to reach that well.

But, oh, he wanted to sleep. He rubbed his eyes and fixed an image of Lizzie in his mind. He had staved off nightmares when he was a child by making himself stay awake. He had to do that now. He must not sleep.

"I will not sleep! I will not sleep!"

His legs didn't want to walk. His head didn't want to think. His body just wanted to collapse down like broken bellows. He grabbed on to some railings by the square. If he closed his eyes, just for a little, it wouldn't matter. Not if he was standing up. He let his eyelids droop...

Whoosh! Air rushed past his face. Robert felt a sharp pain in his forehead just below the hem of his turban. His eyes sprung open. A big white eye looked back at him, the size of a dish. The head drew back and snorted. It was a horse, a stone horse, with a pale twisted horn on its head, tapering into a spike. The unicorn's head butted forward and the spike jabbed Robert's forehead. Just an inch higher and the horn would have smashed through the glass brooch, sending the shards deep into Robert's skin. The beast snorted then leaped away.

Robert blinked hard and looked around. This must be a dream. The pain felt very real, though. He touched his forehead. The drop of blood on his finger was definitely real. Robert was wide awake. It had happened. An enormous stone horse – no, an enormous stone unicorn – had appeared and jabbed him in the head. Many of the mansions nearby kept stables. Was this sickness transforming animals? He tried to peer through the mist that now surrounded him. Were there rats the size of dogs and other giant beasts crawling out of dark corners? He had to get away from here. Robert took a step forward, then threw himself back against the metal railings again. His mouth opened, but no noise could come out.

A stone lion raced towards him. Its giant head rocked backwards and forwards on its gleaming neck, the folds of its solid mane cutting through the gloom. It opened its jaws and a roar bellowed from its throat. Its teeth were like ragged stones and behind them a deep, dark emptiness that could swallow Robert whole.

"Weg sein!" a voice called out.

The lion stopped, reared up and jumped away. Before Robert could move, a huge hand thudded into his chest, slamming his spine against the rails. The cold palm pressed harder and harder, as if squeezing every puff of breath from Robert's lungs.

"Please," he choked. "Stop!"

A giant face pushed through the sickly mist. It was a man's face, twice the size of Robert's own: a statue-man with a high brow and hair curled like a Roman emperor. The face bent towards Robert. The sharp stone nose tapped Robert's own. The eyes were big and grey. The thin lips moved.

"I see you!" it said.

The hand dropped away and the face disappeared.

Robert peeled himself from the railings. He rubbed his chest. His heart was beating so hard again it could burst.

"Have to get away! Have to get away!"

His words used breath that was barely there, but he spoke them like a spell, urging his feet to move. A roar came from the distance and the scrabble and tap of hooves. He looked back towards St George's Church. The giant figures were clambering up the portico towards the steeple. The stone lion and unicorn settled on the base and the statue man walked slowly up the steps to where the spire should be.

"Have to get away! Have to get away!"

And now, Robert ran.

HUSH

Marisee slowly folded Grandma's note.

... there is something I keep that is even more important than the wells. It is called the Freedom of London. If it falls into the wrong hands, the city will be lost again.

... Danger will follow me and I fear that it will follow you too. I need you to be brave.

How could Marisee be brave if she didn't know what she was supposed to be brave about? What *was* this Freedom of London? The knots in Marisee's stomach pulled tighter. Grandma hadn't told Marisee about it. And Grandma was right. It was too late now. Marisee had to find out for herself.

But how? She had to do something, but what? While she was thinking about it, she'd set up her table in the pump room, ready for the customers as usual. It was nearly seven o'clock on a Friday morning and she should already be there.

Marisee wrapped up the bread and piled the crockery by the sink. She picked up a box of empty flasks and some ledgers, and headed out of the house and down through the field.

It took five trips to bring everything down, and each steady trudge, trudge, trudge of her feet loosened the knots in her stomach a little.

Madam Mary(-Ay) Blackwell's pump room was in an old barn. It was long and high-ceilinged, held together with a lattice of oak pillars and beams and beechwood slats. When Marisee was little, she used to lie on the ground looking up at the curved wooden beams and pretend that she was inside a giant fish. There had once been stalls for cows to shelter in bad weather. They were gone now, but Marisee often felt that the cows were still there. Their warmth was absorbed into the walls and, if she breathed in, she could catch the hint of their smell – of old straw and newborn calves.

Down the road at Bagnigge's Wells, Marisee's friend, Camilla, helped care for real cows. Mr Hughes, the proprietor, kept them so he could serve cream teas and offer quarts of fresh milk along with his waters. But Grandma didn't need cheesecake, or an orchestra, or tightrope walkers or ponds with swans on them to bring in customers. Grandma was the Keeper of Wells. Her water would always be the best. And on Fridays, after Grandma made her weekly visit to the Chads, it was at its most potent. There was usually a long queue of customers.

Grandma didn't need a fancy pump, neither, just a pipe, a lever and a faucet. The Chads made sure there was perfect water pressure. Every time Marisee stood near the pump, she felt the thrum of the water beneath the ground. Just one little touch on the lever and it started bubbling up. Grandma always said that they had to look the part, though, or else their fine customers wouldn't believe that the waters worked. So the pump was encased in pale grey stone, as cool as the water itself. The base shimmered with mosaics in every shade of green. The lever was a curve of iron ending in a glass teardrop, just the right size for Marisee's hand and also exactly the right size for Grandma's. Even in the morning gloom, it glowed like sunshine reflecting off the mist over the Turnmill brook. Grandma's great-grandma had dug the teardrop out of the banks of the Fleet. Hundreds of years ago, there had been kilns making glass along the riverbank, but now it was just tanneries and abattoirs throwing carcasses and other stinking filth into the sluggish water.

The pump room was silent. Usually the toll-keeper's dog was barking at the coaches, but not today. The air felt heavy, as if, somewhere above the clouds, a blanket was about to fall across the fields.

Marisee took the first ledger from the pile. These were the regular customers who came three or four times a month. Grandma had placed these ledgers on the top of the pile. Perhaps there was another reason for that. Maybe they held something that Grandma wanted Marisee to know.

The first ledger belonged to Mr Jonas Hanway, one of the governors of the Foundling Hospital. Grandma had made a note that he was due for his monthly pre-order of three quarts for the foundlings but might order double this month to ward off the outbreak of red eye. There was nothing suspicious there. Marisee put it aside. The next was for the Clerkenwell workhouse. The matron didn't come every week, but Grandma had thought she might pay a visit today. Perhaps they were fighting off red eye too. Marisee sighed and placed it on top of Jonas Hanway's.

Next, the Chudley twins from Hoxton. They hadn't paid for three months, but they still sent a footman every other Friday to collect water. They didn't return the empty flasks either. Grandma had muttered plans about having a word with the east-side Chads to see if they'd spring a surprise fountain in the Chudleys' back garden, right in the middle of one of the twins' show-off luncheons. Could her disappearance be something to do with them? Marisee glanced down the columns of figures and Grandma's scribbles in the margins. Grandma had written in large letters in her precious red ink:

Make them wait for the last dregs!

Annoying, but definitely not enough to make Grandma run away and certainly no mention of any Freedom of London.

Beneath the Chudleys' ledger was Lady Hibbert's. Marisee shivered. She'd only met Lady Hibbert in person once when she'd stormed into the pump room to find her footman, shrieking at him for taking far too long. The words she'd used ... Marisee had never heard most of them before, and she'd been frozen solid by Lady Hibbert's fury. Grandma hadn't. She'd promptly escorted the furious woman out of the pump room and banned her from setting foot in there ever again.

Marisee read the ledger from cover to cover. She felt like shoving the pile of ledgers on to the ground. There was nothing here that was helping!

She glanced out of the barn window. The sun was almost fully up. Where *were* the customers? There should be a queue by now, but no one was here. Marisee sat up straight. Someone was coming. That was the sound of hooves. Yes – at last, something normal. Although, now thinking about it, she had better be careful. So little about today had been normal.

Marisse slid off her chair and crouched behind it. She hoped her heartbeat wasn't really as loud outside as it was in her head. The hooves stopped and the horse grumbled to itself while the rider tied it to the post. Then the pump room door flew open.

"Hullooo?"

Marisee knew that voice. She peeked around the chair. She knew those boots too.

"Is no one here?" the voice called. "No one at all?"

Marisee stood up. Mr Jonas Hanway was in the doorway, his face creased and wary.

"Marisee," he said. "Are you yourself? Have you escaped this monstrous sickness?"

"What sickness, Mr Hanway?"

"I fear that we are cursed, Miss Blackwell." He backed away. "I came to warn you. Flee while you can!"

Marisee raced to the door. "Mr Hanway? Mr Hanway! What do you mean?"

He mounted his horse and looked back at her. "Leave, my child! A new plague is upon us. I must return to the poor foundlings. I pray that I don't succumb too."

"Please, sir! I don't understand!"

The horse galloped away. Marisee watched as it disappeared down the path, the empty path with no carriages, no footmen, no one, but ... at last! Her friend was heading across the field towards her.

"Camilla!" she called out. "I'm so happy to see you! What's happen—"

The words faded from Marisee's mouth. The figure

looked like the Camilla she knew from Bagnigge's Wells, but she moved like she was wading through deep water. Marisee frowned and rubbed her temples. Her head throbbed like there were cymbals clashing inside her skull.

Camilla stopped in front of Marisee. She seemed to be the same short girl that Marisee had always known, with her round face and wisps of brown hair sticking out from the lace trim of her bonnet. However, she didn't have her usual mischievous smile, ready to give the gossip on the fine ladies and gentlemen who had visited Bagnigge's that week. Her eyes flitted towards the pump room as if Marisee wasn't there. Her bonnet was inside out, with one ribbon looped round her ear like a shepherd's crook. Strands of hay were stuck to her dress and apron as if she'd been sleeping in the cow stall.

"I must see Madam Blackwell," she said.

Camilla's voice was dull and lifeless and she was blinking hard. As she talked, a shifting yellow mist swirled around her mouth.

"Camilla? Are you unwell?"

"I must see Madam Blackwell."

"Grandma isn't here."

Marisee's head was pounding, the *clang, clang, clang*

of the cymbals clashing against Camilla's words. She edged back into the pump room and rested her hand on the faucet. The ache subsided and her head seemed to clear. Camilla followed her in.

"What's wrong with you, Camilla? You're not … you're not yourself."

"She promised me!" Camilla's wail was so desperate and sad that it made Marisee clutch the pump. "*She* said I can only see my father again if I find Madam Blackwell!"

"I don't know where Grandma is! And who told you that?"

"I need the Freedom! The Keeper has the Freedom and I have to take it!"

The Freedom? Marisee tried to swallow back her rising dread. *Danger will follow me and I fear that it will follow you*, Grandma had written. How could Marisee's kind, funny friend be dangerous? Except, on the outside this girl looked like Camilla, but inside she seemed to be someone or something else. Something that could indeed be dangerous.

Marisee was struggling to keep her voice even. "I think you're sick, Camilla. I think you should go home and rest, and when I see Grandma, I'll tell her that you're looking for her."

"No!" Camilla pushed Marisee so hard she fell back against the table. The pile of ledgers tumbled to the ground. "I need the Freedom now!"

Marisee steadied herself. Fear spread with every thump of her heart. She was angry too. How dare this Camilla-thing shove Marisee in Grandma's pump room! She grabbed Camilla's arm and pulled her out of the door. "I don't know what's wrong with you, or who you even are. You are not you. Now, go!"

"I must see Madam Blackwell," said a new voice.

Mr Browbridge, the elderly miller, stepped out from around the side of the pump room wall. A metal crowbar trembled in his thin fingers. "I need the Freedom."

The air in front of his mouth rippled with yellow.

"Mr ... Mr Browbridge?" Marisee backed away.

The old miller raised the crowbar but was pushed aside by two girls.

"We must see Madam Blackwell." Two voices together. It was the Whitby twins, Cicely and Angelica, three years older than Marisee and much taller. Their father owned the orchards by the tollgate. Cicely dragged a rake behind her, dead leaves bristling between the spokes. Angelica held a mallet in one hand and a wooden

68

stake in the other.

"We need the Freedom." Their tainted breath merged together in front of them. "*She* promised us!" Their eyelids fluttered. "*She* promised!"

"Who promised you, Cicely?" Marisee's voice was trying to hide from her. She cleared her throat. That was better. "What was promised to you?"

Cicely reached out and tugged at Marisee's sleeves. "We must see Madam Blackwell!"

Marisee tried to shake her sleeve free, but the girl's nails were hooked into the linen. Marisee pushed her away and she fell back into her sister.

The mallet thudded to the ground. Angelica bent down slowly and picked it up. It swung backwards and forwards in her loose grip. She took a step towards Marisee. The cymbals clashed in Marisee's head. The fear pulsed harder.

"We must see Madam Blackwell."

Just over Angelica's shoulder, Marisee caught a glint of silver. A young man stumbled towards her with his sword drawn before him. His head was shaven, without a wig. His shirt was fastened at strange angles. He wore the bright orange silk breeches of a dandy, but one shoe was missing and his stockings were torn open at the toe.

There was a page boy a few steps behind him wearing a turban and bright red trousers and jacket. He began racing towards Marisee too. His mouth moved but Marisee couldn't hear the words.

The young man with the sword was moving faster. "I must see Madam Blackwell!"

He tripped on a knot of grass. The sword flew from his hand. He fumbled around as if he could barely see it. Mr Browbridge lifted the crowbar with both hands. The twins lifted their weapons too. The fear had seeped through every part of Marisee. Her body refused to move.

For a moment, the villagers were still. Then their lips tilted upwards and started moving. A yellow cloud bloomed around their mouths. Their voices were not their own. It was one voice, a woman's, singing a lullaby.

"March lamb, walk lamb, follow the sheep,
Open eyes, close eyes, sleep, lambkins, deep.
No sleep, breathe deep, rise sleepers, rise.
Ten years, ten tears, dripping from my eyes."

The cymbals in Marisee's head clanged so hard that everything in front of her shook. The villagers' mouths closed and their heads turned back towards Marisee. The page boy, though, was still running. Marisee must run too, but her legs were so heavy.

She could hear the page boy now.

"I need Madam Blackwell!" he yelled.

The villagers raised their weapons in the air. The stake, the mallet, the crowbar, the young man clutching the hilt of his sword...

"We must see Madam Blackwell! We need the Freedom!"

They came for her, floundering across the uneven grass. The page boy was catching up, running, running...

"She promised!" Angelica raised her wooden stake.

A hand gripped Marisee's arm.

"No!" she shrieked. "Let go of me!"

She was dragged back towards the pump house. The fingers holding hers were brown like her own. It was the page boy.

"Hurry up!" he shouted. "We have to get inside!"

His breath was clear. He wasn't sick. Not yet, anyway.

Marisee tried to make her legs work. The boy pulled her into the pump house. He grabbed one of the doors and heaved it shut.

"Help me!" he yelled.

The words cut through Marisee's fear. She grabbed

the right door and dragged it towards the other one. The boy pulled them together as Marisee shoved the heavy bolt into the barrel. A thud hit the door outside, and another one, as if people were throwing themselves against it. The door was solid. It should hold for the moment. But now she was locked in with this stranger who could be as dangerous as anyone outside.

She and the boy stared at each other. He was around the same age as her, and his skin was the same brown as her own. He was dressed like a prince in red silk breeches, a beaded matching jacket and a turban pinned with an immense jewel. It looked so heavy; it must make his neck hurt. His slippers were soft leather, not fit for walking these roads. He carried a basket over one arm.

"Who are you?" she demanded. Good. Her voice sounded loud and bold even though she didn't feel that way. "And what do you want?"

"I'm Robert Strong." He held the basket out towards her. Blue glass flasks were wrapped carefully inside. "I want some water."

Marisee shook her head. "I've never seen you before. You're not a regular customer."

"You haven't seen me before because Lady Hibbert makes me stay with her coach. She sends a footman for the water."

Marisee made a face. "You're part of Lady Hibbert's household?"

"I am." His voice was without expression. "My friend is sick. I thought I could help her." Robert frowned. "Are *you* Madam Blackwell? I thought that perhaps she was older."

"Madam Blackwell is my grandmother. She ... she's not here."

Another thud. This time it sounded like a mallet smashing the wood. Robert glanced at the door, then back at Marisee.

"I don't understand what's happening." There was an edge of panic in his voice. "Everything is ... *wrong* today."

Marisee wished she could laugh. Grandma had disappeared. The whole village seemed to be trying to kill her.

"Yes," she said. "Very wrong."

"Those people out there. Why do they want to hurt you?"

"They want to find my grandmother," she said. "Just like you. Who *are* you?"

"I told you. I'm Robert Strong."

Marisee looked him up and down. What if this *Robert*

Strong was an excellent actor and had just pretended to rescue her?

I need you to gather ... your wits.

Marisee was going to follow Grandma's advice. She would not trust this strange prince-boy until he had proved himself. She moved towards the table and the box of flasks. She kept facing him, but her hands reached behind her. Her fingers closed around a small earthenware bottle. It was her only weapon, but if she threw it hard enough it might knock him over and give her time to escape.

Escape where, though? And how?

The mallet crashed against the wood again. The door shook.

"How do I know *you're* not making all this happen?" Marisee asked.

Bang! Bang! Bang! Quick and hard, like hammers. Many hammers. There must be even more villagers now. Marisee imagined the houses emptying and a mob trailing across the fields, eyelids flickering, breath turned yellow, weapons raised and ready. She tightened her grip on the bottle.

"Me?" Robert laughed, but he didn't sound amused. "I don't have the power to make anyone do anything. London is sick, though. Nearly everyone in the Hibberts's house is asleep: real, lying-down asleep. They're breathing that yellow mist, but they're not like those people out there." He pointed towards the door. "Those people are like sleepwalkers."

"What about Lady Hibbert?"

"She's still awake."

"No sickness would dare go near her," Marisee muttered.

A smile flickered across Robert's face. Marisee loosened her grip on the flask just a little.

"What else do you know?" she asked.

His frown deepened. "Not everybody falls sick. You and me are awake. And Lady Hibbert, and there was even a gentleman in a coach. He was still awake, though the driver was asleep. And … I think it's more than just a sleeping sickness. It changes things."

A crash and the sound of an axe splitting wood. The door had cracked. The blade of a sword slipped through the thin gap and wiggled around as if trying to slice away the wood. These were people that Marisee had known for most of her life. All of them had come for water before. All of them had their flasks filled for free. Now they did not even recognize her. How could this have happened?

Would they ever be themselves again?

"Yes," Marisee said. "It does change things."

The axe fell again. The hole was now the size of a fist. A face filled the gap. It was Cicely.

"We must have the Freedom!" she whined. "*She* promised!"

The face pulled away and a hand appeared, feeling around for the bolt. It was still out of reach, but it wouldn't be for long. A few more strokes of the axe, and the whole plank would split apart.

Glass smashed above Marisee's head. A rock landed at her feet. It had been hurled through a high window beneath the roof beams. This was the plan! The sleepwalkers must have a ladder. Maybe not just one. Maybe half the village would break down the door while the rest clambered through the window or smashed the slates on the roof to crawl through from above.

Another window shattered. The door shuddered and the plank fell away. The crowbar gripped the wood next to it. In a few more minutes, the villagers were going to be inside.

"We have to get out!" Marisee shouted.

Robert looked from the door up to the rafters. "How?"

If there were secret tunnels below the pump room,

that was another secret that Grandma had kept. Marisee was standing on the old threshing floor, where the grain was beaten to free the corn. Afterwards, the farmers would open a door for the breeze to blow away the chaff.

"There!" She pointed to a small wooden panel behind the faucet. "The winnowing door."

She ran over to it, Robert behind her. It was locked with a hook and eye but the hook was rusted in place. It couldn't have been opened since before Grandma was born. Marisee jammed her fingers beneath it, but it wouldn't shift.

"We need a lever," Robert said.

"Look around," Marisee said. "Can you see anything?"

He shook his head.

"Well, I'll have to try a different way, then."

Marisee drew back her foot and kicked the wood as hard as she could. A panel cracked. A crack wasn't enough! If two of them kicked it, maybe... She glanced back at Robert's feet. He couldn't even kick a buttercup in those slippers. A crunching sound came from the main door. A second panel had been wrenched off.

"I must see Madam Blackwell!" Mr Browbridge's voice wheezed through the gap, echoed by the mob of villagers.

A stockinged foot was thrust between the jagged

edges of wood, the orange silk breeches catching on the splinters. A hand clutched at the broken panel, and a sword clattered on to the pump room floor. Marisee kicked the winnowing door again. Another crack, but it stayed shut!

"I know what to do," Robert said.

She turned back. He was holding the rock that had shattered the window.

"Robert? What are you doing with—?"

He brought the rock down hard and fast. It smashed against the latch, which flew off its hinges and on to the ground. The small door gaped open.

"You go first," he said.

Marisee gave him a quick nod. Her chest was so tight she could hardly breathe, let alone speak. She crouched down and crawled through.

"I need the Freedom." Camilla was standing guard outside the winnowing door. Her hands were clasped in front of her, her eyelids drooping. "*She* promised."

"Camilla?" Marisee kept her voice quiet. "If you let me pass, I'll find Madam Blackwell for you."

Camilla's eyes opened wide. She grinned. The yellow sickness swirled around her mouth as she started to sing. "*March lamb, walk lamb, follow the sheep…*"

There was a scrabbling from the pump room behind Marisee and a tug at her skirt.

"They're getting in!" Robert called. "Move out of the way!"

"Open eyes, close eyes, sleep, lambkins, deep…"

"Camilla, please." Marisee forced herself to her feet. The girls were face to face.

"Ten years, ten tears, dripping from my eyes…"

Was the real Camilla still in there, somewhere? Camilla's eyes stared blankly back at Marisee. But there was a flicker of something else, a deep sadness.

"No sleep, breathe deep…"

"Camilla! Please!"

"Let me out!" Robert yelled.

"… rise, sleepers, RISE!"

The last word was a shriek. The cymbals clashed and clashed inside Marisee's head. When they stopped, she heard the footsteps. Twenty – no, thirty – no, even more villagers, were crossing the field towards them, feet lifting and thudding down like a weary army. Their weapons swung in their hands: broom handles and dyers' poles, shovels and meat hooks. Mr Rand, the cartwright, carried the broken metal rim of a carriage wheel.

"We want Madam Blackwell! We want the Freedom!"

Cicely and Angelica and Mr Browbridge and villagers that Marisee had never seen before shuffled around from the main door.

Strong hands gripped Marisee's shoulders, thumbs pressing into her neck. Camilla shoved her face up so close that Marisee was sure she could smell the sickness; it was sweet and decaying like flowers in ditch water.

"She promised me, Marisee!" She suddenly sounded like the real Camilla again.

"Camilla?" Marisee reached out and touched the girl's face.

Camilla's mouth moved, but there were no words. Her mouth snapped shut and the blankness returned. Her thumbs pressed even harder into Marisee's throat.

"Stop!" Marisee tried to push her away, but the strength was being choked out of her.

An empty flask box dropped over Camilla's head. Robert was standing behind her. Camilla grunted and released Marisee to yank it off.

"Thank you!" Marisee gasped.

"Where is Madam Blackwell?" The dandy was scrabbling through the winnowing door.

"We need the Freedom!"

Cicely and Angelica were just a few feet away.

Cicely shook her rake, loosening the leaves. Every spike seemed to gleam.

What could Marisee do? It was just her and maybe this Robert boy against all these sick villagers.

Ah – but hadn't Grandma said...

"Follow me!" she yelled.

She ran, Robert was following. They could make it, she knew they could. If only she could move faster. The breath caught in her sore chest as Robert slid and slipped beside her. Weapons were flung in their direction. A broom handle caught Robert in the side.

"Ouch!"

"Keep going," she puffed. "We're nearly there."

"Where?"

She stopped by the low well wall and peered between the stumps of melted candles into the shaft. It was completely dark.

"Down here."

She scrambled on to the wall and jumped.

DOWN
THE WELL

Three questions sprang through Robert's head. The first one was: has that girl really thrown herself into a well? The second one was: am I supposed to do that too? The last one was: why am I melting?

One moment Robert was standing by the well mouth as the village mob stomped towards him, and the next, he was surrounded in mist. It wasn't the dank yellow mist of the sickness, but clear, fresh droplets. He held his hand up to his face. It looked like a candle left under the Barbados sun.

Then he was falling. He tried to scream, but he had no face, no mouth, no air.

He saw mossy walls.

Stained bricks.

Falling.

Falling.

He hit stony ground. He was definitely solid again. It felt like the inside of his head had been mixed into a pudding batter and his ears were being poked with forks. He closed his eyes. *That could not have really happened. This is not real.* He rubbed the side of his head hard and opened his eyes. He was splayed on the ground, the well mouth a faint smear overhead. The girl was sitting opposite him, leaning against the wall next to the entrance to a tunnel. He forced his wobbly body to sit up.

It took two attempts to get his voice to work. "Are we really at the bottom of the well?"

The girl nodded.

"We fell down a well and we aren't dead?"

She nodded again.

"Do you know how this can happen?"

"I ... um ... think so."

"Is this part of the sickness?"

"No."

How could she know for sure? She sounded very certain. Though, he supposed *he* was certain he'd been attacked by a great stone unicorn. He touched his forehead – it was still sore. He glanced into the tunnel and could just make out a trickle of shining water.

He frowned. "How can your well be dry?"

The girl gave him a tired smile. "Do you always ask so many questions?"

No, he didn't, though he always wanted to. They bubbled inside him like Mrs Wandle's pie gravy, but there could be consequences if he let them spill out. Back on the plantation, Mama had been strict. *Boys like you must play stupid, Robert. Keep everything in your head if you want to survive. If they think you're clever, they will beat it out of you in case you make plans against them.* Lady Hibbert thought he was stupid. And Mrs Wandle. Only Lizzie let him be himself.

"I've just been chased by your villagers and fallen into a dry well – and lived," he said. "I think it's fair to ask questions."

A rock thumped down on the ground next to him.

"Now isn't the time." She looked up. "We'd better head inside before the sleepwalkers find a way down."

"Inside where?" Robert folded his arms. "And what if

the well fills up with us inside?"

"*That* would be bad manners."

The girl hadn't spoken. The words came from someone else. The voice was deeper, but held a sparkle. Robert peered into the mouth of the tunnel. He couldn't see anyone.

"Is someone else here?" he whispered.

"I hope so," the girl said.

"But who—"

"There'll be time to talk later." The voice again. Robert could still see no one to own it. "I can't hold back my flow any longer."

Hold back a flow? That did not sound good.

Water gushed out of the tunnel towards them. Robert clutched at the wall. The girl did the same.

"It's me!" she shouted into the tunnel. "Grandma said you would help me!"

No one answered. The water licked at Robert's ankles and soaked into his stockings, inching its way up his calves. His nails dug so hard into the well wall, he could feel the mortar flaking away. His heart was banging hard.

"Do you know if there's a way out?" His voice was almost lost in the gurgle of the stream.

"We'll be safe," she said. "I'm sure."

That wasn't what he'd asked! The tunnel was their only way out and it was flooding! There were no ladders fixed to the walls and, even if there were, the villagers were waiting up there with their weapons. But rather that than drown.

Robert pressed his hands against the bricks. There must be a gap, a tiny ledge, a foothold, anything that would give them a chance. Water was lapping around the hem of his breeches now, pressing the silk against his skin. He'd need more than needle and thread to save his clothes if he left here alive.

How could he even think that so close to death?

Robert glanced from the girl to the well mouth so high overhead. They couldn't both escape, but maybe one of them could. It didn't have to be him.

"Stand on my shoulders!" he shouted over the noise.

The girl remained where she was, staring into the tunnel, swaying in the rush of water. It swelled up and up, engulfing her skirt, then sweeping over her shoulders. What was she waiting for? He reached out to her.

"Quickly! Before it's too late!"

Her arms flailed. Her mouth opened like she was about to scream, then she fell back into the torrent.

"No!" Robert lunged towards her, but he was too

slow. She was swept away from him.

He tried to follow her. Water splashed into his mouth and nostrils. He craned his neck back and breathed in, trying to hold the air inside him. Just that one breath in. Then another. Then there would be no more.

"Your turn!" The voice sounded so close its owner should be floating in front of him. But he still saw no one.

"Who—"

His mouth filled with water. It was sweet and soft, not gritty, bottom-of-the-well water. A quick, hard tug on his ankle made him fall backwards. His ears hummed as if every drop was singing. He waved his arms. Wasn't this what you did when you were swimming? It made no difference. The water covered his head and slid down his throat. He coughed it out.

"Relax," the voice said. "It's easier for both of us."

Relax? He was drowning! Still, he would try. He forced his shoulders, arms and legs to go slack. He bobbed straight up and breathed out hard. He was still alive! The stream was bearing him through the tunnel, like thousands of hands passing him from one to the other.

"Watch out!" the voice called.

Robert flattened himself as his nose nearly grazed

the tunnel roof. The end of his turban was flapping beside him and he managed to yank it back and hold on to it.

"And mind the gap!"

The stream twisted a sharp right. Robert's elbow scraped the corner of a brick alcove. Shining, watery hands nudged him clear.

"I said, 'Mind the gap!' Why don't you Solids ever listen?"

"I didn't have time!" He rubbed his elbow. "And what's a Solid? Where are you taking me? Where's the girl? And who are you?"

The stream seemed to shiver. "I've met young brooks with fewer questions than you."

It was the water! The water was talking to him! Or it was something else. "*Am* I dead?" he whispered. "*Have* I drowned? Are you carrying me to the afterlife?"

"Of course not," the voice splashed. "If you were dead, I wouldn't let you anywhere near me. I'd leave you to the Magogs."

"Who?" Robert knew that there were unscrupulous men who dug up the dead and took the bodies to surgeons to be cut apart. He had never heard them called Magogs before, but there were many London words that were new to him.

The stream shivered again. "You Solids know so little! The Magogs are our earth brethren. They'd be happy to take your dead self. You'd sink right back into the London mud."

"Earth brethren?"

"You'll find out more soon enough."

Robert was swept through a wide brick arch and, suddenly, he was sliding across damp ground to a halt. His stomach felt like half of it was still travelling to meet him. He fought away the dizziness. The girl was sprawled a few feet away.

"Not even a 'thank you', then?"

He turned towards the voice. A woman smiled back at him. She was bright, like light bouncing off thousands of drops of water. Her hair, or what looked like hair, was dark green and coiled up around her head, pinned in place by a shard of pottery. Her skin was darker than his and shimmered. She was wearing breeches, a shirt and waistcoat and seemed to flicker between shadow and light. Her hands were on her hips.

"They don't teach you Solids manners?" Yes, it *was* the same voice as before. "I carry you here with no major injuries and no gratitude from either of you."

The girl arched her back and grimaced. "Thank you," she said. "I don't hurt too much."

"I mean injuries to me!" The woman made a face. "Two Solids! I'm not used to that sort of weight." She gave a bow. "But welcome, Marisee Blackwell. It was my honour to bring you here."

The girl was called Marisee. At least Robert knew that now. But that was all he knew. Where was he? And who – what – was this woman? The questions shuffled through his head. Firstly, though, he'd try and stand up. He did so slowly. It still felt like the rest of his stomach hadn't arrived. "What am I doing here?"

The woman considered him. "I thought I would save you from being beaten to a pulp by angry villagers. I can always take you back, if you want."

"No," he said. "I'll stay."

The woman nodded. "Good decision."

Robert hoped so. He looked around. This was not how he imagined the bottom of a well to look. They were in a huge cavern with a high curved stone ceiling. If Robert shouted his name, the echo could be lost for ever. A circle of light in the centre of the roof was like a pale sun, but it must be another well mouth. The tunnel that he and Marisee had just swept through was framed by an arched brick entrance, one of many arches cut at different levels into the cavern wall. Robert counted them. Eight, nine, eleven, twelve tunnels, and more. It was like his ears had blinked because suddenly the world was filled with the sound of water.

A stream shot out of a high tunnel like a cannonball, plummeting over the edge into a muddle of mist and spray. A lower-level tunnel ended in a flight of stone steps, the water flopping over it in a series of mini-waterfalls that ended abruptly before they reached the ground. Robert must be standing on a shelf of stone, because on the far side he could see only the upper curves of tunnel entrances. The water pouring out of them would gather in a pool below where he was standing.

The ground beneath his feet was inset with fragments of dark glass, though the pattern was crusted with sand. Perhaps it was a face. Yes, that was a nose: nostrils below a wide, chipped nose bridge. And was he standing on an eyebrow?

"They're coming," Marisee whispered.

"Who?"

"The Chads!"

"The what?"

Ribbons of mist curled through the cavern, meeting and separating until gradually they thickened into different shapes. Some looked like people, some animals. Others were like sunshine through a smudged window: brightness and strange shadows. Robert thought back to the tales Zeke had told in the close darkness of their cabin. The one he'd like the best was about Mama Wata, who guarded the rivers in their ancestors' homeland. Robert had always believed her to be real. Could these be the same?

"I think I know what they are." Robert realized that he was grinning. "They're water spirits."

Marisee gave him an astonished look. "How do you know that?"

"I've heard stories about them. I've always hoped they were real. I wanted to believe it, but… They are, aren't they?"

"Yes," Marisee said. "They are."

At last, this was something that he might know about.

"The Court will begin soon," the stream-woman said. "So, let me give you a guided tour of my fellow Chads." She peered through the waterfall spray. One of the shapes that had emerged from the spray was solidifying into …

something. "You see that porker over there?"

It looked like a giant boar. Its body was thickset and, as the mists cleared, Robert saw the bristly fur covering its body. It turned its squashed-looking face towards them – two dark, angry eyes, a torn ear and long tusks that curved up from its lower jaw, almost touching its ears. It was very solid for a creature that had been water droplets just moments before.

"He guards Fleet Ditch," the woman said. "And he takes it very seriously. There will probably be a few Fleet river tribs here, but Fleet herself's too sick to attend these days." She sighed. "It upsets Walbrook every time, but that's the way it's always been. London changes and we have to change too. Ah!" She was pointing again. "See her?"

A short, stocky woman, wearing a bonnet and an ankle length skirt and apron, emerged from the spray. She carried a basket over one arm, filled with scrolls of paper. When she moved, she rippled into a young woman in a long black dress, her head covered in white cloth.

"She guards the Tybourne," the woman said. "Or the Westbourne. She's a ballad singer or a nun. It's a very confused river. These days, she tends to stay around Hyde Park to keep an eye on the new waterworks and the

… well, the less said about that the better."

The less said about what? Robert felt Marisee's eyes on him and shaped the question into a different one. "What's the name of your river?"

The woman smiled again. It was a wide, open smile and, just then, Robert's head was filled with the rush of the current pushing against a waterwheel.

"Since I've just hauled you both through London, introductions do seem a bit tardy. Turnmill Brook is mine," she said.

Marisee gasped. "That's near me!"

Turnmill bowed. "Indeed. Me and your family go back a long way, Marisee. Anyway, we'd better shush. We're starting."

The shimmering crowd fell silent. The noise from the waterfalls sank into a hum.

"Here she comes," Turnmill whispered. "Our riverhead, Lady Walbrook."

The water spirits parted as a tall woman glided through. Like Turnmill, she seemed nearly solid and not quite human. Robert imagined her pale skin filled with dark, deep water that flowed through her instead of blood. Her shift was the same colour as her skin, both changing as the light flickered, grey, silver, brown.

Her brow was wide and high, her nose bridge nicked, like chipped china. Robert glanced down at the glass mosaic beneath his feet. It was the same nose. Her hair was twisted into plaits and curled into an intricate style on top of her head. He felt a jab of sadness; his mother twisted and braided his sisters' hair that way.

A pony trotted behind her. Its grey fur was smeared with mud, its matted mane twisted into dirty ropes. It reared back, whinnying, but was yanked forward. Robert squinted and could just see a web of silvery threads tangled around it. The threads tapered into two near-transparent bands attached to silver wristlets on Lady Walbrook's arms. As she strode forward, the pony was pulled behind her.

Turnmill sighed. "Oh! Poor Sadler!"

Robert and Marisee glanced at each other. He wanted to speak, but his thoughts didn't fit words. The cavern filled with a damp chill, soaking through his skin to his bones. Lady Walbrook paused beneath the shaft of light thrown down from the well mouth. The pony stopped moving. Everything stopped moving. Even the waterfalls froze in mid-cascade. Lady Walbrook stared across the cavern, her gaze settling on Marisee, then Robert. Suddenly, Robert felt like his body was bulging with coarse sand. One little twitch and it would burst out and flow away. Lady Walbrook blinked, and the tightness eased. He heard Marisee breathe out next to him.

What happened? You said we'd be safe!

He wanted to shout it at Marisee, but he couldn't bear Lady Walbrook's eyes turning towards him again. His hand brushed against Marisee's. Hers pressed back, so quick and faint he almost missed it.

The air quivered.

"I am ready to proceed," Lady Walbrook said. Her voice filled Robert's head with ghost ships and ancient bells underwater. The pony reared again, its whinny like a scream.

Lady Walbrook glanced down. "Quiet, Sadler!"

The pony still wriggled and cried. The web of silver threads tightened around it, sand scattering from the taut binds. Robert felt his hands clench.

"Stay calm," Turnmill said in his ear.

How could he? The creature was struggling in pain. He looked over at Marisee. A tear rolled down her cheek.

"We have to help it, Miss Turnmill," he said.

"We can't, Robert. Not now."

Lady Walbrook's cold eyes swept across the gathered

water spirits. "Today we must bid farewell to this spirit."

The pony tried to move its head. Clouds of dark sand bloomed around its muzzle and along its flank.

"Please, Turnmill," Marisee said. "You have to stop it."

"It's too late, Marisee. I'm sorry."

Lady Walbrook's gaze returned to Sadler. "We are under daily attack. Our streams are heavy with sludge and filth. We are being culverted and covered over." There were sounds of agreement. "The one thing that can save us is under threat." Angry muttering echoed around the cavern. Lady Walbrook bowed her head towards the Sadler pony. "This spirit was too busy watching ballet dancers and rope-walkers in the music house to guard the Keeper as instructed."

The pony sank to its knees, its eyes rolling wildly. Robert would always hate horses, no matter what Lizzie said, but he still felt for this creature. It could no longer make a noise, but the pain rolled off its flanks in waves. He *would* stop this. He took a step forward.

But Marisee had already moved. "Please don't, Lady Walbrook."

The air rippled as all the water spirits turned to face Marisee. Women, men, children, strange creatures

Robert couldn't name. Some were so solid he could see every detail; others were shades of shadow. Lady Walbrook closed her eyes and pursed her lips, as if whistling for a dog. A tangle of threads whipped out of her mouth and snapped around Marisee's wrists, binding them like shackles. Marisee screamed.

"Don't!" Robert shouted. "You're hurting her!"

Lady Walbrook stared at him. He waited for the threads to whip round him or his body to crumble into sand, but nothing happened. Marisee was silent too, her eyes wide with shock. Robert spun around from Lady Walbrook and tried to rake the threads from Marisee's wrists. They slopped away, loosening then tightening again. Marisee tried to force her hands apart, but the threads dug deeper, her skin swelling out between the wet silver bindings.

Turnmill's cool hand drew him away. "Marisee's the Keeper's granddaughter, Robert. She'll be Keeper in the future. She won't be harmed. The good Lady doesn't like to be challenged in front of the others. She has to prove that she's in charge. Do you understand?"

Yes, Robert knew another "good Lady" like that.

"You, though, Robert, may not be safe. Stay calm."

How could he? Marisee was trembling like the pony.

Turnmill placed an arm around Marisee's shoulders and whispered in her ear. Marisee nodded and let her bound wrists drop in front of her.

"Madam Blackwell has disappeared." Lady Walbrook rose from the ground as she spoke, her shift flowing over her feet to the floor. "She has taken the Freedom. You should have been vigilant, Sadler. The danger should not have come so close. I cannot overlook this."

She jerked her wrists into the air. The pony twisted round and, for a moment, its eyes met Robert's. A hoof flew into the air. The tip of a tail. A blur of darkness streaked with silver. When the dark cloud had dispersed, the pony was gone. Slack silver threads slithered through a puddle of sand and funnelled into Lady Walbrook's mouth. Slowly, she sank back to the ground. Robert looked from the sand to Lady Walbrook. Her eyes were closed, a sliver of silver dribbling down her face.

"Why did you do that?" Marisee cried.

Lady Walbrook opened her eyes and stared into the mist of spirits. "Where is the new guardian?"

A fox-like creature pattered towards Walbrook. Its body was long and sleek and as dark as the night ocean. It bowed its head.

"You will now watch Sadler's Wells," Walbrook said.

"And you will do better."

The creature bowed again and retreated.

Turnmill stepped forward. "May I be permitted to talk?"

Lady Walbrook's head tilted sideways. "You question my judgement, Turnmill?"

"No, Lady." Something in Turnmill's tone reminded Robert of himself when he was "politely" addressing Lady Hibbert. "If we are to find Madam Blackwell, we must understand what pursues her. The streets above are filled with the sleeping and the sleep-walking. Something controls them, and it searches for the Freedom too. If we are not careful, it will find it. We need Marisee and her friend to help us stop this ... this thing. Do you not agree, Lady Walbrook?"

There was silence, and then the threads dropped from Marisee's wrists and slithered across the ground towards Lady Walbrook. They sank away, leaving shiny silver trails across the tiny glass tiles. Marisee rubbed her skin and shot a furious look towards Lady Walbrook.

Lady Walbrook beckoned to Robert and Marisee. "Come close. Both of you."

Marisee thrust her shoulders back like a soldier and marched towards Lady Walbrook. Robert followed. He felt the water spirits around him, a slick of moisture on the back of his hand, a faint bubbling by his ears. He gazed into Lady Walbrook's face. It was not as smooth as it seemed. Robert imagined centuries of tiny stones drawn by tides across its surface. Marisee was staring too, but there was something different in her look. It was an expression he knew well. She was refusing to show that she was frightened.

"Do you know where my grandmother is?" she asked.

Lady Walbrook's tunic shimmered. "No. But it is for me to ask the questions."

"Grandma said that I would find help here, but…" She wiped her eyes. "But you … that pony…" She pulled herself up to stand even straighter. "I will tell you nothing until you answer my questions first."

A tiny silver thread slipped from the side of Lady Walbrook's mouth. She kept her eyes on Marisee as she wiped it away with the back of her hand.

Robert made himself step forward and stand next to Marisee. He must find his polite voice too.

He said, "The sleepwalkers were searching for the Freedom, Lady Walbrook. It will help us greatly if you can tell us more about it."

Lady Walbrook stared back silently. She rubbed her

hands together, smearing her palms with silver.

Turnmill appeared by Robert's side. "Robert, I think you should tell Lady Walbrook what you know first."

"There's a sleeping sickness," Robert said. "Some people catch it while others do not. Those who do can be controlled in their sleep." He risked a look at Lady Walbrook. "Perhaps Madam Blackwell has been infected."

Marisee shook her head. "She was fine when she left the house."

"She cannot be infected," Lady Walbrook said. "The sickness comes from the Ether. Madam Blackwell cannot go there."

"The Ether?" Robert and Marisee spoke at the same time.

"The Ether is part of London." Lady Walbrook stared down at the broken mosaic face. "It rose from the ruins after the last elemental battle. It was the reason why the Romans fled and no Solid would live within the walls for long after. The Ether was strong then. It captured minds and held them. Its power is weaker now. But you can still see it if you look carefully. It's in the mists above the water steps, and in the secret corners of the watchhouses, and in the shadows beneath the workhouse walls. The Ether is part of your dreams."

"Oh," Marisee said. "Dreams. I understand."

A faint smile crossed Lady Walbrook's lips. "You cannot enter the Ether, Marisee, can you?"

"No. Not if it's in dreams. I don't dream."

Marisee didn't dream? Robert realized that he was staring at her and quickly looked away. He had often stopped himself falling asleep so he didn't have bad dreams. Were there people who just never dreamed?

"No Keeper can dream," Lady Walbrook said, as if she'd read the question from his mind. "That is how we know Madam Blackwell cannot succumb to the sickness."

"But whatever is causing the sickness is using the sleepwalkers to search for her," Robert said.

"Yes," Turnmill said. "That was a big crowd of people with a lot of weapons up there."

"And my friend, Camilla, was one of them," Marisee said. "How could it change her like that? It was like she couldn't really see me."

"That, I don't understand." Lady Walbrook's eyes flicked from Robert to Marisee. "If Solids go to sleep hungry, they will find food in the Ether. If they are cold, they'll find warmth and all the clothes they need. You know the Ether, don't you, Robert?"

If they go to sleep hungry, they will find food… The giant pie. The cakes in the hamper. Lizzie falling asleep in her icy room and dreaming of the warm jacket.

"Yes," he said, quietly. "I do. Lady Hibbert doesn't need the Ether. She has everything she will ever want in this world. That's why she isn't infected."

"The Ether has changed," Lady Walbrook said. "Sleepers used to wake remembering the power of their dreams but always knowing it was a dream. But now, when they sleep, the Ether keeps them. Solids stay in their dream world while their bodies wither away in their beds. They smile as they die sleeping. I do not know why."

"I do," Robert said.

Lady Walbrook, Marisee, the damp press of the water spirits – Robert felt all their attention on him alone now.

"Tell me," Lady Walbrook said.

He swallowed hard, lost his voice and found it again.

"My friend, Lizzie, dreamed about her sister, Nelly, last night," he said. "Nelly died before Lizzie came to London. She said that Nelly was so real, it was like they were together. Lizzie fell asleep again this morning, and I couldn't wake her up. But I knew she was dreaming about Nelly because she was smiling and calling out to her. It was the same with the cook who was dreaming about her husband, and the stableboy saw his mother who died when he was small."

"Did you dream of someone too?" Marisee asked.

Robert shook his head quickly. He had not. He knew he would never want to come back to this world if he did. "What about Camilla? Would she dream about someone?"

"Her father died last year," Marisee said. "She still cries about it. And she said something strange. She said 'she promised'. Camilla had to find the Freedom because '*she* promised'. I don't know who *she* is."

"What *is* this Freedom?" Robert asked.

He knew freedom was important. Everyone on the plantation in Barbados had been talking about it for as long as he could remember. But this was something different.

Brown, grey, white; the colours moved beneath Lady Walbrook's skin. "The Freedom of London is the greatest elemental power in this city. Whoever holds the Freedom can call upon its magic to create a new London. Their own London to serve only them."

"And my grandmother had to care for it?" Marisee

sounded astonished.

"It was the fault of that Lord Mayor!" Lady Walbrook's skin rippled with silver. "The one with the cat. He drafted the Whittington Articles and asked us to sign it to make sure we kept the truce. Then the sneak added in the Freedom of London. It was supposed to prove our trust in each other by combining all our magic to make something even more powerful. The Articles state that we are all supposed to take turns to protect it, but…" Her skin flashed pure silver, then dulled into grey. "How can we trust those skulking Dragons? Or those useless Fumis? But it's not them who failed us. It's the Magogs."

Robert rubbed his ear. Had he heard properly? Did she say Dragons? He glanced at Marisee, but her eyes were on Lady Walbrook.

"Yes," Lady Walbrook said. "Those mudlug Magogs. They let the Freedom sink into the earth without a trace. The Fleet Ditch boar found it in one of his tunnels. He should have brought it to me."

"He couldn't," Turnmill said. "We all signed on the inky line. What do the Articles say, Lady Walbrook? *If any elemental fails in their duty to protect the Freedom of London, then possession will be granted to a Solid Keeper.* So it passed to Madam Blackwell."

The silver swirled, bulging beneath Lady Walbrook's skin. "How can a mere Solid be charged with something so powerful?"

"It was charged to us, but we failed," Turnmill said.

"*We* did not fail!" A silver thread broke through Lady Walbrook's cheek and ran down her face.

Robert clutched Marisee's arm. "We need to get out of here. Quickly!"

"It was those clod-creatures that failed!" Lady Walbrook screamed. "They care for nothing! They want everything to turn to mud!"

The silver unravelled from her forehead, her chin, the backs of her hands, knotting together. Threads splashed to the ground or spun away from her. A silver coil landed in Turnmill's hair. She flicked it away. A few grains of sand flew with it.

The noise of water echoed through the cavern again. The spirits quickly sank into the spray and disappeared.

"We should have kept the Freedom!" Another cluster of silver flew from Lady Walbrook's mouth, unspooling around them. Threads glanced off Marisee's hand. She screamed and shook them off.

Turnmill pulled Robert and Marisee towards her. Light shone through her and Robert could see the thousands of droplets that made her. As they merged together, she closed her eyes and collapsed like a wave on to the shore. "Yes. There is a way out!" she shouted.

Robert sank again into the quickening current, gasping at the power of it. He imagined it smashing against a waterwheel, driving the paddles that turned the giant millstones, grinding the grain.

And he was going up, up, up.

LORD
MAYOR

Marisee splashed down on to the grass and breathed out. Robert was lying completely still by the well wall.

"Robert?" Her voice was hoarse from the water. "Are you hurt?"

He clawed at his face. "I can't see!"

"Your turban's slipped over your eyes."

"Oh." He pushed it back and squinted against the light. "Thank you." He touched his fancy jacket and then his breeches. "They're completely dry. Was that... Did that just happen?"

After everything, was he only worried about his expensive clothes? She pushed that away and said, "Do your ears hurt?"

"Yes."

"Then it happened. Swallow hard. That should clear them. I've seen Grandma do it."

Robert sat up. "Your grandmother goes down that well?"

"Yes. Every Friday."

"She must be a strong woman."

Marisee felt a swell of pride. "She is."

She sat up slowly. Her hand knocked against a rake. "Look, Robert."

He grimaced and propped himself up. "Oh," he said again.

The villagers were still there. They were sprawled across the grass as if they had indeed been blown like chaff. The rake lay in Cicely's loose grip, her body completely still. Yellow breath curled out from her grinning mouth.

"The twins' little sister fell from a tree two months ago," Marisee said softly. "She never recovered. Perhaps it's her they see in the Ether."

Robert nodded but said nothing. His eyes, though,

held the same sadness as she had seen in Camilla's.

"We should leave before they wake," Marisee said. "You can collect some water for your friend, if you still want to."

"What will you do?"

"Grandma's in danger." Marisee swept her hand around. "Something or someone has power over dreams. I can't let it take the Freedom. I'm going to find out what it is and help Grandma."

When Marisee had started speaking, she hadn't been sure what she was going to say. But now she *was* sure. That was exactly what she was going to do.

Robert looked at the barn, then back at Marisee. "This sickness can't be cured by your water, can it?"

Marisee shook her head.

"Then, if you don't mind, I would like to accompany you."

"You would?" Did she truly want this stranger with his sad face and flimsy shoes to come with her? Though there was one way that he could be helpful. "Will you be asking lots of questions?"

He frowned, then shrugged. "Yes. I will."

"Good. Because without questions we can't find answers."

"So may I ask…?"

She hadn't meant straight away! "Yes?"

"Where are we going next?"

Marisee rubbed her throbbing wrists. The silver threads had left pale marks. She scrambled to her feet. "We know what the Freedom does, but we don't know what it looks like. I mean, even if it stood in front of us, I wouldn't know it." She narrowed her eyes. "It's not *you*, is it?"

"No," he said shortly. "It's not."

"Well, there was one person that Walbrook mentioned who might be useful to us. She said that the Articles were written by a Lord Mayor of London. What if we could read them for ourselves?"

Robert looked uncertain. "Read them?"

"Yes!" Marisee thought that Robert should be much more excited. This was actually a good idea. "The Articles should tell us much more about the Freedom. I think it's time to visit the Lord Mayor of London."

No one passed them as they headed down the Highgate road towards London. The jumpiness in Marisee's stomach wasn't just because she had been flung up and down the well. She would never forget the cold sting of the silver threads on her skin and the terrified pony crumbling into dust.

She felt angry too. Why hadn't Grandma ever told her about the Freedom? It was even more important than the wells, and still Grandma had kept it a secret from her.

Robert was watching her.

"You want to ask another question, don't you?" Marisee said.

"Is it true that you don't dream?"

That wasn't what she had expected.

"Yes," Marisee said. "I always thought it was like swimming. Some people can dream and some people can't. Most people do dream, though, don't they?"

"Yes," Robert said. "I think so."

"Have you dreamed about anyone who's – who you've lost?"

He looked away from her. "Not since I came to London."

She waited for him to say more, but he was quiet for a moment.

Then he said, "Are there really dragons?"

"Those are the fire elementals, though Grandma says that they're not actually dragons."

"What are they?"

113

Marisee shrugged. "I don't know. I don't think she's ever met one. All their demands come through the Goldsmiths Guild."

"And the Fumis? Are they the air elementals?"

"Yes."

She nodded with certainty, and like Robert she looked up towards the sky. She had never seen a Fumi either. But even if a Fumi was nearby, surely they would never be able to see it. The sky was so stained and murky.

As they neared London, Marisee was glad Robert was with her. She could usually hear the town's clamour long before she arrived. Even when winter snow emptied the roads of most traffic, there'd be the clop of the dray horses and the cries of the desperate vendors walking the streets. There was never this terrible silence. This new London frightened her.

As they passed along Old Street, they saw a mother and her children asleep beneath the bulk of the Three Feathers Tavern. It wasn't unusual; the homeless slept anywhere they could find shelter. Marisee had often seen them huddled together for warmth, the mother or father awake and vigilant against danger. They were never all sleeping like this. The mother's head poked out and she was smiling as if she was on the softest mattress, not shivering in the filthy London streets. The dank yellow mist curled around them.

"The children…" Robert said quietly.

Marisee understood. They would dream and dream and dream until their bodies wasted away.

They both jumped as a carriage passed them heading towards the City of London. The City was almost separate from the rest of London, circled by the ruins of the old Roman wall. For a long time after the last elemental battle, no one had lived here, but now it was the place where secrets were whispered, deals were made and gold and coin were deposited in the Bank of England.

Marisee recognized the coat of arms on the coach. It was the Goldsmiths Guild. Grandma said that they were the richest and most powerful, perhaps they were heading to a guild meeting at the Mansion House to find a way to fight this new threat. She glanced upwards. Were the Dragons keeping guard? The only ones she'd ever seen were the painted wooden dragons used to mark City of London boundaries.

They passed a knot of merchants talking quietly outside a coffee shop in Exchange Alley. The merchants fell quiet, hands reaching for their sword hilts as Marisee and Robert hurried past. A carriage clattered along

Threadneedle Street, a footman in dark blue livery staggering behind it. His eyes were closed. An elderly woman was sweeping the crossroads between Sherborn Lane and Lombard Street, her broom moving in long, round circles that shifted the dirt back around into itself. Yellow sickness curdled the air in front of her. Marisee and Robert moved away quickly.

"This is it," Marisee said. "The Lord Mayor's Mansion House."

The bright stone of the immense building reflected the late morning light back at them.

Robert gazed at it. "I used to think that the white people's houses in Barbados were big. But this…"

The Mansion House was definitely built to look important. Six smooth pillars in front of the entrance held up a triangular stone pediment crammed with sculpted figures. Marisee made out the shapes of children and a bearded, bare-chested man lounging back and emptying water from a vase. An anchor and cable lay close at hand. A stone woman with a tower on her head seemed to be pushing her way out of the building, trampling someone beneath her.

Robert was squinting up at it too. Marisee stared at the statues harder. Had the woman just moved her head? Marisee shook her own head. Strange things had happened today. But moving statues? No.

She rested her hands on the railings in front of the Mansion House. Why was she delaying? The Lord Mayor knew Grandma well. He would be very willing to help her. All she had to do was go through that gate, up the steps and knock on the door. But, there was a feeling about the place … like there was something rotting beneath the shininess. Perhaps it was London itself, already decaying away. She shivered. She must hurry.

"Do you think the Lord Mayor will know who you are?" Robert asked.

"Of course he will! Grandma comes here all the time!"

But never with me, she thought.

Marisee took a deep breath, opened the gate and marched up the steps towards the grand entrance. She had just reached halfway, when a young man slipped out from behind the pillar ahead. He pointed a bow down at her, an arrow drawn back, ready to release.

"Go no further," he said quietly.

His breath was clear, his eyes steady. Marisee stopped. Robert too.

"I … um … I've come to speak to Sir William," she said. "The Lord Mayor."

"You will go no further."

"It's important! He will want to see me!"

The archer drew back the bowstring. He was not alone. Another archer stepped out from behind the next pillar, and then another one.

"I am Madam Blackwell's granddaughter." Marisee's voice was slipping back to its hiding place. All that came out was a mumble. The weapons remained raised. She was sure she heard the bowstrings creak as they were stretched to their limit.

"You will go no further," the first archer said again.

Robert touched her arm. "Come with me. I have an idea."

Marisee made herself walk slowly down the steps, trying not to brace herself for the arrow that might pierce her spine. She opened the gate, turned and shouted, "You wait until my grandma hears how you treated me!"

The archers slipped silently back behind their pillars.

"So, what's your idea?" she asked.

"Who lives here?"

"The Lord Mayor and his family."

"And?"

"And..." She thought hard. "And his servants! Of course!"

There would be a whole household of servants to

keep the Lord Mayor and his family comfortable and take care of their many important guests. The staff certainly wouldn't use the grand front door. They'd have their own entrance. If she and Robert were lucky, the guards would have forgotten about that.

They found the servants' entrance quickly. The guards didn't need to remember it. It was right at the front, below the stone pillars, and the door was firmly closed. Any attempts to break it open would soon be heard by the archers above. Robert didn't seem too worried. He walked past it and turned the corner, out of the archers' sight. Marisee followed.

"A house this big needs a big kitchen," Robert said. "The Lord Mayor often entertains guests, I suppose."

"Grandma says that the Guilds are always eating and drinking."

"Look." He pointed to a window close to the ground.

Marisee bent down and squinted through the dusty glass into a huge, dark room. There was a great long table in the middle strewn with plates, forks and serving spoons.

Robert moved along to the next window. "If we're lucky," he said, "we can find a window that's…" He moved to the next one, gave it a little push and smiled. "Open."

He pushed the pane harder and the window swung inside. Marisee crouched next to him. It seemed like it really was a good idea to bring him with her, but she would still keep her wits about her, like Grandma said. And that window was open to let in fresh air, not people. How was she going to fit through there?

Robert went first, wiggling through the gap, perching on the sill and then jumping. Marisee gathered her skirts as closely around her as she could. She'd often wished that she could wear breeches like a man – or Turnmill.

"Wait," Robert said.

She could just see him dragging a chair towards the window. He kneeled on it and unlatched the other side. That was better! Though still not easy with so much skirt. She squeezed through and sat on the sill, like Robert. The chair made it easier too. She rested her feet on the seat, grabbed the sill and pushed herself through. It was not her most dignified moment, but Robert was making a point of looking in the opposite direction.

Marisee's mouth fell open. This was the kitchen? Marisee reckoned that her whole village could fit in here, including Mr Whitby's orchards. The ceiling was vaulted, like the Chads' cavern, but the hall beneath was filled with benches and tables and a roasting range in a fireplace so huge that Marisee wondered if it could once have housed a real dragon's nest. Meat spits lined a whole wall, though instead of fire, beneath them was nothing but ash. A child was asleep on the cold stones next to them. Perhaps his job was to keep the meat turning. He looked so small that Marisee wondered how he could reach the spit handles. It was too gloomy to see his breath, but his face was stretched into a wide smile. She picked him up and laid him down on a table.

Her eyes followed the rows of shelves bowing beneath the weight of pots and pans, platters and tureens, trivets and trays. The walls were studded with hooks for ladles, forks, tongs and many strangely shaped things that Marisee could not even begin to think what they'd be used for.

"Is Lady Hibbert's kitchen this big?" she asked.

"No, but I'm sure she wishes that it was."

Marisee tried to imagine this place bustling with cooks and maids and footmen, the air thick with steam and cooking smells.

"I wonder where they all are?" Marisee said.

"I suppose the servants' quarters must be upstairs," Robert said. "But look."

He pointed into the shadows. A maid was slumped

next to a pantry door as if she had been standing there when the sickness took her and had slid down to the ground.

Marisee made her footsteps as quiet as possible as she backed away. She sniffed the air. Something was definitely rotting. Maybe it was coming from the storerooms; like a meat a long way past its best.

"We have to find the Lord Mayor," she said.

"Do you think he'll be awake?"

"With a kitchen this big?" Marisee laughed, though it wasn't funny. "He certainly doesn't fall asleep hungry. *He* won't dream in the Ether."

"I suppose he must care for his soldiers better than his servants," Robert said. "The archers are awake while…" He pointed to the boy slumbering on the table.

"Or perhaps those were the only archers that weren't sick," Marisee said. "But it doesn't matter. Now we're inside, we can go to him."

"You're still certain he will see you?"

"Once he knows who I am, he'll see me."

Please don't ask me again if I'm sure of that, Robert, she thought. He didn't.

There were many doors leading out of the kitchen. The first one opened on to steps down to a cellar. The rottenness seemed stronger here. Marisee closed the door again quickly. The next door took them out to a hallway that ended in a narrow staircase. The stairs were wooden and plain, for servants only.

"Lady Hibbert meets her most important friends in the drawing room," Robert said, "and the other ones in the parlour."

A mansion this huge must be full of drawing rooms and parlours, though Marisee reckoned that the room would have to be especially big and grand if that's where the Guild Masters met. She and Robert crept up towards the next floor, stopped and listened. Marisee peeked around the banister along a narrow corridor. She hoped that all the archers were outside. She did not want an arrow in the nose.

"It's clear," she said.

Robert tilted his head. "Listen."

There was the sound of men's voices from the floor above. "It's the Guild Masters," Marisee said. It was perfect, even better than just the Lord Mayor. They would all know who Grandma was because she'd had to negotiate with the river underneath here for this mansion to be built in the first place. Perhaps they even knew more about the Freedom of London. Marisee ran up the last few steps, ignoring Robert hissing at her to stop.

The voices came from behind a panelled door. Her hand was on the handle when fingers grasped her shoulder. A palm clapped across her mouth. There was a flash of muddy, torn red silk.

"Wait," Robert said. "Listen to what they're saying first. You have to be sure you can trust them."

Marisee wanted to go in now! She trusted them more than this boy she'd just met. But it was a good idea to hear what they were saying first and time her entrance for the best effect. She released the handle and pressed her ear against the wood. She wished she owned an ear trumpet, like Mr Reynolds, the village cheesemaker. All she could hear were murmurs and mumbles. They were definitely all men, though, and one of them must be walking around, because suddenly his voice was louder, as if he was standing just the other side of the door. Marisee and Robert quickly pulled away, but the door didn't open. They slipped back into place.

"... bewitched fog," he said. "It is only the poor who succumb..."

So, they knew that much. Good. In a moment, she would open that door and tell them about Grandma disappearing and how this sleeping sickness has something to do with the Freedom. Her hand rested on the handle again. She was shaking. Could she, someone they thought of as a child, stand in front of these men and ask them to help her?

Yes, she could. But she would listen for a little longer. Marisee pushed her ear harder against the wood as the man moved away again and his voice returned to a dull mumble. Then, did someone else say "keeper"? She mouthed the word to Robert. He nodded.

"You keep swearing by the truce, Lord Mayor!" a different voice shouted. "But the Dragons warned us that the Keeper should not hold the Freedom!"

Another man cut in: "You gave a mere woman the most powerful weapon we own! Now she has run away with it!"

"No, she hasn't!" Marisee meant to say it under her breath, but it came out a bit too loud.

Robert shot her a worried look. There was silence inside, and then a man spoke.

"My understanding is that she has taken it to safety."

A chair scraped across the floor.

"But you have no proof, Lord Mayor! Do all the good Guildsmen here know the worth of what has been taken? This woman, this Well Keeper, has stolen away with

125

the Freedom of London! Do you all understand what it contains?"

There were more words that Marisee could not hear, but that was because the Guild Masters were shouting over each other. A voice she now recognized as the Lord Mayor shouted for order, and all was quiet again. The Lord Mayor passed back towards the door.

"... Four elements to rebuild London: Dragon fire, Fumi air, Chad water and ancient Magog clay..."

A bell clanged three times in the chamber. Chairs scraped back.

"I think they're leaving," Marisee said. "Perhaps we'd better wait until he's alone."

"I think we're too late for that, Marisee."

As Robert spoke, Marisee felt the sharp point of an arrow jab the back of her neck.

"Turn around slowly," a man whispered.

She did, very slowly. Robert's hands were already in the air. There were two archers. One aimed his arrow at her. Robert was staring at the second arrow, which was pointing at his chest. The chamber door clicked behind her, sliding across the smooth floor as it opened. There was a bark of laughter.

"Children? We are to fear children now?"

"It seems that my Chief Yeoman is so afraid of children that he must ring the warning bell." It was the Lord Mayor's voice. "He cannot even keep them out of the building."

A flush spread across the archer's face. Marisee bit back a smile. She didn't have time to enjoy his discomfort because this was her chance! She spun around and found herself staring at the Lord Mayor's tightly-buttoned brocade waistcoat. She looked up. His face was round but folded into wrinkles. His eyebrows jutted out as if trying to fly away from his forehead. Beyond him was a long wooden table in a white panelled room. The chairs were pushed aside because the Guild Masters were on their feet, a few with swords in their hands.

"It's me, Lord Mayor!" Marisee's words rushed out. "I'm Madam Blackwell's granddaughter! My grandma is the Keeper of the Wells."

She looked from one Guildsman to the other. None looked pleased to see her. A tall man in a dark curled wig strutted towards her. He shoved his sword back into a black leather scabbard that bore the Goldsmiths' coat of arms.

"So it is your grandmother who has stolen the

Freedom," he said.

"She hasn't stolen it! She's keeping it safe!"

"Is she, indeed? Tell me, where is she *keeping it safe?*"

"I … I … don't know, but—"

The Goldsmith placed a hand on the Lord Mayor's shoulder and whispered in his ear. The Lord Mayor nodded.

"Lower your arms, yeomen," he ordered.

Marisee breathed out. She turned to smile at Robert. *See?* she wanted to say. She'd known that the Lord Mayor would want to speak to her!

"Lock the intruders in the cellar until we call for them," the Lord Mayor said.

"No!" Marisee yelled. "You can't do this! You don't understand! I need your help and—"

The archer grabbed Marisee's arm with more force than he needed. He was obviously not happy about being embarrassed in front of the Guild Masters and the Lord Mayor.

"I want to stop the sickness," Marisee cried. "I want to make sure the Freedom is safe!"

The Goldsmith nodded. "They are spies, Lord Mayor."

Marisee felt her fury rising. "How dare you say that?

We are not spies!"

"Really?" the Goldsmith said. "Didn't we find you outside this door listening for secrets? Who are you working for?"

Why wouldn't they listen? "We are not working for anyone!" Marisee took a deep breath and lowered her voice. She would make herself sound polite. "Lord Mayor, you know my grandmother is the Keeper of…"

"Quiet!" The Goldsmith tapped his sword hilt. "You will tell us who has employed you, one way or another. Perhaps a visit to Newgate Press Yard will loosen your tongue."

THE
CELLAR

The cellar was dark. Robert did not like the dark. He had spent much of the journey from Barbados to England in a tiny cabin below the waterline. He had been given a hammock to sleep in because Lord Hibbert had been very clear: Robert was valuable property and must not be given to his wife damaged. The cabin boy whose hammock Robert had taken was forced to sleep on a blanket on a wooden chest. He'd been furious and would often poke Robert with sticks in the night and once placed a live rat next to his pillow. Robert would rather have slept on the chest. The swaying and sagging hammock had felt like an impossible bed. He'd spend most of the night bracing himself in case he fell out.

He and Marisee could not fight the archers. Two more had appeared, each grabbing an arm and dragging him and Marisee back through the kitchen. They had shoved them into the cellar and locked the door. They had not left a candle.

He and Marisee sat on the cold brick steps with their backs pressed against the door. Beyond was blackness.

"They *will* come for us soon," Marisee said. "They'll realize their mistake."

Even she didn't sound like she believed it.

"And if they don't?" he asked gently.

"They will. They'll realize that they need us to help them cure the sickness."

"What's the Press Yard they mentioned?"

Marisee swallowed so hard he could hear it. "They torture traitors at Newgate prison. They lay them down and put weights on their chest until they say what the warder wants."

"Or they die."

"Yes. But they won't do that to us."

Robert wasn't so sure. That tall man looked like he

enjoyed his power. He reminded Robert of Mr Soothing, the overseer at the plantation. He had delighted in his cruelties. He had beaten one of Robert's cousins so badly her nose and wrist had been broken, simply because a pot of soup had boiled over.

"We can't stay here waiting for them to change their mind," Robert said. "Remember those children we saw sleeping?" And Lizzie, in the broom cupboard. "If they don't wake up, they'll die. We have to stop this sickness."

"Then Grandma can come home too," Marisee said, quietly.

Robert stood up and felt along the door for the handle. He found it and twisted it backwards and forwards as hard as he could. It stayed locked.

"There might be another door at the other end of the cellar," he said. "It would be easier for the tradesmen to deliver barrels there than carry everything through the kitchen and down the steps."

"How do you know this?" she asked.

"I spend most of my time in Lady Hibbert's kitchen."

Marisee made a small puzzled noise, then he felt her dress brush against his arm as she stood up. "Let's go and find it."

They fumbled their way down the steps. For once,

his thin slippers were useful. He could feel the ground beneath his feet, the uneven bricks and slight slopes. Marisee shuffled slowly, slipping and stumbling.

"Why don't you walk behind me?" he said. "Place your hand on my shoulder."

They changed places. He took a few careful steps forward and bumped his knee hard on something wooden. Marisee crashed into the back of him.

"Sorry," he said.

"What is it?"

He reached out his hand and touched it. Curved wood panels, strips of metal, a tap. "A barrel. It's a big one."

Robert felt his way around the giant barrel and then along to the next one. They must be stacked up in a row. That made it easier. He and Marisee moved from barrel to barrel with no sound but their feet on the tiles and hands tapping the wood. At last, Robert reached out and there was just empty air. He edged forward, arms reaching out ahead of him until his fingertips touched brick. He followed a curve of arch across to a wooden panel.

"A door!" he whispered. "Here it is!"

He swept his hand across it to find the door handle.

It rattled and clinked but didn't open. He grasped a heavy chain wrapped around the handle, but it ended in a padlock. He stepped back. Marisee took his place, pulling and pushing at the door. It was followed by a thump and a yelp of pain. She had kicked it. It was much sturdier than the winnowing door in the pump room.

"There must be some way to open it," Marisee said.

The darkness was so heavy that Robert couldn't even see her next to him. There were no windows in the cellar to escape through, but could they hide behind the barrels when the yeomen came and make a run for it? That wasn't the best plan. Did he really want to test the aim of an archer who was already angry with them?

So how else could they get out?

Robert had a thought. When he had first arrived at the Hibberts's, there had been another scullery maid working with Lizzie. Her name was Mary-Anne, and she was the only person Robert had met who would stand up to Mrs Wandle. Late one night, when Robert was curled up on his thin mattress by the dying fire, a candle had crossed the kitchen. It had been set down on the table near the pantry. Mrs Wandle locked it every night and took the key to her room with her. He had watched while Mary-Anne took something from beneath her nightcap and poked it into the padlock. She bent over it for a while, then suddenly there was a click and it opened. She went into the pantry and came out with a bulging bag of food. She retrieved her candle and left the kitchen. If she had known that Robert had seen her, she hadn't shown it. She did not appear that morning, or ever again. Mrs Wandle, however, bought a bigger padlock and thicker chain.

"Do you know how to open a locked door with no key?" he asked Marisee.

"No! I'm not a thief!"

"We're trying to get out, not in!"

"I still don't know how to do it. We've no need to lock our house. But…" She jumped up and he heard her test the lock again. "Do you remember Honest Jack?"

"No."

"*Everybody* knows about Jack Sheppard."

Robert sighed. Marisee obviously didn't realize that he hadn't been in England for very long. "I don't. Please tell me."

"He was a famous thief. They kept putting him in prison and he kept escaping. Once, he even showed the gaolers how to unlock a padlock with a nail. Maybe we can do that."

"Do we have a nail?"

"Perhaps we can find one on the floor. Anything with a spike. That should work."

Anything long, strong and thin… He pulled his turban from his head. The air was cool across his scalp and ears. He unpinned the giant brooch and felt the cloth unravel on his lap. The pin was thick and, like the mount, was made from iron to support that heavy cutglass gem. Lady Hibbert had wanted the biggest possible brooch to show him off to her friends. He felt for the keyhole again and gently inserted the pin. It was hard to hold steady as the glass was bulky. It would be easier to smash the glass from the mount, but he didn't want attention from any guards who might be lurking in the kitchen.

"Can you hold it?" he asked Marisee. "Gently, so I can still turn the pin."

She cradled the glass and he tried again. He felt the pin connect with metal inside the lock. Now what? How did keys work? They turned and something was unlocked. He twisted the pin but nothing happened. He thought harder. When a key fitted into a lock, the cuts in the blade fitted into notches. What if the end of the pin had to fit into a notch to make it unlock? He wiggled the pin around and, for a moment, it seemed to catch in something. He prodded it around again. Yes. A gap. The tip of the pin slid in and he twisted it gently clockwise, but too far. The pin slipped out. He tried again. He had to be very, very gentle. Twisting and – *click*. The padlock opened.

"Yes!" Marisee said. "Well done!"

It seemed such a long time since anyone had said that to him. He withdrew the pin, closed it and clipped it back under its hook. He pushed it into his pocket. It might be useful again. The thick ribbons of fabric that had been his turban were heaped by the door. They could be useful too. It didn't matter. They would stay right there. He never wanted to see them again.

Robert pushed the door open slowly. There was a flash of orange light, then complete darkness.

"Can you see anything?" he asked.

"I can't." Marisee's voice trembled a little. "But that smell…"

He must have been holding his breath as he picked the lock, because how could he miss the stench? It smelled like spoiled meat mixed with the reeking smoke blown across Bloomsbury from a nearby brewer's yard. The stench was so thick it might press through his skin into his blood.

"I don't think we should go in that room." Marisee's

voice was muffled by the hand over her mouth and nose.

"I agree." Robert started to close the door again.

The door banged open above the steps to the kitchen at the far end of the cellar. Lamplight flashed along the barrels.

"There they are!" a man called.

"Get them, then!" It was the Goldsmith. "Alive or dead!"

The air quivered to the side of Robert's face. An arrow bounced off the wall above him. He pushed open the door again. It was their only chance. He grabbed Marisee's arm and they fell into the stinking darkness, shoving the door shut behind them. Robert felt for a bolt or a latch. There was none. He and Marisee leaned with all their weight against the wood, bracing themselves for the Goldsmith and yeomen to force it open. There was just silence, then a chuckle.

"This is even better," the Goldsmith called. "Now the Lord Mayor cannot blame me for your deaths."

Robert heard the padlock click shut. He tugged the door handle, but it was firmly locked – this time with him and Marisee on the inside.

Robert swallowed hard, then wished he hadn't. That stench was in his throat now. What was it? He held his sleeve across his nose. He wanted to speak, but the smell would slip down his throat and curdle in his stomach.

Marisee coughed. "I think…" Her voice was so muffled he could hardly understand her. "A… on…"

"I don't understand," he croaked back.

"I … think…" She was taking a tiny breath with each word. "It's. Dragons."

Dragons?

The floor moved around Robert's feet. After rainfall in Barbados, there were pale, tiny ants that swarmed out from their underground nests. He would think it was just sand until he drew close enough to see the hundreds of tiny bodies scurrying around in the dirt. This felt the same, but there were so many more of them, hundreds and hundreds of tiny moving creatures.

A pinprick of orange light glowed in a corner of the dark room. Then another and another until a fiery orange rippled across the wall. More lights flicked on and still that feeling of swirling and swarming, across the ground, swelling up the walls, covering the ceiling. And as the orange light grew brighter and wider, Robert saw them. Thousands and thousands of dark dots scuttling towards the orange core, then clicking in place like … like snake scales. It was taking a shape. A shortened, stubby body. A long, tapering tail ending in an arrowhead tip. A narrow head with a low, wide brow. The eye sockets were dark and empty. The jaw heavy and strong. It clung to the wall like a giant gecko.

"Dragon," Robert whispered.

"Yes," Marisee whispered back. "Dragon."

Dragon. Dragon? Dragon! The blazing man-eating beast had escaped from legends and was clinging to the wall opposite him. Yes, it was a dragon – and they should run! But all he could do was stare at it. Terror had gripped him too completely to move.

Marisee shook the handle.

"Let us out! Please, let us out!"

Silence.

The dragon's body went dark. Only its head and tail still glowed.

"Once you enter, you are mine." Its voice wheezed like old bellows. The jaws opened wide. A dark tongue snaked out and coiled around Marisee and pulled her towards it. Robert stood there, still frozen. It was a real Dragon. It was taking his friend. All he could do was watch. Marisee tried to slap the tongue away, but her hands passed straight through. Her boots scraped along the tiles as she was drawn closer and closer to those jaws.

"Robert!" she screamed. "Do something!"

But still, he couldn't move. The stench and now the heat made his head swim. His eyes blurred and stung as the cellar filled with smoke.

"Robert!"

The tongue tip seemed to waggle as the dots joined and separated into dark bands that tightened around Marisee's waist. She had thrown her weight backwards, but it made no difference. Her shoes scraped the tough earth floor as she was dragged forwards.

"Stop." One word was all Robert could manage and little more than a whisper. He cleared his throat. "Stop! This is Marisee Blackwell! She is the Well Keeper's granddaughter. You cannot harm her. It's … it's in the truce."

The tongue uncoiled slowly. Marisee dropped to the floor. Instantly, the tongue lashed out again, wrapping around Robert's arm. It was tight as a rope. Robert's jacket sleeve bulged beneath it. The dark tongue was spotted with pinpricks of bright orange that seared through the silk and stung his skin.

Hands grasped his other arm.

"Let go of him!" Marisee yelled. "He's my friend. You're not allowed to hurt him, either."

Marisee was pulling him with her whole weight. The Dragon tightened its grip, pulling him the other way. His arms ached, his shoulder clicked.

"Marisee!" His chest felt stretched too thin to talk. "Make it stop."

"I'm trying!"

"No, you're splitting me in half! Talk to it!"

"Yes," she muttered. "That's a good idea, but say what? I've never spoken to a Dragon before."

"If you don't think of something, I'm going to die."

She still held him but lifted her head to face the beast. "Ummmm … you are failing your Guilds, Dragon." Her voice became louder. "All Guilds will be destroyed if you harm us."

The Dragon's torso burned bright as it drew Robert closer. He could just see the outline of dark wings tucked beneath it. Soon, the heat from its body would scorch his skin.

"The City of London will fall!" Marisee shouted at it. "And it will be your fault!"

For a moment, Robert was still, and then the tongue splintered into thousands of tiny black creatures. They streamed through the folds of his sleeves, dropping on to the floor and flowed back towards the wall. Robert swallowed hard again. His mouth tasted of the stinking room. He could not – must not – be sick.

The Dragon's head turned towards Marisee. The rest of its body did not move, but the neck stretched longer and longer until that head was inches from Marisee's, and those empty eyes were staring into Marisee's own. She took a tiny step back, then straightened her shoulders. She didn't look away. Robert knew he would have. Yes, her grandmother must be a strong woman to go down that well, but Marisee was strong too. Perhaps she didn't know it yet.

"Justify yourself, girl," the Dragon said.

"You guard the Guilds and know everything about them." There was no wobble in Marisee's voice. "You must know what's happening outside. You must know about the sickness in London. People will sleep until they die. Or they will rise and attack. They are like a sleeping army that can destroy everything. And whoever is behind this, they are using the army to search for the Freedom."

"This sickness cannot destroy us," the Dragon said.

It split apart again. Thousands and thousands of tiny glowing sparks rippling out across the ceiling and walls, then gliding back together, darkening into its near-solid dragon shape.

"War, earthquakes, ice or fire. We have survived it all. We can be many or one. We can hide in the tiniest cracks or fight the world with fire."

"But what of the Guilds' gold?" Marisee said slyly. "Will that survive too?"

The Dragon stayed silent.

"How much treasure was lost in the Great Fire?" Marisee leaned towards the beast. "Do you want to lose even more? Walbrook believes that whatever – or whoever – wants the Freedom wants a new London. There may be no place for Dragons there. Do you want to hide in the cracks for ever with no gold to guard?"

The Dragon's jaws opened slightly. Robert could see the flickering tongue inside. The stench of rotting meat rolled over them. Marisee flinched but carried on.

"We must find the Freedom," Marisee said. "Help us. You are ancient, you have seen so much history. Tell us what you know."

There was a silence. *It's going to eat us*, Robert thought. He tried not to imagine how it would happen – how it would feel to be pulled into the void between those fiery jaws.

The Dragon's tail shimmered orange as it twisted and turned. The arrowhead tip cracked against the brick wall as its whole body lifted away. It thumped to the floor and lumbered towards them. Its legs seemed too short to hold its body. Its splayed feet ended in knife-sharp claws. Marisee pressed her hand against Robert's. She was trembling as much as him. Her face still showed no fear.

The tail looped around them both until Robert and Marisee were standing inside a glowing orange circle. The arrowhead tapped the ground in front of them.

"You misjudge us, girl," the Dragon wheezed. "We can outlast this threat. We have been here from the beginning, long before the first Solids splashed their way through the marshes. We know Solids well. They will always seek gold. We just have to be patient." The tail tapped again. "But ... we are bored. There is little to entertain us in this small, fetid room. There are no more battles, no more human flesh – although the Master Goldsmith helps us when he can. He is sly, that one. Now he has given us two, as food and entertainment... We wish to enjoy both." *Tap, tap.* This time the tiles sparked. "First, the entertainment. This is what we will offer you..." The tail coiled tighter. "We will offer you a riddle for your lives."

Marisee and Robert looked at each other.

"Are you good at answering riddles?" Marisee asked.

Robert shook his head. He wasn't even sure what a riddle was.

A strange sound came from the Dragon, almost like laughter. The tail disappeared, then reformed just around Marisee. The arrowhead prodded her heart. The smouldering dark head turned to Robert.

"So you will be the one to answer, boy."

"No!" Marisee shouted. "That's not fair!"

The tail spun her around until she was facing the wall.

"Say nothing, girl, or the bargain will be void."

The Dragon seemed to take a deep breath in. Its head blazed a brighter orange. The eye sockets darkened.

"You have one chance, boy," the Dragon said. "The Goldsmith has no stomach to see how we devour the terrified men he pushes towards us. But if your answer is wrong, you will be the first Solid for hundreds of years to see us feed. Once we have finished the girl, we will feed on you."

It was not just Robert's legs that had frozen. His mouth, his voice, even his thoughts were stuck. Only his heart raced so quickly it hurt. He had to calm down. He had to think properly. He closed his eyes a moment. He must open a place in his fear for other thoughts to trickle through.

He had hated the plantation with everything in him, but there had been moments where he would let his mind wander free. When Zeke had whispered stories into his ears late at night as they sat together in the cooler air outside the cabin. When he had watched the hummingbirds hover above a blossom before darting inside. When he had waited as his mother split apart ripe green oranges, knowing that the segment would burst with juice in his mouth.

His mother, his sisters, his brother, his aunties; their love was as tough as a shield around him. He had promised them that he would survive here. And he would. He'd often tried to explain to Mama why he kept asking questions. He wanted to know how the world worked. She'd said that it was a good thing, but that he should do it secretly. *Watch, listen and learn all you can, my little boy. One day it will help you.*

What did he know about Dragons that could help him? They guarded the City of London. It was the place of money, trade and deals. Robert had no money. The only thing he had to trade was his life and the Dragon had already laid claim to that. But...

"If we are to be your entertainment *and* your food," he said, "then your side of the bargain falls short. The deal must be fair. If I answer your riddle correctly, you will tell us what you know about the Freedom of London. Then you will set us free. Alive."

"Ohhhh." The Dragon shuffled. "You consider yourself a dealmaker, boy. Yes, we will accept your deal, but you have one chance to answer correctly. Remember that."

"I will." Robert stared into its empty eyes. "Now, ask me your riddle."

Marisee glanced around at him. He shook his head slightly.

Please, Marisee. Trust me. Their only hope was that the Dragon would keep to its word. But if Marisee helped him, she would die. She must have understood. She turned back towards the wall.

"This is our riddle," the Dragon said.

Here it came. Marisee still faced the wall. Her shoulders were straight and she seemed to stand tall as if saying, *Be brave. You can do this.*

"I burn every night, but my fire is cold.

I shine like gems, but never pure gold.

I blink and I wink, but I am not an eye.

Answer quick, or your friend will die."

The Dragon laughed another breathy laugh. "And

so will you, boy. We will count to five. Then you must answer. One!"

Robert thought hard. *My fire is cold.* He had once heard Lizzie complain that the ice in the Hibberts's ice house was so cold it burned her hands.

"Two!"

So was the answer ice? *I shine like gems.* Ice sometimes sparkled different colours in sunlight, didn't it? He didn't know whether it ever shone gold. He hadn't seen that much ice.

"Three!"

But, of course, it could be glass. What about the brooch on his turban? It shone like gems, but it was glass! Did it blink? In a way, when the sun caught the sharp edges.

"Four!"

That had to be it. The Dragon would be crafty. They'd choose something that Robert wouldn't expect them to know about. That must be it. His brooch.

The Dragon's tail shifted. "Five! One answer only."

Robert opened his mouth. *My brooch!* Then he closed his mouth again. He watched the Dragon's tail as it coiled and uncoiled, the tiny spots of colour burning and fading. He remembered nights in Barbados, shining spots piercing the night sky, blinking and winking, the colours of gems.

"The answer," he said calmly, "is a firefly."

Nothing moved. Then everything moved. The Dragon exploded out. The tiny black creatures writhing as a column of fire raged through its centre. It whirled across the room towards Robert. The walls themselves seemed to turn with it, the ceiling spun and the floor…

"I guessed correctly!" Robert shouted. "Remember the terms of our deal! You must set us free *and* tell us about the Freedom!"

The floor! A silver circle was etched into the ground, a silver handle pushing through the earth as if driven up from the other side.

"The Freedom!" The Dragon's voice skittered off the walls and ceiling. "It is all our power in one small, golden box. Now go! Before I change my mind!"

"We need to know more," Marisee said. "That's not enough."

"Go!" The Dragon roared.

Robert grasped the silver handle in the floor and tugged it hard.

FLEET

Marisee stared at Robert. He had saved them! He had solved the riddle! One day she would have to ask him what exactly a firefly was. Now, though, wasn't the time.

"Come on, Marisee!" Robert yelled. "Help me!"

Heat flicked at Marisee's skin as the Dragon spun through the room. She crouched next to Robert and grabbed the silver handle, braced herself and yanked. The ground inside the silver circle shifted, loosened, and then cracked apart like the skin of a roast chestnut.

There was a whoosh of air and a smell like stagnant water. They peered down into a dark hole. Threads of silver shone at the bottom. Marisee and Robert looked at each other. They had seen threads like that before.

"Walbrook?" Their words came out at the same time.

They stared back into the hole. Lady Walbrook or the Dragon? What was worse?

"Um…" Robert said.

"Yes?"

"I think the well mouth is shrinking."

She pressed her finger against the edge. Robert was right. It was slowly pushing inwards.

"You broke the deal!" Marisee shouted. "You said you would set us free!"

A head-shape pushed itself out of the spiral, the tongue uncoiled, dripping white hot sparks. "You are free to leave, but the well cannot stay open for ever. It's not our magic. Go now. Or linger with us, if you wish. We would be most happy for you to stay!"

"Er … Marisee?" Robert said.

She glanced back at the well mouth. As she watched, it shrunk even more. Soon, she would not be able to fit through it.

"I won't forget this, Dragon!" she shouted.

It didn't reply, but there was that breathy hiss that sounded like laughter.

Marisee sat on the edge of the hole, legs dangling down into nothing.

"I won't be hurt," she whispered. "I'm the Well Keeper's granddaughter. I won't be hurt…"

The edges of the hole pressed against her skirt. She had to move now, or it would be too small for Robert to follow her. She pushed down on the ground either side of her and let herself drop.

She was in the air for less than a moment, then caught in a damp web of silver threads that drew her silently down. Water closed over her head, soft and bright, with a swift undertow beneath. If the web hadn't held her, she would have been swept away. Somehow, she could breathe and her eyes stayed open. Glints of silver darted around her like silent fish. The web tightened and she rose again, her head breaking the surface.

Robert's head bobbed up next to her. She breathed out in relief. Where were they now? Marisee glanced up at the ceiling. It looked like hardened clay pressed between cracked stone beams. There was no sign of any well mouth at all. She moved her feet. She was standing on stones, waist-deep in a wide channel of water threaded with the silver light. The channel ran the length of a long room. A heavy stone table sat at one end, its surface crammed with glass jars filled with shining water. Nooks of different sizes lined the walls, with a stone bench in each and a jar of glowing water hanging on a hook overhead. More glowing jars lined the edges of the channel. Small high alcoves in the spaces between the nooks were filled with statues of women in long robes.

Robert was already walking out of the water. His clothes turned from dark to lighter as they instantly dried. Marisee followed him, the weight of the water that soaked her dress falling away.

"It's like a church," Robert said.

Marisee nodded. He was right. *It's because of the stillness*, she thought. The glass jars could easily have held church candles and that stone table was like an altar.

"Is that you?" The voice came from behind a nook hidden by a folding wooden screen. It was followed by a fit of coughing. The air turned dank. It made Marisee think of November streets heavy with rotting leaves and mud turned by the wheels of carts bearing the dead.

"Who is it?" Robert whispered.

"I don't know." Marisee wished that she did. If this place belonged to Walbrook and the Chads, she *should* know more about it. But she didn't. It was another of Grandma's secrets.

"Is that you?" The voice came again. It sounded old and weak. "Come to me." The last word was lost in another bout of coughing.

It sounded like gaol fever. Marisee had heard the endless coughs of the prisoners in the basement cells of Newgate prison when she had helped Grandma hand vials of their water through the bars. Marisee had been terrified by the groaning and calls for help from the filthy cells and the dirty, scabbed fingers reaching through the bars for coins. Grandma said that fever killed more prisoners than the triple tree gallows.

"Please." The voice was barely louder than breath. "If you are Madam Blackwell's granddaughter, I must speak to you. But quick, before Walbrook returns."

"You know who I am?" Marisee called back.

"Yes!" Each word seemed to tire the speaker more. "Come!"

Marisee started towards the hidden nook. Robert held her back.

"Is it safe?" he said.

"I'm not sure," Marisee rubbed her wrists. The skin was still sore from Walbrook's binding. "But I think that whoever is there means us no harm."

Marisee walked towards the screen and folded it aside. The rank smell grew worse. An elderly woman lay on a bed, covered by a blanket. Her hands resting on top of it were swollen, her face marked with bruises, or dirt? It was hard to tell. Her bonnet strings were loosened so her head rested back on it. Strands of pale, thin hair were crusted with dirt. Her eyes were closed and, as she breathed, the rancid smell seemed to bloat around her.

She raised her hand and her eyelids fluttered. "Come closer."

Marisee tried to gulp back air as she took a step closer.

"Bring water," the old woman said.

Marisee hurried back to the channel and took one of the jars. She brought it into the nook.

"Dip in your hand," the old woman gasped. "Sprinkle."

The water was cool. As soon as Marisee's fingertips touched the surface, the air around her freshened. She flicked the water around. Beside her, Robert took a deep breath. As the water touched the old woman's skin, it brightened and she opened her eyes. They were the colour of bone, the whites flecked with black. She pushed herself up until she was half-sitting.

"I have been weak for so long," she said. "When I was young, I was powerful. I raced past what you now call Battle Bridge all the way down to Thames Rex. I pushed at my banks like nothing could hold me in."

Now Marisee understood. "You're Fleet," she said.

Fleet's head bowed slightly as if she barely had strength to lift it again. "She was my river, but the poison – who can withstand it for hundreds and hundreds of years? Your tanneries filled me with boiled bones, your butchers with rotting offal and the parts that even the most desperate of you cannot eat. You defiled me by dropping your own waste into my waters. I can take it no more."

"I'm sorry," Marisee said. "I truly am."

Another tiny nod. "I believe you. My sorrow runs deep too. I felt your arrival. I do not know how you came here. Perhaps it is a dying river's luck."

"Dying?" Marisee stepped towards her.

Fleet raised her hand. "I must talk. We have little time. You are in the Mithraeum. No Solid has set foot here since my sister, Walbrook, instructed the Romans to build this temple for her on the banks of her once mighty river. This is where we tend our sick."

"So you *will* be cured?" Robert asked.

"No, child," Fleet said. "My time has passed. That is why I must talk with you. And then you must leave me."

Marisee saw Robert's eyes dart around the nook, looking for a door.

A smile flickered across Fleet's lips and faded. "Remember that this is Walbrook's domain, child. It's made for ones like us to come and go, not Solids. But I will find a way for you to leave. Believe me."

Robert frowned. "No riddles, please."

Fleet sighed, though it may have been a laugh. "*That's* how you came to be here. Riddles!" Another weak laugh. "I had hoped that after so many centuries those Dragons would be less predictable." She heaved herself even further up the bed. Her nails clawed at the blanket. "I hear there is a strange sickness across London."

"It's a sleeping sickness," Marisee said. "It comes from the Ether. Robert and I are trying to stop it."

"We believe that someone wants the Freedom," Robert added. "They're using the sleepwalkers to find it and…" Fleet raised her hand again. Robert fell silent.

A single tear ran down her face. "Tell me, what keeps the sleeping in the Ether?" Fleet's voice trembled as she spoke. Another tear followed the first.

"Lady Fleet?" Robert crouched by her side and took her hand. "Are you in pain? Is there something we can do to help you?"

Fleet breathed out slowly. Marisee caught the tang of decay.

"Yes, children. It is why I ask about the sleeping. I feel that there is happiness, but also great sadness."

"They're dreaming of the loved ones who have passed on," Marisee said. "The dreams are so real, they don't want to wake."

"Now I understand why my heart is so troubled." Fleet paused, as if trying to gather her breath. "No elemental can enter the Ether and no Solid has the power to change it. But this sadness…" She took one jagged breath, then one more. "It is the sadness that Solids feel when a life has ended too soon."

Robert looked away from Fleet quickly and stared at the floor.

"A few years ago in your human time, I tried to help a child. I fear I was too late. It is how I know that sadness. She was filled with it and I felt it too." Fleet's stiff fingers raked through her thin hair. "She had been thrown into my river, already barely alive. How can Solids be so cruel to their own? I carried her to safety. Or, at least, I think

I did. It's so hard to remember." Fleet sighed. "Walbrook brought me here soon afterwards. The sadness about the girl was so strong it spread through me into my own sickness."

"You think she has changed the dreams?" Marisee asked.

Fleet shrugged. The effort exhausted her. "I asked Walbrook to search for her, but she said she found no one. I have always wondered what happened to her. Maybe I really was too late. But then this sickness came and there is something about it, something that is familiar."

Marisee crouched next to Robert. At last! This was something that could really help them. "Who was the child, Lady Fleet? Do you know her name?"

"I am sorry. I never knew it." Fleet's head tilted sideways as if she was listening. "You must go! Walbrook is returning!"

"Do you remember anything about the girl?" Robert said. "Please, Lady Fleet. Anything will help us."

Fleet pushed herself back down on her bed and pulled the blanket across herself. "My sister is not a patient spirit. She will be furious if she finds you here. You must leave by the door above the end of my bed. Be ready."

Marisee stood up. Surely Lady Fleet must remember something else, even a tiny detail. All they had to do was ask a few more questions. But, on the other hand, Marisee did not want to meet Walbrook here in her own temple.

But it was too late. The empty jar in her hand crackled with silver and every trace of decay was blown away. The air that settled smelled of damp fields.

"Sister Fleet?" Walbrook was behind the screen.

Fleet squeezed her eyes shut and clenched the blanket tight between her fingers. Her lips moved silently.

"Look!" Robert pointed. "Up there!"

The faint trace of a circle appeared in the curved ceiling. The screen was shoved aside and it clattered to the ground.

"You! How dare you!" The colours moved beneath Walbrook's skin. Silver-blue, silver-green, grey, silver. Her pale eyes were flecked with dark like Fleet's. "No Solid is allowed here without my permission!" She took a step closer. The colours swirled darker. "*No one* is allowed here without my permission."

"Be still, sister," Fleet said. "They have done no harm."

Walbrook took another step. "Of course they have

done harm." Tendrils of silver snaked through Walbrook's hair. "They divert us. They culvert us. They steal from us and replace what they have stolen with filth. They have made you sick, Fleet!"

The circle in the ceiling was brighter now, as if it was burning into the brick. Marisee's heart was beating hard, the pale scars on her wrists throbbing.

"Lady Walbrook," she said. "We didn't mean to come here! We're sorry!"

Silver dribbled down Walbrook's chin and pooled in a crease below her neck.

"I don't believe you! They sent you, didn't they? The Dragons or the Fumis. They sent you to spy on me!"

"No, Lady Walbrook!"

The hole was wider and darker. There was a bright pinpoint of light in the centre.

"Go through now," Fleet urged. "I can't keep the door open for long."

The edges around the hole looked solid, strong enough for Marisee to grasp and pull herself up and through.

"Come on, Robert!"

"Lady Fleet?" Robert pleaded. "Is there anything else that you can tell us? This child might be important."

"Our time is over." Fleet's lips barely moved. "Try the dead. Ask them your questions. They know everything."

She closed her eyes and the circle flickered.

"Robert! We have to go through before it shrinks again!"

Robert stood up. "Thank you, Lady Fleet."

There was the sound of a whip crack. Robert froze. A thin ribbon of silver water had shot from Walbrook's mouth and wound itself around Robert's body.

"You may be protected, Well Keeper's granddaughter," Lady Walbrook said, "but the boy isn't. You have entered my temple. It is forbidden. It cannot go unpunished."

Fleet's eyes opened. They were completely black. "I invited them, Walbrook," she said. "Let him go."

Robert flinched as the ribbon tightened around his chest. Walbrook and Fleet stared at each other, then the ribbon fell in loose wet loops around Robert's feet.

"Trouble me again," Walbrook said, "and I will ensure there is no one to help you."

She turned her back on them and walked towards the stone table. The silver circle flickered again.

"You go first," Marisee said to Robert.

He jumped towards the hole, grasped the edges and scrabbled his way through. Marisee clambered on to the bed, grabbed the smooth edges of brick and, with Robert's help, sprang through like a jack-in-the-box. A gust of cold air almost blew her bonnet off.

"Where are we?" she asked.

"Where we need to be," Robert said. "Among the dead."

THE FUMI

Marisee was sitting on a stone path. There was no sign of the hole she had scrambled through. She stood up slowly and brushed down her skirts. The path cut through a churchyard. The church itself was topped by a great copper dome and a stone tower. In front of the church, there was a narrow alley and the back walls of a mansion house. Marisee recognized that clean stone. It was *the* Mansion House. The church probably sat right on top of the Walbrook river. Just a few feet away, on the other side of that wall, were the yeomen and a Dragon who would both quite happily kill them. Just below her feet, Lady Walbrook must already be making revenge plans. They had to leave, now.

Robert was studying a gravestone. He turned towards her and waved his arm at the rows of mounds and tombstones.

"*Try the dead*," he said. "But there are so many dead. How do we know which ones we must listen to?"

Marisee nodded her head towards the Mansion House and lowered her voice. "We have to find out quickly. There might be archers patrolling."

Robert moved to the next gravestone. "Lady Fleet made sure we came out here. She must have meant these dead."

"We came to this churchyard because that's where the door opened!" Marisee said. "What if the door opens again and it's Walbrook this time? That's if we aren't shot by the Goldsmith's archers first. We can't stay here!"

"So where do we go, Marisee?" Robert's hands were on his hips. "Lady Fleet was trying to help us!"

"How? She couldn't even tell us the name of the child!"

"Because she didn't know it! I think we're here because there's a clue somewhere." Robert turned away from Marisee and walked further down the row of graves.

Marisee looked around at the gravestones. There were so many. It would take days to check them all and she didn't even know who she was looking for. It was only afternoon, but the sky was darkening. Twilight was coming early, like it wanted to trick more of London into sleep. And they were still no closer to stopping the sickness or finding the Freedom. And she certainly didn't want to be in the churchyard when it was dark. She didn't want to be here at all, but Robert was right. Where *should* they go?

A scrap of paper blew across the churchyard, catching on the brambles. It freed itself, jittering across the tops of the uneven grass, before lifting in the air and floating towards Marisee. It brushed lightly against her nose, then dropped towards a gravestone. She wished she could just flutter from place to place like that.

Kweek!

The sound cut through the stillness. Robert looked around too. Was it a strange birdcall? Marisee could see no birds, not even rock doves.

Kweek!

It came from above her, high up near the church steeple. The weathervane's gold pennant swung to and fro.

"There's no wind to move it," Robert said, coming back to her.

The weathervane spun all the way until it pointed west.

Marisee jumped up. "It's telling us which way to go!"

The weathervane spun wildly again. This time it pointed east.

"Is it?" Robert asked.

"Is that supposed to help?" Marisee yelled up at it. "Because it's not!"

The pennant spun hard again as a cloud of smoke billowed towards it. Marisee could feel no heat. The pennant slowed, then squealed before stopping. The dark cloud stretched wide, like it was spreading its wings, then tipped away from the steeple and glided down to the churchyard.

Oh! Marisee felt a prickle of excitement. Was that what she thought it was? Surely it couldn't be anything else! "It's a Fumi, Robert! An air spirit!"

It was long and thin, like smoke twisting out of a chimney on a windy day. Its head was as wide as a shovel and its body as narrow as a broom-handle.

"That was not enjoyable." Its thin metallic voice scratched at the inside of Marisee's ears. Darkness curled where its mouth should be, two rents in the smoke formed eyes. "I haven't spun myself since 1666. It's something I've always preferred not to do. When that Wren fellow built those new churches, he changed the weathervanes. I really can't get used to them." The Fumi compressed into a thick, black column. "You Solids always make things worse."

Marisee gritted her teeth. How come the first Fumi she met had no manners? Perhaps all the elementals were rude. It was no surprise that they were always so close to war.

"I do not just mean the weathervanes," it said. "There is all your mundungus stink filling the sky. The air above is so heavy that even a Solid could walk on it. And now, even your dreams are sick! Must you ruin everything for yourselves?"

"I ... er..." Robert was staring at the Fumi. He seemed to collect himself. "I'm honoured to meet you." He gave a sweeping bow. Marisee wondered how many times a day he had to bow for Lady Hibbert. "Lady Fleet told us that we should ask the dead to help us stop the sickness, but we don't know how. Can you help us?"

The dark mouth swirled. "No. I cannot."

"Oh," Robert said. His shoulders slumped.

"I am not permitted to help you," the Fumi said. "The Articles confine us to minimal contact with Solids – which suits us well." The Fumi swelled and compressed. "But the Articles *do* allow for favours."

"Favours?" Marisee asked.

"Is that not the correct word?" The Fumi said. "I speak the languages of sparrows and chimneys and weathervanes. My Solid English requires refinement."

"Does that mean you can help us?" Marisee asked.

"It means that we can help each other. A favour for a favour. I have a friend. Their name is—"

The Fumi made a noise like a nail scraping across an anvil. Marisee shuddered and wanted to block her ears, but didn't want to appear rude, even if the Fumi's own manners may be lacking.

"That is their name in Weathervane," the Fumi said. "The first mouth-language we learn. Their true Fumi name is—" A patch of pink the size and shape of a petal blossomed around the Fumi's mouth, then faded. "I believe it beyond Solids' ability to pronounce our names correctly," it said.

"You would like us to help your friend?" Robert asked.

"I would like you to find my friend," the Fumi said.

Robert frowned. "Where did you lose them?"

"They have lost themself." It shook its shovel-head. "They are a nosy sort and decline to follow rules. We are rarely permitted to descend lower than the roofs, but my friend can never contain their curiosity. They go where they should not. They even..." The line mouth puckered into a tight circle and flattened again. "They even go beneath the ground. They were last sighted in the region of Montagu House in Bloomsbury. I believe that there is something called a *museum* there. My friend heard that it is as full of curiosities as they are themself. They wished to see them."

Marisee had no idea what the Fumi was talking about. Robert was nodding, though, like he understood. "There is a museum in Montagu House," he said, "on Great Russell Street, not far from the Hibberts's mansion. Some of Lady Hibbert's friends have visited it."

"Find my friend," the Fumi said. "And I will help you."

Marisee tried to keep her sigh quiet. "We want to help you, but the sickness is spreading quickly. Our friends are dreaming in the Ether and won't wake up unless..." Poor Camilla. Poor Cicely and Angelica.

"Unless they're woken up and used to search for the Freedom," Robert finished for her. "That's what they want. Lady Walbrook says that whoever holds it can create a new London."

The Fumi's smoky body gave another wiggle. "I have no care about London, new or old. *We* will survive. But I miss my friend as you miss yours. I fear that mine has become trapped."

"Trapped where?" Marisee asked.

"I do not know. I never go beneath the earth."

No, Marisee could not imagine this creature of smoke and air wafting around underground. "Do you mean it's stuck in a well or a tunnel?"

"Such words hurt my ears," the Fumi said. "In any language. But yes, I believe that is where they are. They have strayed somewhere that is forbidden and a Magog or one of your beloved Chads is holding them."

Marisee and Robert looked at each other. Did the Fumi expect them to fight another elemental?

"So you won't help us until we find your friend?" Marisee said quietly.

The Fumi turned so pale that for a moment all Marisee could see was its mouth. "We are not like the Dragons! We do not make deals that we try to break. I will help you first. If you succeed, then you must help me."

Oh! This was better!

"Yes," Marisee said, eagerly. "We *will* search for your friend if you help us now. I promise you that."

"Are you sure, Marisee?" Robert asked. "Where would we start looking?"

"In Bloomsbury!" she said. "Where the museum is! And we'll have Grandma to help us!"

She hoped that was true. So much.

Marisee made a sweeping bow towards the Fumi. "We accept your offer." She ignored Robert's questioning look. "A favour for a favour. Now, please tell us how the dead can help us."

The Fumi stretched so thin that Marisee could see the scrap of paper stuck to the tombstone behind it.

"You must follow your nose," it said.

Then it floated away. Just like that! All that was left was a strong smell of beef tallow and wood ash, then that too disappeared.

"No!" Marisee shouted. "That's not help! It…"

The scrap of paper unpeeled itself from the tombstone and drifted towards her, even though there was no breeze. Marisee made a grab for it, but it looped up, then dropped on to her nose. As she reached for it, an airy hand seemed to pluck it off and send it gliding back to the tombstone.

Robert reached for the paper. This time it didn't fly away. He handed it to her. She studied both sides. Each was blank.

"What am I supposed to do with this?" she asked.

She looked up at the weathervane again. It was still pointing east. Was that the way they were supposed to go? Perhaps the writing was secret, written in lemon juice, and she was supposed to smear it with coal dust to see it. Marisee didn't have any coal dust. And, thinking about it, the Fumi didn't have fingers to write with. She hoped it wasn't written in Weathervane language, screechy air on paper. That would not be helpful at all.

"It floated around the churchyard," Robert said. "What if it isn't the paper itself that's important? What if it's trying to lead us somewhere?"

"Yes," Marisee said. "To my nose. And I already know where that is."

Robert tapped the gravestone. "This is where it landed after your nose."

"We're in a graveyard. Of course it landed on a gravestone."

"But why this one? It landed here twice. What does it say?"

"I don't know! You're closest. You read it!"

"It would be better if you did," Robert said, quietly.

Marisee was not in the mood for this. The sky had

turned from greyish blue to dark grey with a sallow tint that did not look like sunshine.

"Why?" she said. "Can't you re—"

Robert stared back at her.

"Oh," she said. Why had she thought that he could read? Not everyone was as lucky as her. Grandma had taught her when she was small. "I didn't mean to... I didn't know."

He shrugged and looked away.

She crouched down next to the gravestone, squinting at the worn epitaph and read it out.

**Here lies the body of
Mrs Mary Heskew,
wife of Robert Heskew,
who left this world while
partaking of an ice cream
in Hyde Park.**

"Oh, poor Mrs Mary," Marisee said. "What a strange way to die." There was so much death in this city, but somehow when it was a Mary, it felt worse. She ran a finger over the words. "Is the ice cream a clue?" Lady Fleet had said they should try the dead. Was there a dead ice cream seller she should ask?

She didn't know of any ice cream sellers. Nobody in her village had ever tasted ice cream, including herself. Then she clapped her hand over her mouth. Of course it wasn't the ice cream that was important. Where did rich folk go to find out about other people's business? She knew *that*.

"Hyde Park," she said. "That's the clue. That's where we must go."

"I know that park," Robert said. "I have to attend Lady Hibbert there every Tuesday. She goes to meet her friends to talk about their other friends."

Marisee knew it wasn't just people who gossiped there. "It's full of streams and rivers," Grandma had told her. "Chattering away and complaining about the new Serpentine lake and the waterworks. There are other things there too, Marisee, best not discussed."

"Like what?" she had asked.

Grandma had thought for a moment and then said, "Ghosts. So many of them I'm surprised there's room for living people. The gallows are just on the other side of the park wall, so some of those ghosts aren't looking their best. They can be useful for a bit of gossip now and again, but they're not my business."

Marisee ran her fingers over poor Mrs Heskew's

gravestone. "It's full of the talking dead too," she said.

"You mean ghosts?"

She nodded. "But if you don't want to come…"

He hesitated for a moment. "Do you know the way?"

"I think so."

"Then let's go."

They crept through the alleyway behind the Mansion House and ran through a barge yard, jumping over scattered planks of wood and coils of rope and out on to a road that led them to Cheapside.

"If we follow the direction of the Thames, it will take us towards Westminster," Marisee said. "But we'll turn north along the way."

And she would make sure to avoid the dark alleys around Covent Garden. London was now completely silent apart from the crunch of her boots on the ground, the soft soles of Robert's shoes and their ragged breath as they hurried west. There were no carriage wheels, no tapping of hooves. The merchants had disappeared. Perhaps they had bolted themselves into their own mansions.

Nor were there beggars pleading for alms. Marisee supposed that they would be like the rag seller Grandma had found on Tuesday, deep in a happy sleep, while their tired bodies wasted away in this world. Had the rag seller ever woken again? Marisee shivered.

A figure suddenly loped out of a doorway towards her. He was a tall elderly man. His striped waistcoat was missing every button so it gaped open, showing bare skin pulled tight over his ribs. A scarlet necktie was knotted at his throat. He blinked as if he was bathed in bright sunlight.

"Missy!" His balled-up hand snapped open and shut. "You have to tell Madam Blackwell to give it up, Missy. You can't win."

Yellow mist curled from his mouth. A dull pain gripped the back of Marisee's neck, spreading up through her head. Somewhere in the distance, a woman's voice sang something sad and tender and the cymbals clashed in time. Marisee tried to edge round him. He blinked hard at her and swayed.

"Missy, please!" He reached out and tugged at Marisee's apron. "Missy, please! *She* promised!"

"Leave her alone!" Robert tried to pull the beggar away.

Another person stepped out of the doorway. She had discarded her broom, but Marisee recognized the old woman who had been sweeping the crossing outside the

Mansion House. Her bony fingers grasped Robert's sleeve.

"*She* knows about you," the sweeper croaked. "*She* knows who you lost. If you help her, she'll let you see him again. *She* promised."

"She knows?" Robert's voice was faint. "She promised?"

"Where's Madam Blackwell, Missy?" The beggar's nails gripped Marisee's shoulder. "Tell me, Missy. Help me, Missy."

The sleepwalkers' yellow breath hung around them and – no – was there a yellow taint to Robert's breath? His eyelids were fluttering. Marisee shoved the beggar away from her and made a grab for Robert's hand.

"Run!" she yelled.

He hesitated, his face confused, then he seemed to snap back to real life. They dodged around the crossing sweeper and ran. Marisee's sides hurt and her chest was tight. A dog bounded out of an alley and ran alongside them.

"Do you think it's sick too?" she gasped as she ran.

"Its breath's clear," Robert said.

Yes, it was, but what if it was a Chad sent by Lady Walbrook to spy on them? The new Sadler was fox-like. A Chad could look like anything! This dog was small, mottled brown and white and had lost half its tail. Marisee tried to outrun it, but her chest felt like it was being pulled apart.

"I need to slow down," she puffed.

Her wobbly legs were only good for walking, and even that was a struggle. Her throat hurt and her feet stung from the pebbles digging through her boots. Robert was wheezing beside her. The dog slowed to their pace, its tail stump wagging. Then it trotted past them to raise its leg on a lamp post. Once it was done, it scampered away.

It really was just a dog. Not everything in this sick London had changed.

"Ready to carry on?" she asked.

Robert wiped his brow on his sleeve and nodded.

Marisee forced her legs to move again. The pale dome of St Paul's seemed to glow through the gloom ahead of them. They cut through the empty cathedral churchyard. It was still a long way to Hyde Park, and she was tired and her head hurt. She felt like a small boat fighting against the Thames current.

At least she knew where they were: on Ludgate Street with the Fleet Bridge up ahead. She'd been this way before with Grandma only two months ago, checking on local wells. The streets that day had been full of noise beyond the usual roar of the city. There was to be a hanging at Tyburn and the mob had been jostling for a view of the cart carrying the condemned folk from Newgate prison. Grandma had muttered words that Marisee was sure she wasn't supposed to hear, her elbows cutting a path through the mass of shouting, laughing onlookers.

Now, Marisee caught a movement out of the corner of her eye. Her brain shouted "wild boar!" just as the beast charged.

"Run. Run! Now!"

Was that her mouth shrieking those words or Robert's?

Her legs wobbled. The creature was so close. She could see every detail of it: the sharp upward point of its tusks, the circle of its snout, black eyes pulling her into darkness – and the smell! It was filthy prison cells, a butcher's abattoir and the thick stink of burning horse bones. The boar squealed as it thundered towards her, the fur bristling between its ears like dressmakers' pins. And she'd seen it before! This was the boar from the Chad court. This was Fleet Ditch, a spirit! It was mist and water. It should pass right through her, but its hooves sparked as it ran and those tusks were sharp as pikes.

Robert was trying to pull her away, but she was so weary. It would take all her strength to take one step.

"You cannot hurt me!" she tried to yell. "I am Madam Blackwell's granddaughter!"

"I know who you are, honey."

That kind, sparkling voice! "Turnmill? Is that you?"

Turnmill had appeared in front of the Fleet Bridge. She gripped the boar by the snout. Marisee felt as if she had been drenched in swift cold water washing away the stench and terror. In the Chad court, Turnmill had seemed to glisten and fade. Now she looked as solid as a pie seller. So did the boar. Its hooves struck the ground and it tossed its head, trying to free itself. It roared even though its mouth was clamped shut.

"Ditch takes his guard duties very seriously," Turnmill said.

The boar snorted, its bristly ears flattening against its head.

"Stop this nonsense, Ditch!" Turnmill said.

The boar shook its head. Dark drops sprayed from its fur and popped as they hit the air.

"Don't you recognize her?" Turnmill said. "It's Marisee Blackwell. You are an excellent guard-boar, but you can't gore the Well Keeper's granddaughter."

The boar backed away and dropped its head. Turnmill clung on to its snout.

Turnmill rolled her eyes. "All Solids do not look the same, Ditch. That's just ignorant. Now, if you promise to behave, I will let you go."

More snorts and head-tossing, a hoof scrape.

"*She* didn't know you were going to stop. All she saw was a great big hairy pig running at her." She glanced at Marisee and Robert. "Isn't that so?"

Marisee and Robert nodded.

"I'm letting you go now," Turnmill said. "But behave!"

Turnmill released the boar.

"What if he charges again?" Robert asked.

Ditch made a noise that sounded surprisingly like laughter. He trotted away, cast Marisee one backwards glance, and then disappeared over the sides of the Fleet Ditch.

Turnmill's attention was on them now. "Our Lady Walbrook is not very happy with you two, is she? Her river surged earlier. Every gutter in the City of London was flooded. Ditch even felt the tremor in his burrow beneath Fleet Bridge. That is pure Walbrook rage."

Marisee backed away from her. "Has she sent you to bring us to her?"

Turnmill laughed. "She knows better than to send me to do her bidding. I try and stay out of her way. You saw what she did to Sadler. You do not want Walbrook as your enemy, though perhaps the warning comes too late for you."

"We didn't mean to upset her," Marisee said.

"It's easily done," Turnmill said. "But you must be especially careful now. Where are you going?"

"Hyde Park," Marisee said. "To talk to the ghosts. We think they might know why this sickness started."

"Good idea!" Turnmill said. "The See-throughs always know what's going on and love new folk to talk at. Ask for Mistress Agnes. She knows everyone. If you keep to the east of the park and away from the Serpentine, you'll be safe. Well, safer. And ignore the lingering monk. I'd be furious if I was him." Turnmill looked up and down the road. "We need to make sure you arrive there safely." She paused, as if listening. "I think our transport problem has been solved."

"Thank you so much," Marisee said. "I know that if Walbrook knew you were helping us…"

She tried not to imagine Turnmill caught in a web of silver threads, slowly crumbling into sand.

Turnmill nodded. "If Walbrook knew I was helping

you, it wouldn't end well for any of us. But how could I not help you? I knew your mother and your grandmother and many of the grandmothers that came before."

"My mother?" Marisee felt that twist from deep inside her. "You knew my mother?"

"Of course! When she was a child, she'd often come and sit by my banks and talk to me. She even came to say 'goodbye' on the day she left. You were so small, a rivulet. It's been such a pleasure watching every one of you grow up. Ah…" She looked along Ludgate Hill. "I believe your carriage approaches."

Turnmill disappeared.

Robert touched her arm. "Do you miss your mother?"

She shrugged. "I don't remember her."

"Yes, but…"

"Can you hear that?" Marisee said. "We should hide. I doubt they're friendly."

Robert held her gaze for a moment longer, then nodded.

Hooves on cobblestones. One horse. The metallic rattle of wheels. A chaise, perhaps. What was she supposed to do? A wealthy person in a carriage wasn't likely to stop for her in normal times, but certainly not now when there was a sleep plague.

"Marisee! Here!" Robert called.

He was crouching behind a large chandler's sign on the other side of the road. She ran over and squeezed next to him. The carriage sounded close, though it was hard to tell. In this strange, silent London, sound moved differently. Those clattering wheels could just as easily be on the other side of the Thames.

The noise grew louder and louder until the carriage appeared. It was indeed a chaise, driven by a gentleman wearing a long black frock coat and matching tricorn hat. The horse stopped suddenly in front of the chandler's sign, almost sending the gentleman flying out of his high seat behind the horse. He was a young man, but his face was folded into frowns so heavy that his forehead nearly met his nose. He was clutching a whip so long that the braided leather almost tangled in the horse's hooves. He cursed the horse and tugged the reins.

"Move, you ignorant beast!"

The horse neighed and suddenly trotted a few steps forward. The carriage skittered across the cobbles.

"Move!" The gentleman raised the whip. "Or I'll ... oh."

Marisee thought he may have glimpsed her, but he was staring back at the Fleet Bridge. The boar was sauntering slowly towards the carriage, head down, each step ringing like a bell. Steam flared from its nostrils. The whip dropped from the gentleman's hand.

"Move," he whispered to the horse. "Please move."

The horse lifted one hoof, then placed it firmly down exactly where it had been before. It tossed its head. Ditch snorted and the horse did the same – yes, almost exactly the same. It was like the animals were talking to each other.

"Be ready." Turnmill had reappeared by Marisee's side. "Any moment now…"

Ditch charged. The gentleman screamed. Marisee hadn't known that men's voices could reach that high. Ditch stopped just before he slammed into the horse.

"Nice piggie." The gentleman's voice wobbled. "Lovely, lovely, nice piggie."

The "nice piggie" turned round and trotted back towards the ditch. Marisee heard the gentleman breathe out in relief. He leaped down from the chaise and picked up the whip.

"You wait until I get you back to … oh."

Ditch had turned around and was staring straight at the gentleman, who was desperately trying to scrabble back on to the chaise.

"Nice piggie?" the gentleman whimpered, and then he fled, disappearing into an alleyway between the houses.

"So now you have transport," Turnmill said sweetly.

Marisee looked at the carriage. She had never been in a chaise before, let alone driven one.

"Can you drive?" she asked Robert.

She picked up the discarded whip and tried to hand it to him, but his hands stayed by his side. "No," he said. "I can't."

Turnmill patted the horse's flank. "Our friend here doesn't need a driver. Who do you think he'd rather carry? You or that cruel addle pate?"

The horse stretched out his head and nuzzled Marisee's ear.

"You see?" Turnmill said. "He likes you."

"What's his name?"

"Red Rum," came a deep, smooth voice. Marisee stared towards the boar, who lowered his head as if he was bowing. "But that nasty Solid never knew that."

Ditch nodded to them, then disappeared over the edge of the riverbank.

Robert opened his mouth and closed it again. "He can talk?"

"Of course," Turnmill said. "Eighty-three different

188

languages at last count, including London Horse. His Anglo-Saxon cursing is next to none."

The cursing boar of Fleet Ditch. Marisee felt a deep sadness that Grandma wasn't with her to meet him. They'd get on so well. Though they were probably already best friends. So much of Grandma's life was a secret.

Marisee stroked the horse's head. "Actually, I thought rum was brown."

"Maybe the name doesn't translate well from Horse," Turnmill said. "But it's better than whatever stupidness that man called it. Come on. You haven't got much time. I'll help you up."

She cupped her hand for Marisee's foot. Red Rum stayed still. Marisee tried not to step too hard, before gripping the carriage side and almost tumbling in. Robert followed with as little elegance as her. She took hold of the reins. The carriage seemed rather fragile for the potholes and gutters of London.

"I hope Red Rum knows the way to Hyde Park," Marisee said.

Turnmill whispered in the horse's ear. "He does now. Hold tight!"

Marisee did – very tight indeed.

THE GHOSTS
OF HYDE PARK

Robert had never sat inside a coach before, though he had often helped to clean Lady Hibbert's landau. He'd travelled on the rear platform, wedged between two conceited footmen, clinging on as the wheels bumped across the uneven roads. He'd also trotted by the side, clearing obstacles from its path. Now, he thought that he would prefer any of those to travelling inside this thing. He had seen these types of coaches speeding around Hyde Park. They made him think of a baby's cradle bouncing around on high wheels. He clung to the sides

190

as it jolted and sprung and wiggled and threw him against Marisee, who sat rigid and upright, the reins slack in her hands. He wished that Turnmill had taught him London Horse for "please slow down before I'm sick".

The early twilight was passing into darkness, with just a smear of orange sky in the west. It was like the sun was fighting the sickness and losing. They stopped by a tavern on the Strand to take the lit lantern that hung outside. Three times, riderless horses trotted out of the shadows towards them. Each time, Marisee had flinched, expecting robbers, but Red Rum had neighed at them and the horse had neighed back. Robert wished he knew what they were saying.

A gentleman in a judge's wig was sitting by a statue on Charing Cross. He'd leaped into the road and yelled "Stop!", but Red Rum had easily swerved round him. Whether he was sick or not, Red Rum wasn't going to stop to find out.

At last, they arrived at a long, high wall. Hyde Park. Turnmill must have given Red Rum specific instructions because they rattled through the gate on the south-east side, rolling north along an avenue. Robert could just make out the dark shapes of the trees on either side. The Serpentine was to the west.

Marisee was looking the same way.

"Grandma said that there used to be many separate wells and streams," she told him. "Queen Charlotte joined them together. Many of the spirits were against it."

Robert's stomach was jumping around too much to reply. He shivered. There was a chill to the air. He imagined the yellow mist from all the sleepers in London curling up and joining together to blot out the light. And he was here to find ghosts. He tried to pull his tight jacket closer around him.

The horse slowed to a walk and finally stopped. It lifted its head and neighed.

"I understand, Red Rum," Marisee said. "I feel it too. This is as far as you go."

She slid out of the carriage. Robert thumped down on the other side. The park was so dark he could barely see where his feet landed.

"We're near Tyburn Road," Marisee swung the lantern towards a high wall at the end of the park. "That's where they've built the triple tree gallows so they can hang twenty-four people at the same time."

Robert knew about it. It had been the talk of the kitchen. Mrs Wandle had even been to an execution there and was very impressed. She'd thought it funny that Lizzie and Robert were so upset about it.

"Grandma hates the hangings," Marisee said. "She says that most of the condemned are just poor and desperate."

Lizzie had said the same, but not within Mrs Wandle's earshot. He hoped Lizzie was safe.

Marisee looked around her. "Do you think the ghosts can see us?"

Robert had been trying not to think of that. The chill in the air became sharper. His own ears must be twitching like the Fleet Ditch boar's as he squinted into the shadow at every sound.

"Miss Turnmill said you should ask for Mistress Agnes," he whispered. Though he wasn't sure if he wanted Marisee to ask for anyone at all. He'd rather follow Red Rum and get far away from this place.

Marisee cleared her throat and cupped her hands to her mouth. "Mistress Agnes?"

In the park's eerie silence, she could be loud enough to raise all the dead people in London.

"I pray for you, my sister." The gargled voice came from on top of the wall. A pale hooded figure huddled there. There was a shine around it as if it was crouching in a tunnel of light.

"Who…" Marisee was much quieter now. But as she held up her lantern, Robert saw her lift her head and thrust back her shoulders. "Who are you?" Her voice was stronger again.

"I pray for you, sister. I pray for all the sinners that sent me to my death."

The figure stood, though there was a thin line of darkness between it and the top of the wall. It was not standing. It floated, clutching its cloak tightly, its hands buried within the folds.

"It's … it's a ghost," Robert said.

He didn't know why he said this. It was obvious. He just needed to say something. It tilted back its head, pushing away its hood, and its face – there was no face. Just a skull held within the fold of the cowl. Its body jerked and the skull rolled sideways. The cloak flew open. Robert saw bony fingers – and then he turned away. The ghostly monk's body had been split open like a hot potato, and everything that was inside it had been pulled out.

Marisee touched his arm. Her hand was shaking, but her voice was not. "It's gone," she said.

"What…" His teeth were chattering too much to speak.

"It's gone," she said again.

Robert remembered Fleet's words. *How can Solids be so cruel to their own?* He had always known that some found it easy. Even when he'd seen Fleet's hands on her blanket, they'd reminded him of the elders in the plantation, finger joints swollen from years of separating cocoa beans from the pods, their nails dirty, ragged and torn.

"Who goes there?"

Robert jumped. His heart hammered. A soldier stood by the wall, carrying the same faint shine as the monk. His red coat flapped open and his pale breeches were stained with mud. A bayonet was slung across his shoulder, though the barrel was pointing towards the ground.

"I'm … I'm Marisee," she said. She lifted her chin. "Marisee Blackwell."

The soldier took a few steps forward. His black leather boots made no sound. "I said who goes there?"

Robert's heart beat even harder. Soldiers had once been called to the plantation. There'd been rumours of a rebellion brewing. They'd marched round the fields, shoulders back, bayonets high. Mama had clutched him and his sisters even closer.

Robert took a deep breath. This was a soldier, yes, but a ghost-soldier. It was only living soldiers that he must fear.

"My name is Robert Strong." He wasn't even sure if the soldier could hear him, but he continued. "This is Miss Marisee Blackwell. We seek an audience with Mistress Agnes."

The soldier marched up to them. He lifted his bayonet and pointed it towards Robert's chest.

"Is that young Marisee?" The voice came from behind them. A woman shone in the darkness, clutching a milkmaid's stool in one hand. Her spectacles were perched low on her nose and her apron pocket was heavy with flasks. A black bonnet lay flat against her head, its strings tied tight below her chin. The light from the lantern shone right through her to the ground below.

"Let them be," she said.

The soldier spun around back to the wall.

"Poor Hans," the elderly woman said. "He was shot. By his own side, if you can believe it. He was meant to be in the barracks, but his wife died bringing another baby into the world. He went off to be with his little ones. He didn't ask no permission so they brought him here." She clutched at her see-through chest. "Straight through his heart. I saw it all."

"Same thing happened to me." Another soldier

appeared by the wall. His tattered shirt hung over his breeches. He stared down at his stockinged feet. His lengthy moustache brushed his chest. "And the rascals stole my boots and jacket."

"Well, it's not like you'll be feeling the cold any more. But I've forgotten my manners, dear." The ghost stretched out her hand. "I'm Mistress Agnes."

Robert stared at the hand. Ghost skin over ghost knuckles and dark ground below. If he didn't shake it, would Mistress Agnes be offended? *Could* she even shake hands?

Mistress Agnes laughed and dropped her hand. "That's not a good idea, is it? What with my hand not really being there." She thumped the ghostly milkmaid's stool on to the ground and sat down. The *thump* made no sound. "You're Mary Blackwell's granddaughter, aren't you?"

"You know my grandma?" Marisee asked.

"Me and her..." Mistress Agnes linked her two forefingers together. "We were as close as that when I was alive. Them Serpentine springs didn't like me having my little spot here." She flicked her nose. "All snooty, they were, just because a queen once looked at them. They said I lowered the class of the place. Your grandma helped me take my case all the way to the Lord Mayor. But then…" She cackled. "That Serpentine got caught up in the new sewers. All them stuck up streams were stinking to high heavens. You really didn't want to walk past it without a peg on your nose. I laughed so much, I…" She sighed. "I died. Heart gave out. But at least I died happy."

"Do you mock us?" It was the soldier without the jacket.

"No, George," Mistress Agnes said. "That I will never do."

Marisee was nodding. "I'm pleased Grandma helped you, but we need you to help us now, and quickly if you can, Mistress Agnes."

The ghost cocked her head. "Ooh, no one's wanted my help for a long, long time."

"No one helped *me*." The soldier with the musket marched up to the stool. "No one."

"Not now, Hans," Mistress Agnes said. "Let's see what the Well Keeper's granddaughter wants, shall we?"

"I don't care what she wants." Hans marched away.

George wriggled his toes and shook his head. "The rascals stole my boots."

"Poor boys," Mistress Agnes murmured. "They

could move beyond this place if they were willing to forget their past."

Mama had always told Robert that they must remember their past, who their people really were before they were stolen to work in the plantations.

Marisee was talking. "There's a terrible sickness across London, Mistress Agnes," Marisee said. "And Grandma has disappeared."

Mistress Agnes pulled off her spectacles in astonishment and dropped them in her lap. Robert expected them to sink straight through, but they didn't. "Mary-Ay Blackwell disappeared! That's against the rules! The Whittington Articles say that no one should ever touch her! She's protected! Do you have any idea who's carried out such an atrocity?"

"No, Mistress Agnes. I believe she ran away to keep the Freedom safe. Did you know that she was supposed to protect it?"

Mistress Agnes slipped her spectacles back on, as if they made her thoughts clearer too. "There was a rumour. Your grandma must have told you much more than I know."

Marisee didn't answer. Robert supposed that Madam Blackwell must have had her reasons for keeping secrets, but it may be a while before Marisee forgave her.

"Tell me more about this sickness," Mistress Agnes said. "It's hard to know what's wrong and what's right with the living world when you're dead. The park's been quiet, not that folk come up this way much unless there's a hanging." She pointed to the soldiers. There was a third one now, barely older than Robert, pointing a musket, his eyes wide and frightened above it. "Them lot make themselves known. So does the monk, especially on a hanging day. He's never forgiven Henry VIII for his wickedness. Most folk can't see the ghosts, but they can feel them."

Robert wondered why he was able to, but he had seen many strange things today.

Mistress Agnes was still talking. "All the lords and ladies are usually down the other end, parading themselves around." And some of them parading servants like him, Robert thought. "We're only busy up here when the poor wretches are heading to the gallows. Some of them misery-gobblers bring ladders, you know, so they can climb on to the wall for a better look. One year, one of them fell off and…"

"I do not need the reminder."

The voice came from the top of the wall where the

ghost monk had been. Robert had to squint to see the newcomer. He was well-dressed, like a clergyman, in a dark frock coat and breeches. He was cradling his wig on his lap.

"Well, don't expect me to feel sorry for you." Mistress Agnes sniffed. "If you weren't trying to get a better look, you wouldn't have fallen off and broke your neck. Now, Granddaughter Blackwell, don't let me be sidetracked. This sickness. Tell me more."

"Lady Walbrook says that it's coming from the Ether," Marisee said.

"Ah," Mistress Agnes said. "The Ether. I miss those dreams. It was the only time I got to taste a proper macaroon."

"Only not just food and clothes now," Marisee said. "People are dreaming of loved ones who have died. And they don't want to wake up."

"It's hard to blame them," Mistress Agnes said. "My first two babies fell asleep and never…" She shrugged. "If I could have kissed my babies again in my Ether dreams, I wouldn't have woken up. So, you want to know what's at the heart of it?"

"Yes, please," Marisee said. "That's the only way we can stop it. Lady Fleet told us to ask the … de—" Would it be rude to remind Mistress Agnes about her condition? "To ask people like you. She said you know everything."

Mistress Agnes laughed. "*I* don't know everything! But there are ghosts who've been here for a long, long time. What do you want to know?"

"Lady Fleet said that you might help us find a girl," Robert said.

"I'll do my best. Is she still warm, or a ghost?"

"I don't know," Marisee said. "But Lady Fleet told us she was badly hurt and—"

Mistress Agnes sighed. "So she may be one of us. Did she come to the park in her last moments?"

"Lady Fleet didn't say," Robert replied.

"But we don't think so," Marisee added.

Mistress Agnes frowned. "I'm not sure how I can help you if she's not here."

Robert thought hard. If he'd asked Lady Fleet the right questions in time, perhaps he'd already know more about the child. Mistress Agnes must have more to say, or else why did the Fumi send them here?

"What if she was here, then went into the Ether?" he asked.

Mistress Agnes shook her head so hard her spectacles flew off. She retrieved them and replaced them on her nose. "We can't get in." She sighed. "Ours is a different kind of sleep. I think all of us have tried at some point, for that very reason. Just hoping to find the people we left behind and turn up in their dreams. But we can't."

After Zeke was gone, Robert had wished so hard that there was an in-between place where they could meet again.

"But what if she found another way into the Ether?" He was sure there must be some connection between the girl and these new dreams. "Lady Fleet said that there was something sad about the sickness, something that she'd felt before."

"As far as I know," Mistress Agnes said, "no ghost can get into the Ether and no Solid can change what's there. But something's changed about some of the new cold bloods here, though. There have been some strange newcomers."

"Like who?" Marisee sounded hopeful.

"Everyone's a bit confused when they're ghosted," Mistress Agnes said. "Especially the ones who didn't realize they had a spot of unfinished business in their lives and thought they'd be on the fast coach to heaven. Then they wake up and they're here. Of course, we get a good share of ghosts from that." She pointed towards where the gallows stood on the other side of the wall. "Those poor souls; this park is the last thing they see. Their ghosts often try and scramble over the wall as soon as they're freed. A few manage it. But these new'uns are different."

"When you say 'different', Mistress Agnes," Marisee urged, "what do you mean?"

"Of course, sorry, my darling. I'm rambling again. It's nice to have warm blood to talk to for a change. I think it'll be easier if I introduce you to someone." Mistress Agnes put her hand to her mouth. "Lou Lou! Come out, love!"

A young woman appeared behind Mistress Agnes's shoulder. She was not even twenty years old, bare-headed, long hair clumped together. Her dress and tatty shawl were muddy. Her feet were bound with rags instead of shoes. Her eyes were open and she seemed to be looking at something no one else could see. She was smiling, the same wide smile that Robert had seen on Lizzie's face.

"The watchman found her by the wall there," Mistress Agnes said. "Just over a week ago. Girls like her don't want to hang around in this world. It's too full of bad memories. But she... You tell them, Lou Lou. Tell the warm bloods who you are."

Lou Lou's mouth moved, but her eyes didn't. "I am a princess. I have silk gowns and a hundred maids and a coach made from gold. *She* promised that me and my baby are going to ride in it for ever."

Mistress Agnes shook her head. "Who promised you this, Lou Lou?"

For a second, Lou Lou's eye flitted to Mistress Agnes, then away. "The Shepherdess…"

The Shepherdess? Marisee and Robert looked at each other. Marisee seemed as confused as him.

Lou Lou started to sing. Her smile widened.

"March lamb, walk lamb, follow the sheep. Open eyes, close eyes…"

"The sleepwalkers!" Robert and Marisee said together.

Robert would never forget the villagers with their poles and hammers trying to smash their way into the pump room.

"It's the ones like Lou Lou that come to the park just to die," Mistress Agnes said. "All of them singing the same song, smiling so hard I can barely understand the words. Watch this. Lou Lou!"

The girl didn't move. Mistress Agnes swivelled round on her milk stool to face the girl.

"You're never going to ride in that coach with your baby, my darling. That shepherdess swindled you out of your life."

Lou Lou's smile switched off. "You don't know nothing, old woman!"

"I know I heard them dump you by the wall over there. They said you were still alive. Why didn't your shepherdess make them take you to a hospital? You didn't need to be dead."

"I didn't need no hospital. I would have fought them if they'd tried to take me. This is where the Shepherdess told me to come. I've got my gold coach and my silks and my baby."

Robert looked at the ragged ghost girl. How could a dream be so strong that it followed her beyond life? Or a life be so desperate that the dream became everything? He thought about Lizzie, usually full of laughter and gossip, fading away into a dream about her sister and never waking up.

"Can you see this living girl here, Lou Lou?" Mistress Agnes said, nodding to Marisee. "Tell her about your shepherdess."

"The Shepherdess gave me a gold coach and silk gowns. She gave me my baby back."

"She did no such thing!" Mistress Agnes's voice was sharp with anger. "She made you dream until you died. We have to stop this. Miss Marisee, here, is going to do just that! She's going to find your shepherdess and stop her from making poor folk give up their lives for a lie."

Lou Lou's eyes widened and her smile faltered. "No!"

"She's hurting people like you, Lou Lou. It mustn't go on."

"You will not harm her!" Lou Lou shrieked. "She's the only one that cares about us!"

Suddenly, Lou Lou was a ball of bared teeth and nails, her deep, glassy eyes full of rage. She shot towards Marisee, a whirl of fury and hate, slamming right through her. There was a screech that made the hairs on Robert's arms stand on end. Then nothing.

Lou Lou was gone. Marisee swayed. She looked like she needed her own milk stool to sit on. Robert wouldn't have minded one either. He breathed in deeply. Even his thoughts were shaking. He had to calm down and think clearly. There was someone called The Shepherdess who seemed to be part of these new dreams. No, it was worse than that. She could do what no ghost or human could do – she could change the Ether and create dreams so powerful they stayed with the sleeper beyond the grave.

But if she was in the Ether, she could do that to any poor person in London. Why did she want Lou Lou to come here?

"You said Lou Lou was brought here just to die," Robert said. "Are there others brought here too?"

"Indeed," Mistress Agnes said. "Those are the strange ones. Some of them are like Lou Lou and fall asleep somewhere else, then get brought here at the last moment. I know some watchmen don't like the inconvenience of the deceased on their streets, but none of them will move a soul on the brink of death. We all deserve peace in our last moments, but dying folk are even making their *own* way here, using all their last strength to pass through these gates before they give up their ghost." Mistress Agnes rubbed the bridge of her ghost nose, then clasped her hands in her lap. "I hear them muttering about their children and their wives and their husbands that they're seeing in their dreams," she said. "They're usually still talking about them when they wake up as one of us. They're just like Lou. The Shepherdess has promised them this and that, and they still believe it."

"But why this park?" Marisee asked. "Why not Green

Park or St James's?"

"That's the puzzle. Once we're here, we can't leave. Those walls keep us in. The charms go back from before the Articles and they're strong! Even him." She pointed to the ghost sitting on the wall. "He can't jump down the other side, as much as he wants to get away from us... I suppose it would be chaos if we could haunt wherever we wanted."

"So people have to stay where they're ... um ... ghosted?" Robert asked.

"That's the rules."

He thought hard. "So the Shepherdess *makes* people come here in their last moments so that their ghosts stay here."

"And you're sure she's not here already? She could be bringing ghosts to her for some reason," Marisee said.

Robert shivered. Was she building an army of ghosts to hunt for the Freedom with the sleepwalkers? He and Marisee could never win!

Mistress Agnes shook her head slowly. Her spectacles wobbled. "There's been a lot of dying going on in these parts for centuries, but I *think* I know all the Hyde Park mob."

"How many ghosts are here?" Robert asked.

Mistress Agnes laughed. "Have you ever been to the Bartholomew Fair?"

Robert shook his head. Marisee nodded.

"This place is like centuries of Barts squeezed together," Mistress Agnes said. "Every type of folk you could imagine, jostling and crowding and hollering at each other. Some of them are so faded that even I struggle to see them." She tapped her spectacles. "Even with these. They've got no reason to make themselves known to the living. That takes effort." *Talk to the dead*, Lady Fleet had said. There were more dead here than Mistress Agnes, many, many more. Some ghost must know something more. But Marisee was already ahead of him.

"Can we speak to some of the other ghosts?" she asked.

"We need to know more about the Shepherdess," Robert said. "Or maybe they might know about the girl who was thrown into the Fleet."

"I want to help you, darling," Mistress Agnes said. "But it takes a lot out of me to summon up a ghost, especially if they're not too willing to come. And Lou Lou – she was a tough one. I can only bring up two more at the most, one if they need persuasion."

Marisee slumped on to the grass. She seemed to have exhausted her supply of questions. Robert hoped she knew how lucky she was to be with him. He always had more.

"Mistress Agnes?" he asked.

"Yes, Robert Strong?"

"The Shepherdess wants the ghosts to be here in Hyde Park; she *must* have a connection to this place," he said. "But you don't think she's a ghost."

"A ghost who makes grand promises and wants to destroy the world. I would know if she was round these parts."

"And what if she was here but had escaped?"

"Oh, no!" Mistress Agnes laughed. "I'd definitely know. The ghost gossip would be so thick you could step in it. Ghost folks are always trying to get out, especially the new ones."

Marisee sat up straighter. "But these new ones want to get in to Hyde Park because the Shepherdess has made them promises, just like she does with the sleepwalkers. Do all of the newcomers get angry if you tell them the promises aren't real?"

"You saw how Lou Lou fired off when I put her

straight," Mistress Agnes said. "I know she looked like a demon, but she can't hurt the living. We *can* make another ghost's eternal life a misery, though." She stared towards the place where Lou Lou had stood. "Yes," she continued. "We *can* haunt each other. And that's what these newcomers are doing! They're turning on any ghosts who talk ill of this shepherdess."

"I think I understand now!" Marisee was on her feet again. "Imagine there's a whole mob of ghosts like Lou Lou. Imagine they've been brought here to torment another ghost."

Robert nodded. "As a punishment."

"Or revenge," Marisee added.

"When you're this close to a gallows," Mistress Agnes said, "there's a lot of ghosts out for revenge. I certainly can't summon all of them up."

"But what about the child that Lady Fleet mentioned?" Robert said. It still hurt to think about it. "It wasn't that long ago, just a few years."

"And no one knows what happened to her," Marisee said. "Perhaps…" She shrugged. "Perhaps she fell into a different kind of sleep, like a magical sleep because Lady Fleet tried to help. Maybe she woke up in the Ether and decided to get revenge for what had happened to her."

"And maybe that's why she's making new ghosts come here. They're punishing the person who hurt her. Could their ghost be here?"

He and Marisee looked at Mistress Agnes. She glanced towards the gallows.

"It depends if they got caught. There's no point me asking around. No ghost admits to the really bad stuff."

"I don't think you'll need to ask," Robert said. "It will be the ghost that all the new ones are … haunting."

Mistress Agnes stood up. She rolled her shoulders like they still hurt her. "I can't promise I'll find the right ghost, but I'll do my best."

Mistress Agnes disappeared. For a moment, Robert worried that she wouldn't return, but she reappeared straight away. She was accompanied by an angry-looking ghost-woman whose face and dress was smeared with – were those rotten tomatoes? And egg yolk? Robert was glad that the smells in the ghosts' world didn't seep into real life. The woman glowered at them and picked a lettuce leaf off her simple bonnet. The skin around her neck looked red and sore.

"What do you want?" she barked at them.

"We have guests," Mistress Agnes said. "Please be polite."

"I don't have to!"

"I just freed you from those stocks," Mistress Agnes said. "So keep a civil tongue."

"I don't care about them stocks. I'm not sorry for what I did. She was a silly little girl. No one would have known if Mrs Lowrigg in the house next door kept her nose in her own business."

"Known what?" Robert said, quietly. "What did you do?"

The ghost held up her wrists. "Lock me in the stocks! I won't answer your questions."

"Why were you in the stocks?" Marisee asked. "Did you hurt the Shepherdess when she was a child?"

"Shepherdess!" The ghost laughed so hard Marisee thought her head might tumble off. "She wasn't no shepherdess. She was a lamb. Those fools in the Hospital sent her to me. It's their fault. They shouldn't have been so trusting."

"I know this one!" The shout came from the ghostly clergyman sitting on the wall. "That's Mrs Broxbourne. I saw her up there on the gallows. I helped her over the wall!"

Mrs Broxbourne jabbed a finger towards him. "I didn't ask for your help! I don't need no do-gooders doing anything for me."

"If I remember correctly," the clergyman said, "you were *begging* me to help you into the park."

Mrs Broxbourne made a face. "Oh, shut your ugly cakehole!" And she disappeared.

"Come back!" Robert yelled. She'd hurt a child and that made him furious and sad at the same time. And she knew more! The least she could do was tell them the poor child's name.

"Can you get her back, Mistress Agnes?" Marisee asked. "Please!"

"Sorry, darling. She won't come willingly and I'm too old to wrestle ghosts like her these days."

Robert wasn't going to give up. He must know that child's name. He was sure that she was the centre of this. He walked towards the wall where the clergyman sat. Hans and George were there too, but they ignored him. The third young soldier pointed a musket at him, then away again.

Robert called up to the clergyman. "What was Mrs Broxbourne's crime, sir?"

Close up, Robert saw that the ghost was floating

just above the wall.

"How can I remember?" the clergyman said. "I've seen so many swing."

"She seems like one that would be remembered," Robert said. "If she was hanged because she hurt a child, wouldn't the crowd be angry with her?"

The ghost sniffed. "I told you. I've seen so many – um – events, I can't remember specific ones."

"Yes, you can," Mistress Agnes called over. "You've got the best seat in the house there, John. You never miss a hanging day."

"There's too many, I tell you!"

"Think hard, sir," Robert said. "You do remember helping her, don't you?"

"I certainly do! She was the last one I ever reached for. She was so rude and disagreeable, I didn't help anyone after that."

"You remember her name," Robert said. "You remember helping her. It's important, sir, for you to tell us everything you can."

"Come on, John!" Mistress Agnes said. "This is the Well Keeper's granddaughter. I need to help her for her grandma's sake."

"Right! Right!" John stretched his wig. "I think… I

think… That's it! I remember now! The mob cheered the hangman when the noose dropped round her neck because … she'd had a foundling girl. That's it! A foundling girl from the Hospital was apprenticed to her. She treated the girl harshly, very harshly, and the child didn't survive. She … I believe that she threw the child into the Fleet."

When Robert was still on the plantation, he had hoped that cruelty there did not spread beyond. When he'd arrived in London, he'd soon realized that his hopes were unfounded. He had seen the thin women with babies tied to their backs, begging for money in Bloomsbury Market. He had seen the children themselves, shivering in the alleys off the Strand, barefoot in the wind and sleet. But what Mrs Broxbourne had done was a cruelty beyond even that.

He felt Marisee by his side. "Children leave our village to be apprenticed in London," she said. "I always hope that they'll be met with kindness."

Robert nodded. He must remember that there was kindness too; Lizzie's kindness had kept him alive. If he was to find a way to wake her, he must live up to the name his mother had given him. Strong. He was supposed to be Hibbert. But no, he was Strong.

"When did this happen, sir?" he said.

"And answer the boy's question properly," Agnes said. "Not in our eternal time. In the living's time."

"I know *that*." John sounded very certain. Robert felt a spark of hope. "The church bell had struck midday." He smiled proudly.

Robert waited for more. John plucked at his wig and said nothing else.

"That's very helpful, sir." Robert forced a grateful smile. "Thank you. Do you remember the month or, perhaps, the year?"

John thought for a moment. "I believe it was a Monday."

"What year?" Mistress Agnes said. "Was it Farmer George, Soldier George or Blockhead George on the throne? Or poor Queen Anne?"

"It was Soldier George!" John shouted in triumph. He wobbled on the edge of the wall. "Yes! The soldier!"

He tipped forward and disappeared. Robert stared at the empty space.

"There you go, love," Mistress Agnes said. "It was in the reign of your second King George. That's all we're going to get from him. But I'll keep my ear to the wind in case I hear more. I wish I could have been more help."

"But you have helped us!" Marisee said. "The Shepherdess was that poor foundling! She died when she was apprenticed to Mrs Broxbourne and the wicked woman threw her in the river." She looked thoughtfully at Robert. "The second King George died four years ago. The Foundling Hospital opened on Lamb's Conduit Fields in 1745." Marisee grinned at Robert. "I know because that's how far the ledgers go back. If we can see the Hospital's records, we'll find out who she is." She gave Mistress Agnes a little bow. "Thank you so much! I know exactly where we need to go next."

Mistress Agnes picked up her stool. "I hope so, my darling. I really do." She held a finger to the air as if testing the direction of the wind. "We have unwanted visitors."

She disappeared. The soldiers were gone too.

"Mistress Agnes?" Marisee called.

"Listen," Robert said. "Can you hear it?"

March lamb...

He wasn't sure. Was someone singing or was the lullaby inside his head? His eyelids had become heavy. It had been such a long day. He needed to rest. It was only fair.

Marisee shook him hard. "Don't you dare go to sleep!"

"Leave me alone," he groaned. Couldn't she just let him be?

"If I leave you alone," Marisee said, "they won't."

THE
SERPENTINE

Robert turned around. The sleepwalkers stood on the path behind him. A butcher's boy was closest, slightly swaying, his basket still loaded with sausages. He held a lantern. The light was weak but enough for Robert to see that the boy's eyes were open but unmoving.

Just behind the butcher's boy, two girls stood in the shadows, their bonnets pulled low over their faces. Wisps of yellow escaped from their lips. There was a man carrying a flaming torch. He looked like a farmer. Beside him was a gardener still pushing a wheelbarrow, and two men in sturdy boots and neat jackets – sedan chairmen. Standing between them was a thin man in torn checked breeches. Robert counted perhaps ten or eleven more sleepwalkers in the shadows behind them. Some held lanterns, others torches that made dark shapes flick across the path. They didn't blink, or speak. Robert wondered if, just beyond his sight, the ghosts were watching.

The man in checked breeches opened his mouth. His sick breath merged with the glow of the lantern. "Robert Strong, *she* has something to give you."

"Do you know this man?" Marisee whispered.

"No."

"Then we won't stay long enough to find out how he knows your name and what *she* has for you."

But Robert did want to know. He was suddenly sure that the man had something very important to tell him. And *she* … whatever *she* had for him, it *was* important. He knew that.

"Robert!" Marisee was pulling at his arm. "Let's go."

"Robert Strong?" The two girls stepped forward on each side of the man. Their voices were too old for their faces. "You know what *she* has, don't you?"

Robert thought he did. He *hoped* he did. He wanted

it more than anything else. He felt his head sag. Staying awake was too much effort. Sleep was so much better, softly squeezing wakefulness out of him. When he next opened his eyes, would he be standing outside the pie shop again? He didn't want to smell mutton and potato and gravy. He wanted oranges, green Barbados oranges, when the fruit was only just ready to pick. Their scent was so strong, he could almost taste them—

"Fight it, Robert!" Marisee yelled in his ear, jerking him awake.

"I don't want to fight it!" he yelled back. "I want to see my brother!"

It had slipped out. He hadn't wanted anyone to know about Zeke.

"Brother?" Marisee gave him a surprised look.

The sleepwalkers were moving, closer and closer.

"But you want to save your friend, Lizzie, too," she said. "Don't you?"

Lizzie? Who was…? Oh, yes! She was the person who had been kind to him. That's why he was here. Of course he did. How could he have forgotten?

"I do," he said.

Marisee brought her face close to his. "Then we run after three," she whispered. "One. Two."

She didn't wait until "three". She snatched the lantern from the gentleman in checked trousers, grabbed Robert's hand and ran.

They veered off the path that was blocked by the sleepwalkers, swerving between the trees and across the grass. Robert's slippers tried to slide away from him, catching on the knots of weeds. Every time he stumbled, Marisee held him.

The sleepwalkers were following, though. They weren't fast, but they were steady.

Robert and Marisee leaped from the grass on to a narrow gravel path.

"I hope this leads to a way out," Marisee wheezed.

Robert did too. Everything in his body was begging him to slow down. He glanced behind. The butcher's boy had gained speed, his basket swinging from side to side. The chairmen too, running with a heavy, lumbering gait as if they were being pulled by an invisible rope. Marisee lunged off the path and towards a thicket of trees. Robert could just see a stretch of low grass beyond it. He ducked below a low-hanging branch. He flinched. Stockings were no protection against the thorns.

Marisee stopped suddenly. "Did you hear that?"

He strained. There had been something. It came

again. This time he heard it clearly. He knew exactly what it was. It was a scream, but not a human screen. It was like the noise from the stables this morning.

"Horses?" he asked. "Red Rum?"

"Please, no!" Marisee was running again. "But we have to help."

They fell over tree roots, their feet catching in rabbit burrows and tangles. They emerged on to another gravel path, wider than before. Just beyond was the inky glisten of water. It must be the Serpentine, the place where Turnmill had told them they must take care.

Another scream came, louder now. Marisee sprinted towards it. Robert tried to follow, but his body was so heavy. His head ached and that lullaby... It was in his head. The Shepherdess was singing just for him. He dropped down into the grass, panting. As he breathed out, the air was stained pale yellow.

Fight it! Marisee had said. *For Lizzie.* He'd made himself stay awake so many times before, all those nights swaying in the hammock in the ship's hold, his few moments of sleep filled with nightmares. He could stay awake again. He sniffed. Oranges.

Oranges meant...

Oranges meant his mother and...

Oranges meant that he could fall into a dream and maybe never wake.

He staggered to his feet. His breath was clear again. He followed Marisee towards the water.

"I'm sure the noise came from here," she said. "But I can't see anything."

Nor could Robert. The Serpentine was smooth and dark, but the air felt muddy, as if the lake had been turned inside out.

Then the scream came again, like a knife on a grinding stone. Still, he could see nothing, not even the sleepwalkers. Perhaps they had returned to their dreams.

"There!" Marisee shouted.

Robert sensed her before he saw her. His head was filled with whispered prayers and wistful ballads about the lives of the hanged. The water spirit Westbourne-Tybourne was standing by the lake, her shape rippling from the older woman to the younger, then back again.

She held up her hand. "You should not have come this way." She spoke in two voices, one echoing the other.

"We heard a scream." Marisee looked around. "We thought our horse was in trouble."

"You brought the trouble with you."

The butcher's boy stumbled through the copse.

He was now carrying a sharpened wooden stake over his shoulder like a spear. He gathered speed, hurtling towards them, trailing yellow breath.

"No!" Robert shouted, pushing Marisee aside. She pushed Robert at the same time. They fell backwards, away from each other. The butcher's boy ran past them, thrusting his stake into the river bank. Westbourne-Tybourne appeared next to him.

"You cannot do this." She spoke as the young, timid woman before rippling into the older, shriller seller. "You must not do this!"

She shoved the butcher's boy aside and tugged at the stake until it was free from the mud. Heavy footsteps crunched across the gravel path behind her. She spun around: it was the two girls. Their eyes were open, but they moved with clumsy, ragged movements. They carried buckets, a rank stink rising from them. A gardener wheeled a barrow loaded with spades, rakes, canes and sharpened gateposts. The sick yellow mist congealed in ribbons around them. More sleepwalkers arrived, a long winding queue with barrows and bags, buckets and boxes. They unloaded axes, hammers, sharpened pikes and sticks, gathering by the edge of the lake.

"What are they doing?" Marisee asked uneasily.

Robert couldn't answer. The Ether was pulling at him. It was *her*. She was impatient.

"Leave!" Westbourne-Tybourne cried.

The sleepwalkers ignored her. They were still now, poised, as if waiting for a signal. The gentleman in the checked trousers stepped forward. He held a torch.

He lifted it to the sky and dropped it. "Rise!"

"No," Westbourne-Tybourne screamed. "Not this! You must not do this!"

"Rise! Rise!" The sleepwalkers pounded the banks with their pikes, churning up the soft earth.

"Rise!" The two girls reached for their bucket and tipped its stinking mess into the river. It was animal fat and bones and intestines, fresh from an abattoir. A chairman rolled a barrel to the edge of the bank, prised off the lid and pushed it into the lake. It bobbed on the surface, a dark substance like treacle spilling across the water.

Westbourne-Tybourne was flicking between nun and ballad singer, nun and ballad singer. "Stop. STOP!"

The butcher's boy picked up an axe and cleaved great chunks of earth from the banks. Westbourne-Tybourne pushed him away, ripping the axe from his hand and hurling it past him into the water. He returned to the bank, picked up a stake and started stabbing at the ground.

Marisee shook Robert's shoulder. "We have to go NOW!" She released him so suddenly, he staggered. "What's that?"

A small circle had formed in the water near the bank, rippling quickly outwards. Voices rippled with the water. They were calling his name! They were calling for him!

"This is not good!" Marisee had grasped his shoulder again. "We must leave."

He was tired of her pulling him this way and that. He would stay here. *Robert! Come to us!*

She wanted him to stay.

A finger broke through the surface of the water. The skin was grey and cracked like old leather, and it was tipped with a hooked brown nail. It rose, but there was no hand, just an arm, an arm without bones that curled round and back on itself. Higher and higher it pushed through the water until it swayed above the lake.

Wait, the voices told Robert. *You'll be with us soon.*

Another arm rose, and another, each one crusted with pustules which bulged with tiny creatures jumping inside. Fleas. The reek of it made Robert want to retch. It was the smell of a city plagued by death. It was the smell of London if the poor weren't raised from their sleep. Marisee was shouting at him, but the babble of the voices beneath the water was too loud.

Robert stared at the lake. Another arm broke the surface, and another. The voices were louder. They weren't calling for him. They were crying, pleading, praying.

The arms slowly sunk back beneath the surface of the lake. As the voices quietened, Robert realized that those were not arms. They were…

A tentacle whipped out from the lake. Its curved nail hooked the butcher boy's shirt, drawing him towards the water. The axe fell to the ground as the boy struggled. The sleepwalkers chanted, dug at the river's edge, emptied stinking slop into the lake. No one helped him. Marisee ran towards him, but Westbourne-Tybourne stepped in front of her, shaking her head. She walked towards the captured boy, reaching out her arms. She lay her hands on the tentacle.

"Rest, rest."

The tentacle slackened, the hooked nail tearing through the butcher's boy's shirt until it was free. The boy fell backwards. He lay for a moment on the grass, then clambered to his feet. He picked up a pole and started digging again.

Another tentacle shot out, but this time it flew past the boy and wound around Robert's waist. He opened his mouth to shriek, but he was being squeezed so tight that only a trickle of breath came from his chest. He tried to brace himself, but the creature dragged him with ease. He slid through the grass towards the water's edge.

"Robert!"

Marisee was running towards him, Westbourne-Tybourne by her side.

"Help me!" he gasped.

He was answered by a sound like a fresh wound being pulled apart.

A head emerged from the water. The cracked, leathery skin stretched over a skull that would seem human if it wasn't so immense. There were no eyes, only dents in the skin where sockets should be. The head rose and rose, now no longer human as it tapered into a long curved beak. For a moment, Robert thought of hummingbirds in Barbados, dipping deep into blossom. But this wasn't a hummingbird. It was a plague squeezed into the shape of a monster.

Robert heard the wet slap of another tentacle as it wrapped around his legs. This time the shriek burst out of him as he tried to push it off. He pushed it hard.

Marisee had grabbed one of the sleepwalker's stakes, and now she plunged it into the tough, grey hide.

The creature's beak opened and it screamed. It was the same scream they had heard from the other side of the park then a scream that echoed through the earth itself.

The monster began to slide back beneath the water, drawing its tentacles with it. Robert tried to dig his heels into the earth. Reeds whipped at his skin. His slippers caught in the churned up mud and were left behind. As his bare feet skimmed the water, the creature thrust him up high, as if he was a trophy.

Distantly, he could hear Marisee screaming, see Westbourne-Tybourne running towards the water's edge. Then the tentacle was plummeting, and Robert was plunged into the lake.

The freezing water stopped his breath. He tried to hold what was left in his chest. He forced his eyes open. What was he expecting? People calling him from the bottom of the lake? He knew now that those voices were part of the monster itself. All he could see was the writhing bulk of its snake-like body and tentacles moving like dancers.

Was this the way he would die? Robert pushed and

wriggled, but the tentacle gripped him tighter, crushing his ribs. His last breath was going to explode out of his chest.

He thought of his mother and his sisters still on the plantation in Barbados. When they had said "goodbye", he had known that they would probably never see each other again. But while he was still alive, there had been hope. That hope was gone now. He thought of Zeke. Would he now follow where his brother had gone before?

Robert let the air leave his mouth and closed his eyes. His head filled with the scent of oranges. He let himself sink into it.

THE
SLEEP

Sleep wrapped around Robert like a sea-monster pulling
a ship below the surface.

Sinking.

Sinking.

Deep, deep down, a mermaid was singing.

"March lamb, walk lamb, follow the sheep,
Open eyes, close eyes, sleep, lambkins, sleep.
Ten years, ten tears, dripping from my eyes.
No sleep, breathe deep, rise, Robert, rise."

Robert woke up. He breathed in and sighed. He smelled warm pastry and meaty gravy. He was standing in front of a pie shop. His stomach gurgled as if it was trying to sing its own song. The shelves inside were jammed with pies, and the oven must be baking a fresh tasty batch because the fragrant heat crept out beneath the door towards him.

Robert pushed open the door and walked towards the counter. He could hear the shop owner moving around the room at the back. It didn't matter. Robert could still choose anything he wanted. Yes, there were chicken, mutton, beef and oyster pies, but there were sweet pies too! Cherry, apple, damson!

"Do you need help, my brother?"

The shop owner emerged from the back room. He was in shadow, light shining behind him. He was short. He wasn't wearing a wig. His voice... Robert knew that voice.

He shouldn't be here. Not in a pie shop. Not in London. Not in this world ever again. But the Shepherdess had promised and her promises were true.

"Zeke?" Robert said, quietly. "Is that you?"

"Do you remember my other name?"

235

It *was* his voice! The shadow came towards Robert, hardening into a real body, arms, legs, a face that was in Robert's earliest memories.

"Remember what Mama called me?" the figure said.

"Akan," Robert whispered. "To remind you who we once were."

Mama had said it over and over again, even after Zeke couldn't fight the fever any longer. But – here he was! Strong and alive and standing in front of Robert.

"Did you miss me, little brother?" Zeke said.

"You…" Robert shook his head. "You can't be here."

"But I am. Just for you."

Robert looked at the outstretched hand. Zeke's fingers were long and smooth. The cuts and splinters and torn nails from the endless work had disappeared. Robert was pleased. He'd always hated seeing Zeke scratching at the ragged skin. He reached out his own hand and clasped his brother's. It was warm and strong.

"And there's much more to my world than a pie shop," Zeke laughed.

There was a burst of heat, then the pie shop shimmered and dissolved. Robert was out on the street. London was bright and shining. No smoke or fog or dark corners. And Zeke was still right next to him, holding his hand. But… He stared at his brother. It had been six years since Zeke had left this world. He should be six years older, not the same fourteen-year-old boy.

Even as Robert thought it, Zeke was taller, his face narrower and his chin covered in a beard.

It's a dream, Robert! Remember that!

"Are you all right, Keke?" Zeke asked.

Keke. Zeke's special name for him.

"This looks good on you." Zeke pulled at Robert's shirt. The silk jacket was gone. He was wearing the dark grey shirt that Mrs Wandle had burned. He stretched it out for a better look. Here was the faded patch that Mama had tried to scrub clean after Robert spilt soup on it. It was as loose on Robert now as it had been when Zeke had first given it to him, when Robert was a small child.

But I've grown! Even when I arrived in London, it was tight. The sleeves tightened around his arms and the fabric pulled a little more across his chest.

"It's been a long time since I saw you, Keke," Zeke said.

"I tried to dream about you," Robert said. "But they were always bad dreams. I tried to stop myself sleeping at all."

"I know," Zeke said. "I saw your suffering, but there was nothing I could do. I've come to take care of you, Keke. I can make a new London for you. Do you see?"

Zeke swept his hand around.

Yes, it was London, but not the London Robert knew. They were in Leicester Fields, but the iron railings around the grass were gone. Children were clambering over the statue of the horse and dipping for fishes in a pond. A cheer went up as a sedan chair was carried on to the pathway. The chairmen set it down and opened the door. A man was helped out, followed by footmen in gold uniforms. Surely, they all couldn't have fitted in there! Mistress could barely fit her dress and hat in the Hibbert chair.

Lady Hibbert! In this London, surely there is no more Lady Hibbert!

The man's hair was pulled back and tied with a ribbon; his skin was as dark as Robert's own.

"Is that the king?" Robert asked.

"We're all kings here," Zeke said.

"But *the* king."

"If you wish."

The king dipped into his pockets and started throwing candy in the air. The crowds moved towards him, hands raised. Pieces of candy dropped into their palms. Others spun away, sprouted wings and arced over Robert's head into a bush full of bright red flowers, long beaks delving between the petals.

Robert grinned. "They're hummingbirds!"

"Of course," Zeke said. "I remember how much you used to love watching them."

Robert touched his heart. It was beating faster. Mama had cried for weeks after Zeke passed.

None of this is real. It can't be. It's part of the sickness. Does it matter?

Yes. Robert had to leave. There were reasons why he had to leave. He tried to remember what they were. What was more important than him and Zeke being together again?

Zeke gripped Robert's hand tighter. "This world is better for us, Keke. You can see it, can't you? This is what you want."

Robert wiggled his hand. If he could free it from Zeke's, he could think clearer. He was supposed to be looking for something. Stopping something.

"All these lonely months," Zeke said, "with that wicked woman beating you for nothing. No food. No big brother to fight back for you."

Robert tried to pull his hand away again, but with less force.

"No family," Zeke said. "No friends."

Friends? Friends! Zeke was wrong! Robert did have friends! He had Lizzie and Marisee!

"Who are you?" Robert yanked his hand free. "You can't be my brother!"

Leicester Fields had become silent. The children sitting astride the horse statue were staring at him. The king and his footmen too. Even the hummingbirds were hovering without movement.

The hurt in Zeke's eyes made Robert want to cry. "I am your brother, Keke," Zeke said. "Look at me. You know the truth in your heart."

"I do know the truth." Even though Robert's own heart felt like it was splitting apart, he knew it. "You aren't really my brother." He held Zeke by both shoulders. The cloth shifted beneath Robert's fingers. Zeke's shoulder blades were as hard as real bone. "Who are you and why are you really here?"

"Ten years, ten tears, dripping from my eyes,
No sleep, breathe deep, rise Robert, rise."

Zeke's mouth was moving but a woman's voice sang the words.

"I've been waiting for you," she said.

Zeke was gone. Robert's dream-brother. The brother who had died so long ago. The brother who had given him the name "Keke" as a special gift that no one could take away even when the plantation owners called him by other names.

Leicester Fields was gone too. Robert was on a busy street. Chairmen hoisting sedan chairs on long poles barged their way through the crowds with the passengers gripping the seat inside. There were hackney coaches and wagons laden with barrels. A porter pulled a handcart crammed with bulging sacks, weaving between the carriages and the merchants hurrying between the coffee houses. All of the London bustle Robert knew so well was there just for a moment, emerging from a mist of colours, then disappearing again. But it was a silent bustle. The only sound Robert could hear was the lullaby.

"March lamb, walk lamb, follow the sheep…"

A street porter fell into step beside Robert and tipped his hat.

There is no porter. You're dreaming, Robert.

The dream-porter selected an orange from a basket hanging from his arm and offered it to Robert. When Robert accepted it, the porter tipped his hat again and faded. Robert dug his nails into the thick skin of the fruit, the pith giving way and juice bubbling over his skin. He held the fruit to his nose and breathed in.

"Keke?" Dream-Zeke was beside him again, but this time he looked like a drawing where the coloured inks had run outside of the lines. "Don't send me away, Keke."

"You're not real!" Robert dropped the orange and tried to run. London streamed past him. That must be Temple Bar arch looming in the mist. He recognized the spikes poking out from the gloom on top. What were those dark, round shadows on their tips? Sometimes they displayed heads there after public executions. Robert tried to run faster, but a man in checked trousers stepped in front of him, conjuring hummingbirds out of a pie.

"March lamb, walk lamb, follow the sheep…"

Robert dodged into a narrow alleyway, the crumbling buildings leaning so closely into each other that the garrets touched. Everything was darkness and shadow.

His feet made no sound on the cobblestones. He walked through the door of a ruined coffee house, up crooked stairs…

"Open eyes, close eyes…"

He passed one landing and then another. He could smell bitter coffee and hear laughter and faint music, but the doors to the rooms were closed. The song was now so loud it could be coming from Robert's own throat.

"Sleep, Robert, sleep."

The song stopped. The silence seemed to vibrate with the echo of the lullaby. He was standing in front of a closed door that hung slightly crooked in its frame. There was no key or handle. He paused, then tapped on the battered wood.

"Come in, Robert."

He pushed open the door and stepped into a meadow. The grass was softer and greener than Bloomsbury Square. A flock of sheep were grazing in the distance. The air was still, though, as if he hadn't left the landing. He glanced back. The door was still open and he could see dirty plaster and the glassless window that looked down on to the alley below.

"I'm here, Robert." It was the voice from the lullaby. "I know you've come all this way to look for me. I won't hide from you."

A woman appeared suddenly, as if the air had been slit by a sharp knife for her to step through. Her dress was light blue, and he recognized the shine of silk. The skirt fell in folds from her waist to the ground, making him think of the winter ice on the stairs down to the coal cellar. One wrong step and he would fall and break a bone. Over the dress, she wore a sleeveless waistcoat of dull, dirty linen, like those worn by the Hibberts's stable-hands. It was pinned together with a small brooch with a lamb engraved on it. Her straw hat was wide, threaded with gold around the brim and laden with roses. Her long, thin fingers were wrapped around a crook. It was wrought iron instead of wood, twisted like candy, but tarnished with rust.

She lifted her head so he could see her face. And it was … just a face. A face that he wouldn't remember unless he carried on looking at it. She stared into his eyes. Her eyes were as green as the meadow he was standing in. No eyes were truly that colour...

Because this wasn't real. He must remember that.

"Who are you?" He sounded like a child. "What do you want?"

"You know who I am," she said. "I am the Shepherdess. I want to help you."

"Why?"

"Because from the moment you were born, the world has been unfair to you, hasn't it?"

The plantation overseer's wife had had a baby and one of Robert's cousins had been taken into the house to care for the new baby. He'd sometimes see it toddling around on the overseer's porch, or on his cousin's hip. Robert knew that the white child would never starve, never be beaten, never be pulled out of its mother's arms and sold to someone on the other side of the island.

He tried to damp down the memories. This was a dream. They were looking for the Shepherdess and she was standing in front of him.

"What are you?" Robert's voice sounded less hollow this time. "Are you the foundling child?"

The Shepherdess tapped the crook against the ground. "I am the one who cares about lost lambs."

She drifted towards him, then passed him, waiting on the landing.

"Come, Robert. I want to show you something."

She seemed to glide down the rickety steps and he followed her, feeling, rather than hearing, the creak of the floorboards. They left the coffee house and turned on to a street filled with a bitter yellow fog.

"You know the pain of losing someone," the Shepherdess said. "You will understand."

She moved her hands through the fog as if she was rolling up twine. The fog bunched around her, clearing the space before it.

"Look, Robert," she said. "This is the real London."

Robert peered over her shoulder, through the doorway of another garret room. How had they got here?

It's a dream, Robert. Anything can happen.

The room's four walls were bare brick, flaked with peeling plaster, and the ceiling bowed as if a giant foot had stamped down on it. The small fireplace was thick with old ashes. Robert couldn't see a coal scuttle or wood. That hearth had been cold for a long, long time. A ragged coat and bonnet hung on a nail. Beneath it was a small table with a jug, three mugs and a piece of old bread. As Robert watched, a rat scuttled along the edge of the wall and up on to the table. It crouched there, nibbling at the crust.

A bed took up the most space in the room. At least eight people were asleep on it: two mothers, maybe, and their children. The floor was heaped with straw and covered with sleeping people. Some were curled into themselves; some were stretched out flat on their backs, boots crushed against bonnets, arms flung across others' faces. This was almost worse than the plantation cabin where they all had to sleep foot to head, carving out any tiny space they could. But no one in the cabin had smiled in their sleep. The few faces he could see here were relaxed and content. One old man was sitting upright, back against the wall, his neck crooked sideways. As Robert watched, the man slowly slid sideways until he thudded on to the straw. He chuckled loudly but didn't wake.

"Who are all these people?" Robert asked.

"These are all the people that live here."

"In this house?"

"In this room."

"Will they wake?"

The Shepherdess's eyes sparkled in the gloom. "I've helped them find their lost sheep. They may not want to lose them again."

"They'll just dream until they die?"

"Perhaps. But what life do they have to awaken to, Robert?"

He looked again at the Shepherdess. She was no older than twenty, perhaps. There was a fading bruise on her forehead, its square edges raised like it had been branded on to her.

"You asked me what I want," she said. She gestured around the filthy room. "I want an end to *this*. Have you never wondered, Robert, why there is food in your dreams but not on your plate in the Hibberts's kitchen? Why there is warmth and kindness in the Ether but not in the world where you must all labour?"

Yes, of course he had. But he'd known that if he thought too hard about his life, he'd have curled up in a corner and never woken up again – just like the people who filled this room.

"It's always been this way." As the Shepherdess spoke, the garret faded around her and Robert was standing on a deserted street, peering at her through the mist.

"You know Fleet Street," she said. "Feet have trodden this road for thousands of years, Robert, building, destroying, building again. There have always been commanders and foot soldiers." She turned to him, a faint smile on her lips. "And slaves, Robert. There have always been slaves."

He felt the heat rise in his face. Mama had told him for as long as he could remember that "slaves" was what happened to them, not who they were.

"I can change that, Robert."

"By making people die in their sleep!"

"No!" The Shepherdess gripped his wrist. "I can use the Freedom of London." She brought her lips close to his ear. "When I have it I will remake London, Robert. I will bring both Londons together. The Ether and the Solid world will be so close you could flit between the two as you wish. You will be with your brother. Your friend, Lizzie, will be with her sister. You will eat and be warm and never have to walk through the Hibberts's door again."

Never walk through the Hibberts's door again... How?

"In the Ether as it is now, you dream of the life you wish for. But then you must wake to this harsh world. Imagine living in the Ether for as long as you wish. Days, weeks, years. You would live the life you dream of. That is your real London."

"But it will just be a dream!" A good one, though, such a good one! "What will happen to the other London, the one I live in now?"

"Bring me the Freedom, Robert. I have waited until I have the strength to control it. But you saw! I am strong enough to wake the plague monster, to shape its thoughts, to make it take you." She rolled her crook between her palms. Silver spots sparked and faded. "We will remake London so that it serves the poor. You have seen how I can control the sleeping. Imagine if I had the power to make Lady Hibbert serve *you*, Robert. You would sleep on a soft feather mattress and she would scour the pewter. There would be no more cold kitchen corners for you or anyone like you. Lady Hibbert would make sure you were fed in Solid London and that you slept in comfort. Then your dreams would bring you back to the only world that matters, here in the Ether, with your brother."

"Do you mean she would be *my* slave?" Robert could not even imagine such a thing.

"What is your future, Robert? Lady Hibbert will eventually tire of you. You will be sold on like brick dust to some other monstrous woman or back overseas to another plantation to work until you drop dead from exhaustion. Let her clean her own hearth. Let her darn her own stockings. Let her beg for the rotting apples in Covent Garden. Let her feel that pain, Robert. Let all the cruel people feel the pain."

A question darted through his thoughts, but it wouldn't stay still long enough for him to catch it. It was about a woman who was hanged … and a child … and a river. The Fleet river, that was it. A girl thrown into the Fleet.

"She was a foundling." The question dashed closer. He reached for it. "A foundling girl! She was an apprentice and treated badly. Do you know of her? Is … is she you?"

"There is so much cruelty, Robert," the Shepherdess said. "But we can end it. Find it, Robert. Find the Freedom and bring it to me. I'll be watching you, Robert, and waiting."

She pushed him and he fell backwards.

"And, Robert?" She was fading away but her eyes were as bright as emeralds. "I wouldn't have let the monster kill you."

He was falling faster now. Perhaps he would never stop.

A TITHE

Marisee dashed towards the Serpentine, screaming Robert's name as he disappeared beneath the surface.

A tentacle flipped out and flicked her away. She landed with a thump on the grass. Marisee scrambled back up, rubbing her sore back as Westbourne-Tybourne ran among the sleepwalkers, pushing them away from the water's edge. The sleepwalkers, though, were relentless.

"Please!" Marisee slithered down to the water's edge. "You have to save him!"

The Serpentine was greasy with oil and streaked

with muck. The guttering flames of the torches showed the surface as it swelled again. Suddenly, a tentacle broke free. It was holding Robert! His arms dangled, his head flopped from side to side. Marisee had to do something, but what? She had drawn him into this adventure; if she didn't help him, he would die.

The tentacle dropped back into the lake, taking Robert with it.

"No!" Her scream sank away into the water.

Suddenly, everything was still. There were no more barrels or buckets. No more pounding and hammering.

Westbourne-Tybourne stood on the Serpentine bank, between the sleepwalkers and the water. She was stretched so thin she was almost transparent. She was not alone. Other Chads had joined her. They must have been drawn from the wells and tributaries nearby. Perhaps some came from the original springs that had been broken apart to create Queen Charlotte's Serpentine. Many were pale things that barely hung together. Others were small and solid, as if they were made from mud. They sparked with silver that threaded through them all as if that was what held them together. Water sprung from the earth around them, making many sleepwalkers slip in the darkness. Fountains rose from the earth and toppled others over. Ribbons of water curled almost invisible in the dark and knocked weapons from hands. It wasn't enough. It wasn't saving Robert.

"We have to make that beast give Robert back."

Westbourne-Tybourne shook her head. "We cannot. The Articles decree that we must guard it and…"

"The stupid Articles!" Marisee burst into tears. "They're going to kill my friend! Can't anyone help me?"

"A favour for a favour?" The words screeched like the twist of a weathervane.

It sounded just like… Could it be? Marisee squinted into the sky. The air was heavy with the rank smell of burning coal. She clasped her hand over her mouth, coughing. Then the night seemed to split itself apart and settle over the lake. The darkness stretched across the water, a blanket pressing down on the filth. The stench was stronger now, the stink of the putrid slop mixing with the acrid, sulphurous fumes of the soap-makers and tallow-melters.

"A favour for a favour?" the voice called again.

Did she want to owe the Fumis another favour? Without even knowing what it was? They hadn't paid back the last one yet. But Robert was beneath that water, drowning.

"Yes!" she shrieked. "A favour for a favour!"

"A favour for a favour!" The dark smoke curled across the surface of the water towards her. "Use fire!"

Fire? But water couldn't burn! A chairman slithered down through the reeds and was shoved back by a watery jet. He dropped his torch. A little flame still glowed.

Marisee froze. Water itself didn't burn, that was true – but what if it was filled with a mess of things that *did* burn? She had seen a picture in one of Grandma's old books of a warship from long ago set alight during a battle. It blazed with such power that even the sea burned around it. She picked up the torch. This could barely light a candle.

Westbourne-Tybourne glanced back at the lake, then at Marisee. "Please don't hurt it," she begged. "It was woken. It was hurt."

Marisee blew gently on the tiny flame. "If I don't do this, it will kill my friend."

Smoke twisted away from the lake and spun past Westbourne-Tybourne towards Marisee. It curled itself into a hollow bowl.

"Give me the fire," the Fumi said.

Marisee held the flickering wick up to it and the smoke closed around it. The torch light was snuffed, but the smoke itself was streaked with red. It spun back towards the Serpentine, twisting across the lake.

The Serpentine erupted. Shards of bright red flame pierced the churning water, flecking the air with red spume. The creature screamed. It was the sound of pure pain. A tentacle broke the surface, and through the smoke Marisee saw Robert hurled back towards the bank. His body spun through the air. Surely his back would be broken when he hit the ground – if he wasn't dead already. Marisee's hand clamped over her mouth. He stopped, hanging in mid air. Then he drifted slowly down to land next to a willow tree.

"A favour for a favour!" a voice screeched, fading away.

There was a thump as the stake dropped from the butcher's boy's slack hand. He backed away from Marisee, eyes wide and ran away down the path. All around her, it was the same. Poles and staves, axes and hammers fell as the sleepwalkers awoke. Some screamed, others silently surveyed the scene and ran as fast as they could.

Soon, just Marisee and the Chads were left by the lake. The silver threads that drew the water spirits together seemed to pull tight until they were spinning like a bobbin. Their spray splashed against Marisee's face as they lifted from the bank and skimmed the Serpentine, extinguishing the fires. The bobbin became thinner and thinner until it was only Westbourne-Tybourne hovering on the lake.

"She is too strong … strong…" the spirit said, the words echoing each other.

She dissolved into the water.

But Robert? He must be injured or… She wasn't going to believe that he could be dead. She backed away from the lake and ran towards the still figure. Someone was crouched next to Robert, a girl in a blue dress and wide-brimmed hat. She must be a sleepwalker suddenly woken from her dream. There was a thinness about her. She wasn't a ghost, but she reminded Marisee of damp blotting paper, easily torn.

"Is he alive?" Marisee asked. "Please tell me he's alive."

The girl nodded. She stood up and walked away.

Marisee dropped to the ground in front of Robert and touched his forehead. Thank goodness! It was warm.

"Robert?" His eyelids flickered, then opened.

"It's me! Marisee! I thought you were dead."

"I'm not?" He closed his eyes again. Even still, tears escaped. She wished she could wipe them for him, but perhaps he didn't want her to see him crying.

"Can you walk?" she asked gently.

Robert tried to sit up. He winced. "I don't know."

The park had fallen so silent that the clatter of carriage wheels made her jump. She stood up, checking the paths. Yes, there was a chaise bouncing towards them. It was *their* chaise, pulled at speed by Red Rum. It stopped close by on the path. Marisee ran over to it.

"Thank you, Red Rum! Thank you!"

The horse nuzzled Marisee's neck.

"Can you take us to the Foundling Hospital?"

Another nuzzle. Marisee hoped it meant that he understood her. Maybe Red Rum was like the Fleet Ditch boar and secretly spoke several languages.

Marisee helped Robert to his feet and into the carriage. He was soaking wet and shivering. She picked up two discarded lanterns from the banks of the lake; between them, there was enough wick for their journey. She clambered up next to him. His face was smeared with lake weed and his eyes just stared ahead. She wished that she knew a way to console him.

"The roads are empty," she said. "We shouldn't be travelling for too long. I know Mr Jonas Hanway. He's a governor of the Foundling Hospital. He can give you some dry clothes and the Matron can tend to your wounds." *Unless they've become sick too.*

Robert didn't answer. He seemed to have gone deep inside himself. Perhaps she would do the same if she had come so close to death, but she felt so lonely. She missed Grandma so much it felt like her bones were being pulled out of her. And now Robert had gone away too.

She touched his hand. "I'm sorry the monster hurt you. I wouldn't have asked you to come with me if I'd known all these bad things would happen. But once we get to the Foundling Hospital, we'll know who that poor girl was. Then we'll find out how to stop the sickness."

Robert closed his eyes and turned his head away.

She sighed. "I don't know if I can do it without you."

It was hard to see the road ahead, but Marisee presumed they were taking a straight route, heading east along Piccadilly. The lanterns flashed across the closed gates of Burlington House. Marisee wondered if the rich folk who owned it were wandering around their massive mansion trying to wake their slumbering servants. Or perhaps they'd run to the country, leaving their servants to dream to their death.

So far, they had seen no sleepwalkers. Marisee knew she should be pleased about that. But it made her uneasy, as if this was still part of the trick, a plan that she and Robert didn't understand.

The houses and shops gave way to the dark sweep of fields. Marisee wished that Red Rum would keep going on to Clerkenwell where Grandma would be waiting to tell Marisee that everything had returned to normal. They would drink hot chocolate and finally eat toast with butter and plum jam, and Grandma would tell one of her funny stories about the Chads. But the carriage turned off to follow the road through Lamb's Conduit Fields. This was where they must go.

Marisee knew the Foundling Hospital well. Their account with Grandma had been opened soon after the building had been completed. Grandma had been called upon to check the springs before new wells were built on the land. She'd said there were a few small water spirits, but they kept themselves to themselves, and the bigger springs had been diverted many years before and their spirits moved on.

The carriage halted by the gates. Marisee tapped Robert's shoulder. His eyes were still closed, but his body was too rigid to be sleeping. She grabbed her lantern, slid off the seat and on to the ground.

"Robert? We're here."

He opened his eyes, stretched, and then clambered

down from the other side. He had lost his slippers at the Serpentine and his stockings had been shredded. His feet must be so cold. Soon, he'd be warm and dry. Marisee held up her lantern and peered through the gate.

Robert spoke at last. "The children must live well here," he said.

The Hospital did look like a mansion, with two large wings and a chapel between them. Candles burned in many of the windows. Marisee wondered whether those inside were infected by the sleeping sickness. She hoped not. A grand carriageway led up to the entrance, with strips of grass either side and gardens at the rear. On Sundays, Marisee knew that the carriageway was busy with wealthy folk come to watch the orphans sing in the chapel. Sometimes there were concerts held here, but Grandma had never brought her to one.

"I suppose they do live well," Marisee said. "It's better than being left in a workhouse or having no place to live at all. They even send the babies to live with families in the countryside for a few years because it's healthier."

Marisee *didn't* tell him that she had seen the little ones soon after they returned to the Hospital. They'd be crying for the only families they had known.

She stroked Red Rum's neck.

"Thank you. Will you wait here?"

Red Rum lifted his neck, straining at the harness.

"He must be tired and hungry," Robert said. He unbuckled the harness and Red Rum trotted away.

"You're good with horses," Marisee said.

He shook his head with a hint of a smile. "I'm not. But I'll make an exception for this one."

Marisee smiled back at him. He was returning to her.

She unlatched the gate. As her boot crunched on the gravel, shadows pulled away from inside the courtyard wall. The figures carried no light, but Marisee's lantern revealed the brown uniform of the foundlings. These were older children, boys and girls, the ones who would be leaving soon for apprenticeships. The taint of yellow breath swirled around them.

"You will go no further."

Marisee took another step forward. "Let us in. You're sick. We want to help you."

"You will go no further."

The children crowded towards the gate. A woman dressed like a nurse pushed her way through to the front. She held a warming pan, its heavy copper base thumping against her side. The children clutched their own makeshift weapons: chisels and spades, meat mallets and thin logs from the woodpile.

The nurse took another step forwards. Marisee held her ground.

"*She* says you can't go no further," the nurse said.

"But I must—"

The woman's eyes fluttered and her arm jerked backwards, smashing the warming pan against the wall. Marisee jumped backwards. Robert remained still. The nurse moved towards him.

"*She* says that you want to see him again, Robert Strong," the nurse said. "*She* understands."

Marisee looked from the nurse to Robert. He lurched towards the nurse, as if being reeled in to her.

"*March lamb…*" the nurse sang. The children crowded further into the gateway, blocking the entrance. "They sent her to the slaughter, Robert," the nurse said. "There will be no more lambs."

Robert lurched even closer to the nurse.

"*She* says he's waiting for you. When you're ready."

Robert nodded as if his head was jerked by a string. Marisee grabbed his shoulders and pulled him away. She may not have saved him from the monster in the

Serpentine, but she would do everything she could to keep him from the sickness.

The children opened their mouths, tipping their faces upwards. The familiar ache gripped the back of Marisee's neck.

"Ten years, ten tears, dripping from my eyes,
Ten years, ten tears, dripping from my eyes,
Ten years, ten tears, dripping from my eyes."

They sang in tune, but their voices were flat and without feeling. The same line over and over again. *Ten years.* Ten years? That was the last thing they needed to know to find out who the girl was. The terrible thing that happened to her was ten years ago. The answer was inside the Foundling Hospital, Marisee was certain.

Robert wriggled free from her and took another step towards the gate.

If Marisee let him go, he would be lost to her. He could barely walk. His clothes were ripped and torn, his body sagging. Perhaps she should let him lose himself in his dreams.

As Marisee reached him, the foundlings moved in front of him, barring the way. His head jerked upright and his eyes widened. He lifted his bare foot and winced. He looked around and then back at Marisee, turning his back on the Hospital and walking away from the gate.

"What happened?" Marisee asked. "I thought you were going to change into one of them."

He limped past her, not meeting her eye. The nurse and the children stayed by the wall. Then the singing stopped and the gate clanked as the nurse closed it. They returned to the shadows.

Robert was still walking. Marisee hurried after him. Now it was her and not Robert who had so many questions. What had the nurse said to Robert? *She's waiting for you, when you're ready.* She? All the sleepwalkers said that *she* promised. They meant the Shepherdess. The Shepherdess was waiting for Robert? Marisee didn't understand. She had been sure that Robert was on her side until…

Until he'd changed. What had happened to him at the bottom of that lake?

She wanted to trust him so much! But she should have remembered what Grandma said. She should keep her wits about her.

The way ahead was pitch-black. The wavering flame in her lantern barely lit the path around her feet. But there was a small light further along the road – a lamp hanging from a building. Marisee ran to catch up with Robert. She would be very careful from now on.

"The people who live there might have a ladder," she said. "If we can't go through the gate, perhaps we can climb over the wall. The sleepwalkers can't be everywhere at the same time. There might be dry clothes inside too, and shoes…"

Robert kept walking. He didn't even look at her.

"Robert?"

There was no answer apart from the slap of his bare feet on the stone path. She took a deep breath to keep her voice calm.

"Robert, I want to trust you, but how can I if you won't talk to me? Something happened at Hyde Park, didn't it? I know you were hurt, but it was more than that."

He glanced at her and then away again. "I can't really remember much. It was mostly dreams."

"Were you in the Ether?"

Robert finally stopped walking and turned to face Marisee. Her lantern cast deep shadows beneath his eyes. There was a graze above his eyebrow that she hadn't noticed before.

"Yes," he said.

"Did you see who's causing the sickness? Is it the foundling girl? Did she tell you her name?" She should stop, but she couldn't. "What does she want to do with the Freedom?" *And what about Grandma?* Marisee longed to ask. *Did she say anything about her?*

Robert waited while the questions tumbled out, then started walking again. The splash of light ahead grew closer.

"Was she in the Ether, Robert? Was the Shepherdess there?"

"Yes."

She waited, but he stayed silent. She wanted to scream at him. She held her hand over her mouth and her words quietened.

"I just want my Grandma back," she said quietly. "If you know why this is happening, please tell me."

Robert sighed. "I think she's sad, Marisee. Angry and sad. That's why she wants to change things."

This time the words burst out. "She wants hundreds of people to die because she's angry and sad? She must hate everyone in London, and you sound like you feel sorry for her!"

"You don't know anything about me!" Robert's voice

caught in his throat, but Marisee felt his anger pushing back at hers. "I know what it's like to hate people. I still do. Before I even came to London, I hated Lord Hibbert and Mr Soothing and all of them on the plantation. And when I thought I'd hated them as much as I could, they took me away from Mama and my sisters and I hated them even more."

Marisee looked away from him. Grandma had always told her that "hate" was a bad word to use. This quiet, serious boy was suddenly so full of hatred that it frightened her.

"Why were you on the plantation?" she asked.

"I was born there. So was Mama. Her grandma was stolen from her family thousands of miles away. She told Mama that all her family were tied together and locked in the ship's hold. There were hundreds of people down there, all tangled together, and she couldn't tell who was alive or dead."

Marisee had heard the stories of people taken to the West Indies to grow sugar and cocoa. Grandma had said that even Marisee should be careful walking through London in case someone kidnapped her. Grandma had seen posters in coffee shops asking for information about girls that looked like Marisee who had run away from cruel homes. There were rewards if they were captured.

"Mr Soothing was the overseer on the plantation," Robert said. "He was even crueller than Mrs Wandle, the Hibberts's cook, and *she* hates everyone. Lord Hibbert had a whip made from manatee skin and Mr Soothing flicked it at my sister. She was only seven years old. He said it was because my mother wasn't working hard enough. I miss Mama. I hate being here. I don't think you could ever understand that."

Of course Marisee understood! *I can't remember my parents, Robert. You don't understand what it's like to miss someone you never knew.* But she had to keep that to herself for now because they'd reached the inn. The door was closed. She hammered on the locked door as hard as she could and it made her feel better.

A curtain twitched in the window, but the door stayed shut. She looked up and down the road. There was a scattering of houses, but all were in darkness. She wished she was brave enough to break a window and climb in.

Only a few hours ago, the sleepwalkers had smashed their way into Grandma's pump room. So much had happened since then. They had solved a riddle from a Dragon, escaped Walbrook's fury in the Mithraeum and survived an attack by a plague monster in Hyde Park.

They couldn't give up now. Just on the other side of that Foundling Hospital wall she would discover who was causing this sickness.

"I'll have a look around the back," Marisee said. "In case there's another way in."

Robert followed her. As they moved away, a curtain fluttered in an upstairs window. Marisee knew that if she herself was in there, she certainly wouldn't welcome strangers.

Marisee opened the gate to a small garden. Her light fell on some chairs, a skittles board and something else. A well. Marisee's stomach gave a little jolt. A *well*...

Wells led deep underground. Grandma had said that there had once been watercourses across these fields. Could there be water from the well to the Hospital? If Marisee couldn't go through the Hospital gate or over the wall, could she creep in from beneath?

She straightened her back. There was only one way to find out. She would have to do it. She would have to jump in.

Robert would have to stay behind. Turnmill wouldn't be there to catch him. And she wasn't sure that she wanted him with her now, anyway.

But Robert was already peering down the well.

"I've found a ladder," he said.

Marisee dangled her lamp over the side. A rope ladder was nailed on to the inside wall. She could not see if there was water below it.

She found a pebble and dropped it in. There was silence, then the tap of it landing on something solid.

"The well's dry," she said.

"Perhaps there's a tunnel at the bottom," Robert said. "Like the one that Turnmill carried us through. I think we should have a look."

He didn't wait for an answer. He climbed on to the ladder and disappeared into the darkness. Marisee had no choice. She would have to follow. The Hospital gate was guarded. The walls were too high. If there was a tunnel at the bottom, it was her only way in.

She waited until the ladder stopped moving and picked up the lantern. The wick was nearly burned out, but any light was better than none. She clutched it tight with one hand and the ladder with the other. Luckily, the rough rope stopped her hand sliding. It may have been the one thing that was easier in bare feet. Her boots glanced off the narrow rungs and the ladder twisted and swung with every step. She moved slowly and steadily, clinging with her lantern-arm around the ladder each time her grip moved down. Jumping into a well full of water was much easier.

Suddenly, there were no more rungs. She stretched her leg right down and it touched the ground. She breathed out, long and hard. Instantly, she was plunged into complete darkness. The wick had been burned away.

"Here." There was a noise beside her, metal striking metal, then a sprinkle of sparks. "Hurry!"

The cold waxy curve of a candle knocked against her hand. She took it, felt for the wick and held it ready. Robert blew gently on to the tinder and a tiny flame flickered.

"Now," he said.

Marisee dipped the wick into the flame as Robert blew a little harder.

So this was how people started fires without Dragon fire!

"Light!" she pleaded. "Light!"

The candle glowed and the flame fluttered and flared. Robert was holding another candle that he lit from hers. He placed it into a small iron candelabra.

"There are boxes of candles here, and candle holders," he said, looking around. "And another tinderbox. The innkeeper must come down here often."

Marisee jammed her candle into the candelabra next to Robert's. They lit two more candles and a new lantern that was already half-filled with oil. The bricks were dry and free from moss. There hadn't been water in here for a long time. But there had definitely been people. A tunnel led away from them. It was lined with barrels and boxes. Robert lifted the lid from one of the barrels and sniffed.

"Coffee," he said. He checked a second one. "Coal."

Many containers were marked with the names of different boats. They rummaged through the containers. One box held rolls of silk, while another filled the air with the scent of spices. Marisee peered into an unmarked box. It was crammed with bolts of heavy brown fabric, the same one used to make the foundlings' uniforms. The ends of each bolt were ragged as if a length had been torn away. Another box contained jars of flour and sacks of oats. Marisee pushed back the lid of a trunk. It was packed with brown dresses and trousers, white aprons and a few pairs of shoes.

"I think the innkeeper is a receiver," Marisee said.

Robert was pushing his feet into a pair of shoes.

"What's a receiver?" he said.

"They buy stolen things." She tapped the barrel

of coal. "This must have come from the boats on the Thames. Some of the porters like to help themselves. And a shameful person must be stealing the orphans' clothes from the Hospital. The innkeeper must store it all here before selling it on." She held up a small white bonnet. The strings were so short they would have barely tied beneath a small child's chin and a hole was cut from the crown. "These are made for the foundling girls, but it's strange. It's like someone has cut a little bit from all of them." She shrugged. "Perhaps they were made by someone still learning to sew."

Robert looked down at his shoes. The laces were too short and the heels were uneven, but they seemed to fit. "I don't want to steal from orphans."

"You can give everything back afterwards," Marisee said.

Robert nodded. He started to peel off his damp shirt. She turned her back. When she looked around again, he was wearing several shirts layered on top of each other. One was missing a sleeve, the other a collar.

"None of them are complete," he said.

It was strange. Marisee knew that the Foundling Hospital needed every scrap of clothing, even the damaged ones, to mend and wear again. Mr Jonas

Hanway had always told Grandma how careful they had to be with money. It was hard to persuade people to feel sorry for the children of poor, unmarried women.

Marisee stared down the tunnel. Perhaps there used to be a stream here, one of the ones that flowed through the fields before they built the Hospital. Now it was used by a thief to steal from the foundlings.

She picked up her lantern and started to walk.

The tunnel was wide enough for Marisee and Robert to walk side by side. The ground was deeply rutted by the barrels and boxes that had been dragged though it, many now stacked against the wall. The wall itself was solid clay held back by wooden struts that gradually gave way to brick. The brickwork was neat and precise, though there were gaps where the clay showed through as if bricks had been removed to make a pattern. There was something about it – how regular it was – that bothered Marisee, but she wasn't sure why.

"Look," Robert said. "There's light."

The tunnel narrowed to a small archway ahead. The light flickered on the other side, a flame that was more white than orange. They stopped, listening.

"I think someone's there," Marisee whispered.

"Of course we are here," a voice replied. "We are

always here. If you wish to pass, you must pay us. Those are the rules. The watchman knows that. The innkeeper knows that. You must know that."

Marisee and Robert looked at each other.

"Who are you?" Marisee called out.

"You walk through our tunnels and you don't know? For shame! Come through so we can see you."

It was a strange voice, high and brassy like a trumpet but with a snort at the end of each sentence. Marisee wasn't sure if she wanted to meet its owner. What lay ahead? But still she had to go forward.

The tunnel widened into a room. The walls were lined with shelves, and each shelf was crammed with jars and boxes. A neatly labelled tag dangled from each. It reminded Marisee a little of the pump room. Only that morning, she had been sitting at her table, thinking about the labels for the water. There was a table here too and someone sitting at it, scribbling in a ledger, his thin hand clasping a pen made from a long, white feather.

It was a man. His slick white hair fell in feathery wisps around his ears. He looked up. His face was smooth and unlined and his eyebrows as black as ink. His eyes were the brightest blue and seemed to flash in the strange flickering light. There was a lantern on his desk and others scattered around the shelves. The candles within were black and the reflectors behind shone back white light. They looked like blinking eyes.

"Oh," the man said. He sounded happy. "We see you."

He pushed back the chair and stood up. He was no taller or shorter than most men that Marisee had met, but he was different in other ways. His neck was just a little longer and, as he studied her and Robert, his head bobbed down and up again. His nails were white and in the centre of each was painted an eye. But it was his cloak that Marisee could not look away from. It was made from swans' skins, complete with heads, necks and wings. The cloak moved around the man, the birds' necks all stretching the same way, glassy eyes fixed on Marisee and Robert. Marisee shivered.

"You are the Well Keeper's granddaughter," the man said.

Marisee nodded. Her mouth was too dry to talk. The cloak fluttered. How many swans were there? Ten? There were ten. A wing tip poked out then disappeared. As the man walked towards her, the cloak rustled to the side as the swans tilted their heads to keep her in view.

"Quieten," he said.

The cloak drooped back in place.

"And you are the boy from Bloomsbury," the man said.

Robert nodded. "How ... how did you know?"

"We see you," the man said. "We see everything." He reached for two jars from a high shelf. As he stretched, Marisee glimpsed bright yellow stockings and shoes that were wide and flat. "How do you intend to make your payment?"

"Payment?" Marisee said.

The man's head bobbed down and up. "The tithe, of course! I am the tithe-master! Even the Keeper of Wells herself must pay to pass through. No exceptions. I must take one tenth."

"One tenth of what?" Marisee didn't understand. "I have nothing for you to take one tenth from."

The tithe-master shone his blinking lantern around the room. "There is always something to take from." The light rested on a stack of crates in a corner. "There's your traditionals: your coal and your wool and your coffee that gets taken off the boats on the big river. Sometimes we get fruit. We like a fig or two. Our masters let us have that. Fruit don't keep and we hate waste. Me and the birds like an apple or a fig, but not too many. You can't feed a swan cloak fruit and not have consequences. My birds might be a bit flat-like, but that fruit's got to come out somewhere."

"Your masters?" Robert asked.

The tithe-master nodded. "They see everything, my masters. You can't hide from them. Everything goes back to them in the end. I just collect their dues."

Everything goes back to them in the end. Marisee had heard that before. "Are your masters the Magogs?"

The tithe-master snorted. "Please show respect. Messrs Gog and Magog are currently indisposed, but they have eyes everywhere. We watch for them. We take what's theirs."

"So to pass you, we must pay a tenth of something?" Marisee said.

The tithe-master nodded. The swans nodded too. "A tenth of something of value to you."

"What if we haven't got anything?" Robert said.

"We told you," the tithe-master said, "there is always something." He waved his lantern towards the higher shelves. The top one was lined with clear glass jars. They looked empty.

"Some folks give me ideas," he said.

"You take a tenth of their ideas?" Marisee said.

"We do if they wish to give them to me. We have taken

a tenth of breath. A tenth of a year." On the shelf below the seemingly empty jars was another crowded with jars that Marisee wished were *not* clear. One – tall and column-shaped – was half-filled with a dark liquid. Was that blood? The bell-shaped jar next to it held something stumpy, with a nail at the end. A toe? Marisee took a deep breath and tried to keep her face blank, though her stomach was churning.

The tithe-master grinned. His mouth was as wide as an open beak. "Bodies have always got extra bits they don't need."

"What's in here?" Robert was standing by a tall vase that reached almost to his chest. The glass stopper was sealed in wax. At first, Marisee thought the vase was shimmering glass. But as she looked closer, she realized that the glass was clear, and its dark contents were swirling up and around. For a moment, Marisee saw a smudge of pink, like a petal, before it dissolved back into the eddy of grey.

A *favour for a favour?* A petal of pink in a cloud of smoke – the name that only another Fumi could pronounce… The Fumi at the churchyard had been sure that their friend was trapped below ground. Robert was staring at it, thoughtfully. Was he thinking the same thing? Marisee had to push that to the back of her mind now. The important thing was to find a way into the Foundling Hospital. When she found Grandma, they would come back.

Robert rested his hand on the stopper and asked again. "What's in here?"

"That is none of our business today," the tithe-master said. "Our business is your payment." He sat back down at the table and picked up his white feather pen. "How will payment be made?"

Marisee looked down at her dress and boots. They could lose a tenth easily.

The tithe-master was nodding slowly as if he had read her mind. "Dress, boots, apron, bonnet. It seems so much, but I need more. What else can you give? Something truly valuable to you."

What else could there be? She glanced around the room again. A mannequin's doll was draped in strips of jackets, each with one dangling sleeve. Behind it was a row of upright poles that ended in bulbous wooden heads. They were criss-crossed with the remains of periwigs of all styles and colours.

"You can take my hair," she said. "A tenth of my hair."

The tithe-master rubbed his hands. "A tenth of your

hair?"

Marisee nodded. It had taken her so long to be happy with her hair. When she was little, she had longed for it to dangle out of her bonnet like the other girls in the village. She had even once tried to cut off her curls with Grandma's candle-wick trimmer. Now, though, she loved the way her thick braids filled her bonnet.

"That will line our nest nicely," the tithe-master said.

Neither of them moved, but she felt a weight lift from her head. One of her thick braids dangled from the tithe-master's fingers. He dropped it into a jar.

"Will it grow back?" she asked.

"Oh no." The tithe-master's pen scratched as he wrote out a label. "What would be the value of a tithe if it grew back?"

Marisee touched the place where her hair had been. It was soft stubble, not one curl left. It was just hair. She had to remember that. Only one braid, a small price to pay.

The tithe-master looked up. "You are free to pass," he said. "But only you. He has given nothing."

Robert bit his lip. Marisee eyed him. How could he pay anything? The clothes weren't his. Hair, perhaps? But it was short, and she was sure it wouldn't be enough for the tithe-master. Perhaps this was where she and Robert parted.

"Go back," she said. "If I find a way into the Hospital, I'll help you in too."

"I want to come with you now, Marisee," he said. "I must."

"Then pay your dues to pass," the tithe-master said.

"Sometimes you take breath or ideas or years?" Robert said.

The tithe-master nodded more eagerly than Marisee liked.

"What about memories?" Robert asked. "Can you take a tenth of my memories?"

The tithe-master leaned forward. His blue eyes glittered. "Ohhh, that is a most acceptable payment."

"No, it isn't!" Marisee said. "Robert, you don't have to come."

"I do," Robert said. "I have few memories that I will miss."

"But there must be ones that you want to keep?" Marisee turned to the tithe-master. "Can he choose which ones go? Can you just take away the bad ones?"

"We take a tenth!" The tithe-master was out of his seat again. The swans writhed around him. "That's the rule! If you wish to pass through we take a tenth. Good memories and bad memories, we take a tenth." He grinned at Robert again. This time Marisee saw that his mouth was empty of teeth. "Are you ready?"

Robert touched the tall, cloudy vase again. "What's in here isn't a tenth, though, is it? This is a whole and you cannot keep it trapped here."

The tithe-master's eyes narrowed. They were like the edge of two blades. "That is not your business. It didn't want to pay. You cannot pass through and refuse to pay. You cannot linger where you are not wanted." The tithe-master stepped towards Robert. One by one, the swans' beaks opened and snapped shut. "Do you understand?" The tithe-master's voice was low. "You cannot linger where you are not wanted. Pay your dues and leave."

"I understand." Robert said and kicked the vase hard.

The tithe-master dived to catch it, but the squirming cloak made him clumsy. The vase fell to the ground and shattered. The air became a dark wind sodden with smells of the city. Lime kilns and breweries, candle makers and forgers. Then it rushed past Marisee back towards the well.

Marisee and Robert hurtled in the opposite direction. Marisee didn't have to look back. She knew that the tithe-master and his swans were watching them.

FOUNDLING

The Fumi swept past Robert. For a moment, Robert's head seemed to be full of white feathers, then it cleared again. He was so tired. It was hard to move faster than a shuffle. Shoes were better than bare feet, but the uneven heels made him stumble. It was hard to think properly. He needed to think.

Marisee seemed sure that the answers lay in the Foundling Hospital. If the Freedom of London ended up in his hands, what would he do? After all, the Shepherdess was right. London was often a cruel place. Robert did want to make it better. But could he really betray Marisee?

The tunnel ended in a flight of steps and a small door. Marisee flung herself at it and it gaped open on to an even steeper flight of steps closed in by another door. Robert dragged himself upwards after her. The second door needed both of them to push it open. Then they were in a kitchen. It was nowhere near as grand as the one at the Mansion House, though it was still far grander than the Hibberts's. There was so much of everything. Enormous pots and kettles, rows of bread bins and grain barrels. Cups of milk were lined up on a tray as if waiting to be shared out.

"How many children live here?" Robert asked.

"About six hundred, I think," Marisee said.

An army of sleepwalkers, Robert thought. *Or even worse, all those children who would stay lost in their dreams until the end.*

"Where do we go now?" he asked.

"We have to find the records," Marisee said. "The details are taken by the steward, so we need his office."

They padded through the kitchen and up another flight of stairs. They arrived at a small hallway with three doors in front of them. The first opened into a large squarish room filled with tables and benches. Tall windows looked on to a courtyard, and a row of lamps cast light on the enormous faces of serious-looking men in the portraits on the wall.

"The dining room," Marisee said.

If this was just where the orphans ate, what was the rest of the Hospital like? It must be a palace. Perhaps the Shepherdess was wrong. Perhaps London wasn't as cruel as she claimed.

Marisee closed the door quietly. "The Committee Room is near the entrance." She pointed. "I think it's that way; it's next to the waiting room. I think the offices are at the back near the chapel. It must be one of these." She studied the two doors. "It's this one." She tapped a copper plate screwed into the door. "It says 'Steward's Office'."

Reading seemed so easy to Marisee. One day, Robert would learn.

Marisee twisted the handle and they both stepped into the office. Robert had often glimpsed inside Lord Hibbert's study in Barbados. It had been painted white and featured a heavy wooden desk that had been shipped to the plantation especially from Bloomsbury. Several portraits of Lady Hibbert were hung on the panelled walls, faded in the sun. When Lord Hibbert wasn't patrolling his plantations with Mr Soothing, he was hunched over the desk, wiping his forehead with his handkerchief and ordering his maid to fan him quicker.

This office was also panelled in wood, with paintings on the wall. There were more serious-looking white men, but also paintings of fields and rivers. A large engraving of a coat of arms hung over the window. It showed a naked baby on a shield and a lamb with a sprig of something in its mouth. There was also a woman sweeping back her cloak to show six breasts.

"It's the Hospital coat of arms," Marisee said. "Grandma says she blushes every time she sees it."

Robert was blushing too.

Marisee opened the top drawer of a bureau that had been pushed against the far wall. She lifted out a thick book. "Yes, these are what we need."

"What are they?" he asked.

"Billet books." Marisee flicked through the pages and eased the book back in the drawer. "Records of when the babies were admitted. Remember that lullaby the Shepherdess sings?"

There was still a faint echo of it in his head. *Ten years and ten tears.*

"Something bad happened ten years ago," Marisee

said. "It must have been when Mrs Broxbourne did that terrible thing. And ten years ago…" She thought. "1754. That was definitely the second George. She would have been apprenticed when she was twelve or thirteen." Marisee opened another drawer. "So she would have been born around 1741 or 1742. We need to find the billet books from then. The Hospital hadn't moved here yet. I hope they brought those old records with them." Marisee looked up. "How old did she seem to you?"

"Older than fourteen," he said. Much older.

"Do you think people get older in the Ether?"

Robert could picture … someone… Their face narrowed and a beard spread across their chin and— it must have been such a small part of his dream because he couldn't remember.

"Perhaps," he said.

"It must be her, Robert. She was thrown into the Fleet ten years ago, and somehow she's come back and wants revenge." Marisee pulled two more books out of the drawer and laid them on the desk. One fell open. The scratchy black marks made no sense to Robert, but there was more to this page than words. The patch of pale blue cloth and a small paper packet sealed with black wax had its own story to tell.

"What's this?" he asked.

"The Hospital cuts a patch of fabric from each baby's clothes to give to their parents," Marisee explained. "Another piece is placed here, in case the parents return for their baby. They can match the patches."

"What's wrapped in the paper?"

"Sometimes the parents leave tokens with their babies for the same reason. So they can find them again."

"Why don't they just ask for their children by name?"

Marisee looked back at the page. "The babies don't keep their names. They're given a number and a different name." She held up the book she was holding. "This was a girl, baby number 8073. The Hospital baptized her Desdemona Wilkinson."

Robert ran his finger across the scrap of blue cloth. "Why did they take their names away from them?" he said.

Marisee closed the book. "I suppose it was to help them. To save them from shame."

"They took away who they really were," Robert said. "That's what they did to us in Barbados. Mama had to call me by the name that Lord Hibbert gave me, whether she liked it or not. Robert Hibbert. That's who I'm supposed to be, but I'm not."

"No," Marisee said. "You're not. You are Robert Strong."

Yes, he was. But didn't he have another name, a special name? Someone would call him it, someone he loved. He wasn't just Robert, he was ... Ke... It wasn't important. He closed the book.

"Wait!" Marisee said. "Can you find that page again?"

He opened the book, turning the pages carefully, each one heavy with secrets.

"This one?" he said.

Marisee held up a token packet from the book in front of her. "Look at the seal."

It was the same as the red wax used in the Hibberts's household.

"Look at yours," Marisee said.

The wax was black.

"Black is the colour of mourning," Marisee said.

Robert rubbed the packet between his fingers. "It feels empty."

"Perhaps it's a slip of paper, or lace."

Robert looked at it more closely. He could see flakes of red wax as if the original seal had been broken. Perhaps the token had been taken out and the packet resealed with black wax. He held the packet closer to his eyes. There were tiny numbers written below the seal along with some letters. Robert did know numbers, as he'd learned to count cocoa pods with his mother when he was a tiny child. They said 1741 and 1754.

"I think it's her birth year and death year," Marisee said.

This child would have been thirteen when she died, the same age as Robert. He held the small, flat packet on the palm of his hand.

"Should we open it and look?"

Marisee thought for a moment. "It doesn't feel right, does it?"

"No." These were packets of hope and sadness. It would be wrong to tear them apart.

"I would like a closer look at the book, though," Marisee said.

Robert handed it over.

"The baby was a girl, admitted in 1741 when the Hospital was on its old site in Hatton Gardens," Marisee said. "She was registered as baby number 33. Her mother died in childbirth and her father couldn't care for her."

Robert couldn't understand it. Didn't the baby have an auntie or a cousin who could take her in? How could there be no one? Death came often to families on the plantation, but there was always someone to care for the children.

"What was her name?" he said.

"Her new name..." Marisee squinted at the spidery writing. "The name the Hospital gave her was Sally Blake." She looked up and her eyes were shining. "I think we've found her. The dates fit... Sally Blake must be the Shepherdess, Robert."

"But there might be others who—"

Robert glimpsed a flash of movement in the doorway – the brown sleeve of the Hospital uniform. A furious shriek made his breath stop. Sleepwalkers!

"They are not sleeping!" a man shouted. "Do not attack!"

The foundling halted, his weapon raised. It was a soup ladle. The man had entered behind him. He was older, his clothes dark, his wig white and curled. His breath, like the boy's, was clear. He touched the boy's arm.

"Go back to the chapel, Erasmus."

Erasmus glared at Robert, then strutted away, the ladle dangling by his side.

"Mr Hanway!" Marisee ran towards the man.

"Miss Marisee Blackwell?" Mr Hanway surveyed the

books spread open across the desk and folded his arms. "Miss Blackwell! How dare you intrude on our children's secrets! These are desperate times, but this can never be excused." He gently closed the books and beckoned towards someone unseen outside the door. "Mr Carper, take them to the chapel!"

Mr Carper was very tall and very wide. He wore the long dark coat and hat that Robert knew from the watchmen in Bloomsbury. He carried a wooden staff in one hand and a fire poker in the other. He scowled at them from beneath thick, grey eyebrows.

"Come with me," he said. "And don't even think of no tricks."

Robert had only ever been inside one church before and that was St George's in Bloomsbury. He'd been baptized there, and every Sunday it was his duty to dress in his most impressive costume to attend Lady Hibbert. It was the very same church where the unicorn had leaped from the steeple and the statue had stared into his face. That seemed even more like a dream now. He touched the sore spot on his forehead. Had that really been from a stone unicorn's horn? Perhaps he had jabbed himself and forgotten. His tiredness was making him forgetful.

The chapel of the Foundling Hospital was well lit with candles jammed into anything that could hold them – saucers, clay pots, even an old shovel. There were no statues, but there was a tall wooden pulpit and wooden galleries, like those in St George's. He imagined the lords and ladies sitting up there, watching the orphans singing. The pews were full of children. Some wore the Hospital uniform, others looked like children of the street, ragged and coated with dirt.

A girl in a bright blue bonnet sat on the floor by the font. She held a penny whistle to her lips but did not blow it, her eyelids heavy and her breath hanging in a cloud around her mouth. An older girl with a kind face flitted between the children, offering words of comfort. She carried a big handbell. She stopped by the girl in the blue bonnet and rang the bell hard. The girl jerked fully awake again.

Robert's eyes passed over them to the altar and stopped. A painting hung above it. Right at the front of the picture, was him, Robert. He closed his eyes and opened them again. But the figure who looked like Robert was still there in the painting. He walked towards it. Dimly, he heard Mr Carper threaten him and Marisee plead with Mr Hanway to let them go. He let their words wash past him. The painting was all that he could see. He stood and stared.

Close up, the painted figure was older than Robert but had the same dark skin. He wore a white turban and matching robes edged with blue. Jewels hung from his ears and around his neck. He bore a chalice of gold, or some other precious metal that he was offering to the baby Jesus. This man was not a servant or stolen to be made a slave. He was a king. Something leaped inside of Robert. The man who looked like Robert was a king! Mama had said that their people were kings and queens and warriors. He had wanted to believe it, but really it had just seemed like stories. But here, in the palace for orphans, he saw it. In a different time, maybe in a different London, people like Robert could indeed be kings.

And he, Robert, could make that happen. If he gave the Freedom to the Shepherdess, together they would make London so much better. Poor people would never be cold or hungry or treated badly again. Rich people like the Hibberts would know how it felt to be like Robert. Would he – could he – betray Marisee? He made his decision.

"If you can hear me, Shepherdess," he whispered. "I will do what you ask."

Thank you, Robert. The words were like a lullaby in his head.

He felt the weight of sleep push down on him. His eyelids fluttered and his head filled with her song.

"March lamb, walk lamb, follow the sheep…"

The song wasn't just in his head. It was in the chapel too. Everyone fell silent.

"Open eyes, close eyes, sleep, lambkins, deep…"

There was more than one voice. The Shepherdess, yes, elegant and soothing, but also children's voices, high and flat. The clash of metal on metal beat time to the song.

"Ten years, ten tears, will I let you wake?"

"Bolt the door!" Mr Hanway shouted.

It was too late. The girl in the blue bonnet ran past him and threw the door open wide. She put the penny whistle to her lips, and it was almost hidden in the cloud of yellow breath. The shrill sound bounced off the chapel walls.

"Ten years, ten tears, will I let you wake?"

The nurse entered first, bashing the warming pan with fire tongs. Her mouth was open wide with song, each note a blast of yellow. She was followed by the children who had been with her by the gates, making their own noise. Sticks tapped against writing slates. A boy had taken two pots from the kitchen and was slamming them together. A girl hit a saucepan lid with a gardening fork.

"Ten years, ten tears, will I let you wake?"

And now *she* came, behind all of them. He glimpsed the icy blue of her dress first, then the waistcoat of dirt-streaked linen. Her straw hat was gone. It was replaced by the same simple white bonnet worn by the foundling girls. He noticed then that the brooch pinned to her waistcoat was made from beaten copper. The image engraved on it was one he had seen before: a lamb holding a sprig in its mouth. *She* banged her twisted, rusty crook on the chapel doorstep.

The noise stopped.

"Ten years, so many tears, will I let you wake?" Her voice had sunk so low, Robert had to lean towards her, leaning and leaning, so far he was falling. Drowsiness was closing in on him, his knees giving way. The dreams were circling, but he heard the last words of the lullaby.

"Yes, dears, wake and hear" – the Shepherdess's voice rose – "who killed Sally Blake?"

THE
FORGOTTEN FACE

Marisee stared at her. So this was the Shepherdess! She didn't look anything like Marisee had expected. Robert was right, she was older than thirteen or fourteen. She was maybe twenty or more, but the white bonnet made her face seem younger. Her eyes were bright green and her face – Marisee thought that if she closed her eyes she would forget it instantly, except for the raised mark on her forehead. The mark was shaped like a rectangle and looked like it had been caused by a burn.

But of course! Marisee had seen that face before!

And she *had* forgotten it. This was the woman who'd been bending over Robert after the Serpentine creature had thrown him from the lake. She glanced at Robert. He was watching the Shepherdess intently, as if she was saying things to him that only he could hear. Her heart pulled. She'd wanted to trust him so much, but how could she when the Shepherdess had spoken to him in his dreams and he wouldn't tell Marisee what she'd said?

The Shepherdess's voice was almost a whisper. "Yes, dears, wake and hear – who killed Sally Blake?"

Robert dropped to the floor with a thud. A smudge of yellow breath escaped from his mouth.

The Shepherdess raised a hand. "Waken."

Robert stayed sleeping, but the chapel echoed with the clatter of wood and metal on stone as the weapons fell from the sleeping foundlings' hands. They looked around them, their eyes wide with shock, before running towards the pews and away up to the gallery.

Only the nurse remained. The warming pan had crashed to the ground. Her arms were crossed in front of her as if tied at the wrist, yet there was nothing binding them. Or was there? Marisee looked more carefully. Was that a thin silver thread digging into the skin on the nurse's wrists? Or was that a trick of the candlelight?

Jonas Hanway was staring at the Shepherdess.

"Mr Hanway?" Marisee said. "We … we came here to find out who was causing the sleeping sickness. We think it's a girl called Sally Blake. Do you remember her?"

"Poor Sally was the victim of terrible cruelty." James Hanway was still staring at the Shepherdess. "She was murdered ten years ago. Her murderer confessed that the poor child was thrown in the river and therefore not even permitted a Christian burial. Her body was never found."

"Is this Sally Blake?" Marisee said.

He shook his head. "No. This is an even worse devilment. I'm sure I knew this woman many years ago. She has not aged. I had forgotten her, but now I see her again… She looks exactly as she did then. She is—"

The Shepherdess thumped her crook on to the floor again. Silver sparks bounced from the stone around her, then stretched themselves into taut threads that tangled at her feet. She smiled at Mr Hanway. The smile reminded Marisee of Lou Lou, the ghost in Hyde Park, who even after death believed that she would be a princess. It was a smile ready to shatter into rage.

"Be quiet, Mr Hanway." Her voice was a dry whisper. "I can speak for myself. Sally Blake cannot. *I* came to tell her tale. And you" – she tapped the nurse's shoe with her crook – "can add to the tale if you so wish." She turned to gaze at Mr Carper, the watchman. "You, sir, as well."

The watchman moved quickly. He ran to the chapel door and it slammed behind him. The Shepherdess laughed. "I fear he does not want to be reminded of his part. But he will be. His time will come."

"I remember Sally Blake," Jonas Hanway said. "My heart still breaks when I think of what she endured at the hands of that monstrous Mrs Broxbourne."

"I told you to stay quiet, Mr Hanway." The silver threads writhed at the Shepherdess's feet. "Sally Blake was given to you in trust." The Shepherdess tapped her brooch. "Her father left this token with her in case he took another wife who would be content to care for his daughter."

"But no one came for her," Marisee said quietly.

"They did not," Jonas Hanway said. "She was a happy child, I believe. Perhaps some said she was a little wild, not always good at following instructions."

The Shepherdess stared at him. She did not blink. Eventually, Mr Hanway looked away. "But, of course," she said, "the governors want all the children to be as one. Is that not so, Mr Hanway? The foundlings must wear the same clothes. They must follow the same rules. They must know their place. But, Mr Hanway, perhaps you would like to tell us why Sally Blake left the Hospital."

"Yes … um…" Jonas Hanway looked away from her. "Sally was apprenticed to Mrs Broxbourne, a midwife. We were not familiar with her, but she was recommended to us by…" He broke off.

"Ah," said the Shepherdess softly. "Who recommended her?"

The nurse flinched. The silver threads rustled again.

"Do you have something to say, Nurse Page?" the Shepherdess said. "It is not yet your turn to speak, but you may correct my story if I am wrong. You and Mr Carper, the watchman, were already busy stealing from this Hospital. You take food and even these children's clothes to sell to the innkeeper in the village."

The nurse opened her mouth to speak, but the Shepherdess shook her head.

"You spoke well of your friend, Nurse Page. You advised the matron that Sally would be well taken care of by Mrs Broxbourne. It is a pity that you did not care to mention that Mrs Broxbourne had employed two girls before from the Clerkenwell workhouse who were treated most harshly. The magistrate believed Mrs Broxbourne when she said that they had run away, but if Mr Carper was still in the room, he could tell us otherwise. He already knew of the crumbling house in Chick Lane with the trapdoor in the basement."

Jonas Hanway covered his face with his hands. "I wish I had known this. I am so sorry."

"And, Nurse Page, you did not mention that Mrs Broxbourne paid you five pounds once Sally Blake's apprenticeship was secured."

Jonas Hanway shook his head. "Was poor Sally the only one? Were there others?"

"Sally was the only one from this hospital," the Shepherdess said.

Jonas Hanway sighed. "Even one is too much."

"And you know who I am, Mr Hanway. The devilment, as you called me." The silver threads reared up, flicking out sparks. They coiled together again.

"You look like her." Jonas Hanway rubbed his eyes. "You are identical to her. Her name was Caroline Lamb, but you should be older."

"That was my name." The Shepherdess chuckled. "I told you that I was named after the Mr Lamb who built the conduit through these fields. Though perhaps that wasn't the real story. Perhaps the fields were named after me."

"I thought you came from the village," Jonas Hanway said.

"I was here *before* the village, Mr Hanway." The crook clattered against the chapel floor again. There were more silver sparks, but these seemed to scuttle across the ground towards the nurse. Her eyes widened as the sparks spread out in a circle around her. "Before this mighty hospital of yours was built on these fields."

"Then who are you?" Jonas Hanway stood tall. "And what are you?"

"Do you really want to know?" The Shepherdess looked him in the eye.

"We are in God's house," he said. "I will not fear you."

You should fear her, Marisee thought. Because now she knew exactly what Caroline Lamb was. It was not a trick of the candlelight that made it look like Nurse Page's hands were tied together. They were indeed bound by a thin, watery thread.

"I know what you are," Marisee said, looking away from the nurse, straight into the Shepherdess's strange green eyes. The Shepherdess cocked her head slightly.

"As you should, Marisee Blackwell. You would have known me sooner if Walbrook had been paying attention. But she only has interest in the big rivers. She wants to break free and flow through London again. She never had time for little springs like mine. She thought we were weak and had no power."

"I don't understand." Jonas Hanway pointed at the Shepherdess. "What *is* she?"

Would he ever believe it? *Caroline Lamb isn't human, Mr Hanway, she's a Chad, an elemental water spirit.* But now she was more than that. She was the Shepherdess who had cast London into an enchanted sleep. And Marisee was face to face with her.

What should she do now? This may be Marisee's one chance to stop her. She had to calm down and follow Grandma's advice. She'd use her wits and find out everything she could about why the Shepherdess wanted the Freedom. Then, Marisee might know enough to stop her.

"You knew Sally Blake?" Marisee said.

"Know her?" The Shepherdess twisted the crook between her palms. Marisee felt it grind into the chapel floor. "I was Sally's friend."

"How did you become friends?" Marisee asked.

The Shepherdess looked across the pews and up to the galleries. The children stared at her. The smaller ones were crying, comforted by others who looked afraid. For a moment, her eyes rested on Robert, who was curled in a ball by the altar.

"I noticed a little girl one day," the Shepherdess said. "She was standing by the drying ground, frightened and alone. She had recently returned from the countryside and was pining for the family that she had lived with there. I understand how it feels to be ignored and lonely."

Once again, the Shepherdess glanced at Robert. "Lady Walbrook had little interest in us quiet springs," she said. "So many once ran through these fields, but no one cared if we were covered over with slabs and bricks. We were never mighty rivers. Even when the wells ran dry, the houses and taverns and this Hospital were built over us. My family faded away; there were no springs for them to care for. Only I remained, a small trickle running between the brambles and cobnut trees on the woodlands at the edge of the field. So when I saw that girl, I wanted to be her friend." The Shepherdess turned her gaze back towards Jonas Hanway. "I had never taken a human shape before. I had never taken a shape at all – there was no one to see me. Then I became a foundling. There is no record of me, Mr Hanway. No number or billet book or new name. When I wore the same brown dress as the other girls, I was like everyone else. I am good at being forgotten."

Marisee kept her eyes on the Shepherdess's face. She wanted to remember everything about it and know everything about her.

"Sally and I were like sisters," the Shepherdess continued. "I would sneak into the orchards to play with her or we would sit in the alcoves around the courtyard and talk. When she was older, I would go to the wash-house and help her with her tasks."

"And then Sally was sent away to be apprenticed," Marisee said.

The Shepherdess nodded. "I was heartbroken. It was sudden, with no chance to say goodbye, but I believed the governors. They said she would be cared for. I decided to stay. I liked it here. Perhaps I would find new friends."

Mr Hanway grunted but said nothing.

"I was good with the younger children," the Shepherdess said. "I comforted them, the ones who had returned from their early years in the country. I would nurse them and sing to them until they settled again. I even made up a song for them."

"March lamb, walk lamb…"

Marisee realized that she was singing the words

beneath her breath. She couldn't even dream! Somehow, the Shepherdess's power was seeping into her. She clenched her mouth shut.

"Nurse Page," the Shepherdess said. In spite of the candles, her eyes seemed as dark as coal. "Would you like to continue this story?"

The nurse shook her head. Her eyes darted left and right as the circle of silver closed tighter around her feet.

"Then I shall relay the next part," the Shepherdess said. "Sally was forced to live in a hut in Mrs Broxbourne's yard with the pigs. Her supper was the same swill given to the pigs. You were sent to check on her welfare, Nurse Page. You reported that all was well. Then you pocketed the guinea that you were given for your silence."

Mrs Page wrinkled her nose in disgust. "I had my own children to feed. Do you really think the money here is enough?"

"A child paid for your food with her life," Jonas Hanway said.

The nurse spat on to the floor next to her. "Don't think you're better than me until you know what you'd do if your own children were starving."

"I try to stop children from starving," Jonas Hanway said. "That's why I do my work here."

"You didn't stop Sally from starving," the Shepherdess said. "When she was found unconscious, Nurse Page was summoned to the pig yard. She brought Mr Carper with her because no one will question a watchman carrying a sick child through the streets, will they?"

Jonas Hanway moved close to the nurse. He clenched his hands together as if to stop them trembling. "What terrible deed did you commit?"

Nurse Page jerked her head away and refused to look at him.

"You and Mr Carper took Sally to a certain house in Chick Lane," the Shepherdess said. "One with a secret trapdoor."

Chick Lane. Marisee must remember that, though it would take all her bravery to go there. Even Grandma would only travel through Chick Lane in daylight and accompanied by people who knew the area well. It was where the desperate people lived.

"And there you fed her to the Fleet river," the Shepherdess said. "But this time, the magistrate didn't believe Mrs Broxbourne's story that the apprentice had run away, especially when her neighbour, Mrs Lowrigg, described how Sally had been mistreated."

"The magistrate came here," Jonas Hanway said. "He

told the governors that Mrs Broxbourne had confessed. She…" Jonas Hanway scratched at his wig. "I believe that she named Nurse Page and Mr Carper as accomplices. There were no witnesses and the governors refused to believe it. We swore that you, Nurse Page, and Mr Carper, were good, honest people." Jonas Hanway's next words were very quiet. "The magistrate often gave money to help the Hospital. We didn't want him to suspect anyone here of wrongdoing. We all swore on God's name that Mrs Broxbourne was lying to save herself from the gallows."

"I know," the Shepherdess said. "I heard you all in the Committee Room squabbling about who was to blame. Later, I took Sally's token and refolded the empty billet, stamping it with the dark seal of mourning." The Shepherdess tapped the lamb brooch again. "I wear it close to my heart."

Marisee tried to imagine Caroline Lamb picking the brooch from the folds of waxed paper and fixing it to her waistcoat. Sally's father had left that token. Did he ever know that he would no longer need it?

"Erasmus!" Jonas Hanway called. "Lock Mrs Page in the Sunday office. We will take her to the watch-house tomorrow. Mr Carper will follow when he is found."

The Shepherdess tilted her head. "Oh, he will be found," she said softly.

"Erasmus!" Jonas Hanway cried. "Erasmus! Where are you?"

The pews were still and silent. Erasmus was huddled with three other foundling boys on the steps, leaning against the altar. The girl in the blue bonnet was slumped by the font, her fingers brushing the penny whistle that had dropped to the floor. Children lay across the benches and on the floors as the candlelight flickered a dirty, smoky yellow.

"No!" Jonas Hanway ran to a small boy curled by the altar steps and shook him. "Wake them! Have mercy! They've done nothing to you."

He took the bell from the loose fingers of the older girl who had fallen asleep, sprawled awkwardly on a pew. She was smiling widely. They all were. Jonas Hanway rang the bell as hard as he could. No one woke.

"Please!" Marisee cried. "Wake them. They haven't hurt anyone."

The Shepherdess bent towards Marisee. She was so close that Marisee could barely see. Instead, there was just water trickling through furrowed fields, the sweet scent of thyme and spring sunshine still too weak to warm old bulbs. Marisee blinked. The Shepherdess was once again a young woman dressed in blue silk, a young woman with a face that was so easy to forget.

"Sally Blake didn't hurt anyone," the Shepherdess said. "But the world hurt her. Imagine if she could have slept safely – enjoying beautiful dreams – until there was a new world, one where she could do or be anything she wished. One where she was not just a lowly apprentice sent to live in a pigsty."

"But you will kill these children!" Marisee cried. "They will starve while they dream."

The Shepherdess's green eyes glinted. "No, Well Keeper's granddaughter, *you* will kill them. The longer you hide the Freedom from me, the longer these children will sleep. Once it is in my hand, I will wake them up."

"But I don't know where it is," Marisee said.

"Don't test my patience." The crook tapped the ground. A bubble of water rose and burst. "It is with your grandmother. You will find her eventually, I know."

The Shepherdess returned her attention to Jonas Hanway. Her hands moved. The silver sparks swirled away from Nurse Page, stretching into threads and entwining between the Shepherdess's fingers.

"Did you believe that you could escape justice?" Her voice was a murmur.

The threads shuttled and spun until they were the thickness of rope.

Jonas Hanway stood still as stone, his eyes fixed on those weaving fingers. He did not look afraid.

"If you wish to take me," he said. "Do so. But save the children. Wake them. They have done no harm."

In and out, loops and twists, the rope grew thicker, then snaked upwards. It slid through the space between two spindles in the banister in front of the gallery, wrapped around them and dropped to the ground. Marisee watched as the end of the rope twitched and coiled around itself. The rope pulled tight and it rose into the air. It was a noose.

The noose swung back and forth in front of Jonas Hanway's face.

"This is not justice!" Marisee tried to grab the rope, but the watery thread slipped through her fingers.

"It is my justice."

The rope whipped back in the air. The noose stretched like a yawning mouth and dropped over Nurse Page's head. It hovered for a moment, no part of it touching her skin. Then, it started to tighten.

"No," she whimpered. "No, no, no."

She was clawing at the rope, trying to pull it away, but it slipped through her fingers. The noose began to rise.

"Please!" Nurse Page screamed. "Have mercy!"

She was standing on her tiptoes. Just a few inches higher and she would be hanging.

Jonas Hanway grasped Nurse Page, trying to support her weight.

"Stop this!" he shouted.

This is what befell Mrs Broxbourne. The Shepherdess laughed. "Isn't this justice?"

No, Marisee thought. *This is not justice*. She knew that she would never be part of the jeering, laughing crowd who headed to Tyburn for execution days. She never wanted to see anyone die. She ran to Jonas Hanway, and tried to support the nurse's legs. The rope pulled taut, tightening its grip. The nurse was growing weaker. Marisee was sure that she could see every single watery thread wriggling against the nurse's throat.

The chapel door banged open. "Justice is due." The voice was deep, but with a sparkle beneath it. "But not by you."

Turnmill stood there. The Fleet Ditch boar was on one side of her, the fox-like Sadler on the other. A wave of water rushed past them, snuffing out the candles that lit the nave. The water glowed with its own light. The noose dissolved and Nurse Page tumbled down. Jonas Hanway grasped her arm.

"I promise that justice will still be done," he said, pulling her towards the door.

"By me!" The Shepherdess laced her fingers together. A silver thread whipped away and caught in Nurse Page's hair. Her head jerked back.

"Marisee!" It was Turnmill. "She's strong. We can't hold her for long. Red Rum is waiting for you. Go!"

The Sadler fox shot towards the Shepherdess. It was as slick as onyx, with the speed and talons of a falcon.

Marisee splashed towards the door. "Go where?"

"To where it all started!" Turnmill stirred the air with her finger and water followed, spinning across the chapel towards the Shepherdess, engulfing her within it. The Fleet Ditch boar roared, its snout drawn back, teeth bared. It galloped towards the whirlpool.

To where it all started… Marisee tried to think. This had all started when a girl called Sally had been thrown into Fleet river in a house on Chick Lane.

"But Robert…" Marisee started. She looked around. Robert was lying in a pool of water, asleep.

"Go!" Turnmill yelled. "Go!"

THE TRAP

Robert was floating. It was like hands rocking him backwards and forwards. He was tilted up and held firmly until he was steady on his feet once more. He opened his eyes. This time there was no pie shop. No aroma of meat and gravy. Robert wasn't hungry. He didn't need to eat. He was in a field. The grass was so green it made his eyes hurt. *She* was here. He could hear her singing, but he couldn't see her. He sat down. He would wait.

The green field faded, shaping itself into houses, a statue, a grassy square. A man in a checked suit ran across

Robert's path, leaped into the air as if on springs, turned upside down and landed on the ground in a forward roll. He bowed.

"Greetings, Master Robert Strong."

The acrobat grinned at Robert and ran into the crowd. A crowd? Yes, there was a fair in full flow in ... where was he? The place seemed familiar. This was the dream place he'd been to before. Leicester Fields. That was it. He would enjoy the show while he waited.

Actors strutted on raised stages, their towering wigs wobbling as they moved and their wide skirts knocking each other over. Robert laughed. Many of Lady Hibbert's friends could barely fit in their sedan chairs because their dresses were so wide. Their hair often poked out of the roof.

Stalls were piled high with fruit and pies and all manner of toys. A small child picked up a miniature wooden cart with wheels that turned and a horse with a tail that swished as she held it. She waved it at Robert then skipped away. No money changed hands. People bustled from stall to stall, but all stepped aside when Robert passed them. They smiled at him. They called his name.

He passed two boxers throwing punches at each other in a makeshift ring. The crowd only cheered when the blows missed. The boxers turned to Robert and punched their fists in the air.

"You made the right decision, Robert!"

He smiled at them all and waved. A cheer rippled through the crowd. This was his place. This was where he belonged. Something brushed against his head. He touched it. He was wearing a turban again. He knew that this was not from Lady Hibbert's dressmaker. This was one like the king in the painting. He lifted his arm. The sleeve of his robe was white edged with blue.

He passed a wooden table with baskets piled high with oranges. He paused. Did he like oranges? He couldn't remember. The young man behind it called out. He was dark-skinned like Robert. He reminded Robert of someone.

"Keke!" the young man called.

Keke? Was that him, Robert? Did he know this man?

"It's me! Zeke!"

Zeke? A thought was trying to shape itself, but it kept blurring. Robert quickly moved away from the stall, and he was back in the green field. Where was *she*?

A hand touched his shoulder. "You have paid a price to come here, Robert."

The Shepherdess was standing next to him. She was

resting heavily on the rusty iron crook. He realized now that her waistcoat wasn't linen. It was the heavy brown drugget of the Foundling Hospital uniform.

"You didn't know Zeke?" she asked Robert.

Zeke. Robert was sure that he did know that name. He strained hard, trying to remember the face that matched it. The memory hovered out of reach.

He shook his head. "I don't know him."

The Shepherdess touched his head. He felt the coldness of her fingers through his hair.

"Did you follow the tunnel beneath the wall?" she asked.

"Yes, we did."

"Then you met the tithe-master. He took his dues from you," she said. "I am sorry."

"The tithe-master?" Robert said. "No, I was lucky. I told him that he could take a tenth of my memories, but I escaped without paying him."

The Shepherdess sighed. "I wish it was so, Robert."

But it was so! Hadn't Robert and Marisee raced away before anything could happen? So why did Robert feel that he should know who Zeke was? Why was there a blur inside his head as if something had been wiped away?

The Shepherdess's finger pressed hard into Robert's head. "When you give me the Freedom, I will make sure that whatever the tithe-master has taken will be restored to you."

Her finger lowered. Robert rubbed the place where it had been. Was the Shepherdess right about his memories? He recalled the Hibberts and Mrs Wandle and Lizzie. He remembered Mama and his sisters and… And something important. *Someone* important. It had gone. *They* had gone. He wanted them back.

"How can I give you the Freedom?" he asked. "I don't know where it is."

The Shepherdess laughed a light, happy laugh, though her eyes were as hard as rock. "The Magogs are not the only ones who have spies all over London," she said. "My sleepers bring news to the Ether. Madam Blackwell has the Freedom and I know where she is."

Suddenly, Robert realized that he was laughing too. "You know where it is?" Everything he had hoped for could come true now. "Where is it?"

"It has returned to where I first found it." She pushed back her wide-brimmed hat and surveyed him. He could see the faint rectangle of the bruise on her forehead more clearly. "Come with me. I'll show you."

Robert took her hand. They were standing on the corner of a narrow lane near the banks of the Fleet Ditch. The water was solid with filth and stank of decay. The Shepherdess led Robert down the lane, away from the water. The houses tumbled into each other. The doors hung from their hinges, and most of the windows were covered with rough wooden shutters, nailed shut.

The Shepherdess pushed open a door. Robert followed. The ceiling in the front parlour had collapsed. Only the beams remained in place. The floor was filthy with plaster and dust. There was a dampness too, as if the river had sunk into the walls.

"This is where they brought Sally," she said. "That nurse and that watchman. There are houses like this all along Chick Lane, but this one is marked."

She pointed to the wall above a glassless window. There was a hole as if the bricks had crumbled away.

"Thieves removed the bricks," the Shepherdess said. "It's a sign. This is a house where secrets can disappear."

They walked through the ruined house to a staircase at the back. The smell of stagnant water was heavier, the wooden banister split and flecked with mould. The Shepherdess released Robert's hand and stepped on the first stair, pausing as if waiting to see if it would hold her weight. Robert knew that beneath the house was darkness and water. He didn't want to follow her.

Nothing in dreams is real. He must remember that.

The Shepherdess disappeared. Robert heard the creak of old wood, then silence.

Nothing in dreams is real.

He took a deep breath and walked down towards the basement, keeping his tread light on the rotting wood. Neither he nor the Shepherdess carried a lantern, but the air shone with a silvery light. He could see everything. He wasn't sure if he wanted to.

The basement floor was brick, more solid than the walls and roof of the house. The Shepherdess was standing by a trapdoor that had been fitted into the middle of the floor.

"Sally Blake's body was never found," the Shepherdess said. "I wanted to find her. It hurt to think of her alone. I went from tavern to sponging house, listening to talk of the secret places near the river. One innkeeper told me about this house, whispering quietly into my ear in case he was overheard. He said that this hatch is still used. When the tide is low, thieves escape through here, or hide their stolen goods in boxes below. When the river is high, anything that is dropped through here will quickly be swept away."

Suddenly, Robert wanted to leave this sad, stifling place. The Shepherdess bent down and laid a hand on the heavy wood of the trapdoor. Robert hoped with all his will that she didn't open it. Beneath it the darkness would swallow everything. Even in a dream.

"I lowered myself into the water." The Shepherdess said. She rested her cheek against the trapdoor as if listening for sounds from below. "It was just shallows. There had been little rain that summer to fill the rivers. I crawled through the mud calling Sally's name. The only answer was the rats scurrying by. The air grew danker and danker like it carried death itself. But I carried on calling for her. Then I saw it, Robert. A golden box, sticking out from the mud, glowing in the darkness. I dug it free. I knew it straight away, the Freedom that was lost somewhere in the earth beneath London. I held it to my face to feel the power inside it." She touched the raised bruise on her forehead. "It marked me. I knew then, Robert, that this box could change everything. I was no longer just the spirit of a small spring that no one noticed or cared about. I could do anything and go anywhere."

The Shepherdess straightened up. "But I was so tired, Robert. I fell asleep and I remember nothing more until I woke up in the Ether. My hand was empty. But the power the Freedom had given me…" She laughed. It echoed around the airless basement. "The Ether is not a place for elementals. It was created after the last London elemental war. The mix of leftover magic is like a poison for us. But there I was. That's how powerful the Freedom is. The magic of the four elements let me enter the world of human dreams."

She waved her arm. Robert returned to Leicester Fields. The Shepherdess was still by his side.

"It took me a while to recognize what it was," she said. "But the Freedom has made it safe for me here. I saw Solids, humans like you, yearning for simple things, like food and warmth. But so many of them carried an extra sadness. They grieved for someone dear that they had lost. I didn't need food or warm clothes, Robert, but I was full of fury. I wanted to see Sally again; I wanted to tear down whatever wall separated my world from hers. I wanted every sad and cold and hungry soul who came to the Ether to see those who they had lost, those who had loved them. I wished so hard that the power of the Freedom made my wish become part of the Ether." She let out a breath. "It is why Solids come here but do not want to return to the harsh, lonely world outside."

Again, Robert felt the tug of a memory. The scent of oranges. The whir of a hummingbird. He pushed the thought away.

"I was here for ten years, Robert," she said. "I watched. I waited. I grew my power. I planned. But for all that time, I looked for Sally in the Ether. If Solids could meet the ones they had loved and lost, why couldn't I?"

"But you didn't find her," Robert said.

A man cried out from behind Robert. A table had tipped over, scattering cakes across the grass. A pack of stray dogs fed on them, ignoring the stall-holder trying to chase them away. A shout arose from across the fields. A moment later, a boxer stumbled past Robert. There was a bloody gash above his eye. He did not appear to see Robert at all.

"I searched and searched," the Shepherdess said. "I couldn't find her anywhere. Perhaps she has travelled so far from pain that no one can reach her now. But you were here, Robert, you and all the others, brought to the Ether in your dreams. You needed more than food and warmth. You needed true happiness. You needed to feel love again. I gave you that."

"And now the tithe-master took it away," he said.

The Shepherdess touched the sleeve of Robert's

white robe. Her eyes were as bright as the grass around the stalls. "You will remember him again, Robert, when we have the Freedom. I held it for so little time, but even so I changed all this." This time she held both arms wide. "Imagine what I – *we* – can do, if we can keep the Freedom for always."

They had walked towards a fountain. Robert hadn't noticed it before. The water sprung from the mouths of ten small stone lambs, their heads tipped back. The drops fell like scattered rainbows. The water arced higher and higher until it was cascading around him.

"Go with her," the Shepherdess said. "Go with the Well Keeper's granddaughter. She will help you find her grandmother. When the time comes, I will make sure that you continue alone. Once the Freedom is in your hand, call for me."

"If you know where the Well Keeper is, why don't you just find her and take it?"

"The magic is protected. It will only work if the Freedom is freely given. It is to stop the elementals trying to seize it from each other. It is why I couldn't bring it to the Ether when I fell asleep. The magic binds it to the Solid world, in case an elemental tries to take it to a place that no others can reach. Now return, Robert. I trust you.

I trust you to do this for me."

The stone lambs tilted towards him and their mouths opened wider. Robert closed his eyes and felt the spray grow heavier and heavier, beat harder and harder until he too was scattered into drops.

He woke up standing on the hard gravel path outside the Hospital chapel. There was a chaise with a horse about to pull away. It was Red Rum! Marisee was perched on the seat above the horse. The chaise started to move away.

"Marisee!" he shouted. "Red Rum! Wait for me!"

Marisee must have heard him, but she didn't look back. Luckily, Red Rum stopped, and Robert stumbled towards the carriage. He scrambled up on to the seat next to Marisee.

"Were you going to leave without me?"

She gave him a long look. "You were asleep in the chapel. How did you get outside?"

Robert shrugged. "I'm here now. The water must have woken me up."

She nodded but didn't reply.

"Where are we going?" he asked.

"Chick Lane."

There are houses like this all along Chick Lane, the

Shepherdess had said. He must stay with Marisee until the Shepherdess told him otherwise.

"Did *your dream* give you any other ideas about where we should go?" Marisee asked him.

"No," he said. "I'll follow you."

Marisee stared straight ahead as the chaise rattled down to London. She seemed unusually quiet – but Robert wouldn't worry about that now. He had enough to think about.

It was the early hours of Saturday morning, dark as night but with a yellow mist staining the darkness above the fields. Lamps burned outside the Holborn watch-house, but Robert could only see one watchman standing by the gate. As they drew closer, they saw his face.

"It's Carper!" Marisee said. "He's been tied to the gate!"

Robert watched as the man writhed and struggled. He knew those bonds would not come undone. The watch-house door was flung open. A dark crowd surged out: women, men, children. They stood in a row beneath the lamp, the light throwing their shadows against the wall. They carried weapons – cudgels, pikes, shovels – thrown over their shoulders. They ignored Carper, as if they had urgent business elsewhere.

"Do you think we should help him?" Marisee said. "I know he did terrible things, but I don't want the sleepwalkers to hurt him."

Why should Robert care what happened to Carper? He had thrown a child through a trapdoor into a river.

"I think it's more important to find the Freedom," he said. "Once we have that, no one will be hurt."

"No one should be hurt anyway!" Marisee said. "She's taking her revenge on people who did nothing to her!"

He stared at his knees. "I told you," he said. "She's sad and angry."

"She's *sad* and *angry*. Is that all you really know?" Robert felt Marisee's eyes on him. "She was with you in Hyde Park. You were sleeping in the chapel. Did she speak to you, in your dreams?"

"Why do you keep asking *me*? She was in the chapel talking to *you*, wasn't she?" Robert's words spilled out quicker than he wanted. He made himself slow down. "Or else, how would you know about Chick Lane?"

"Because Turnmill told me." Marisee looked away from him as if she'd decided that the conversation was over. "Maybe she did. I think the sleepwalkers are heading towards Staples Inn. The well there is a favourite of Grandma's."

"Why?" If Robert let Marisee talk, hopefully she'd stop asking him about the Shepherdess.

"Staples Inn is a school for lawyers. The springs like to follow all the correct rules. It makes it easier for Grandma." He felt her eyes on him again. "I miss her, Robert. She's my only family. If we don't stop the Shepherdess, I'll never see her again."

Robert bit his lip and stared into the night ahead. He caught the reek of animal pens.

"We're near Smithfield market," Marisee said. "Chick Lane isn't far."

The chaise stopped. Red Rum whinnied, his head shaking from side to side.

Marisee leaned out of the chaise. "Can you hear it?"

Robert could hear it. The silent city suddenly shook with noise. The clang of metal against wood, bricks smashing through glass. An orange glow flared across the road ahead. A column of sleepwalkers passed in front of them, armed like the others, many bearing flaming torches. The sleepwalkers didn't notice the carriage. Robert wondered if the Shepherdess had directed their attention away.

"She's not even waiting for London to destroy itself," Marisee said. "She's making the sleepwalkers do it. Then when she's finished with them, they'll sleep until they die. We have to stop her."

Robert gave a tiny nod. When the Shepherdess controlled the Freedom, she wouldn't let the poor die. Robert was certain.

Red Rum started moving again, the trot slowed to a walk. He turned sharply into a narrow, dark road and stopped again so suddenly that Marisee and Robert were thrown forward.

"Chick Lane?" Marisee wondered.

Robert wasn't sure. Was this the place where the Shepherdess had brought him? He couldn't tell because the street was blocked with barrels stacked three high. They climbed down from the chaise and stood in front of the barricade.

"The barrels are too heavy to move," Marisee said. "But maybe we can go back and enter Chick Lane from the other end."

"We can't," Robert said. "Look. The sleepwalkers are coming."

"So many of them," Marisee whispered.

Yes! But Robert knew they weren't coming for him this time. He would be safe. Was this the moment the Shepherdess had meant? Marisee had brought him to

Chick Lane. Should he go on alone?

An old woman staggered out from a doorway. She wore the black clothes of a widow and held a fire poker high in her hand. Behind her was a man in a bloodied apron, a butcher. He grasped a bone-saw in one hand and a meat hook in the other. Sleepwalkers emerged from every door, women with sticks and fire irons, men with axes and long heavy poles. An old man was so bowed over he struggled to walk, but dragged a sword behind him. As they opened their mouths, the yellow fog of sickness threaded between their faces.

"March lamb, walk lamb, follow my sheep,
Close eyes, never wake, sleep, lambkins, sleep.
Ten years, ten tears, dripping from my eyes,
Freedom comes when sunlight comes and cruel London
dies."

The butcher loped towards them, waving his saw.

"Cheap cuts!" he called.

Robert's body was screaming at him to run. *Now, Robert! Go and take the Freedom!* Was that his own head shouting at him or the Shepherdess?

"Robert?" Marisee's voice shook.

She had flattened herself against the barrels. Her hands were scrabbling around between them as if looking for something to fight back with. The butcher was close now. He stopped and lifted the meat hook in the air. Red Rum's hoof flicked out and caught the butcher's thigh and he crumpled to the ground.

Now, Robert! Go! It was like the Shepherdess was shouting at him from inside his own head. It *was* the sign. He glanced at Marisee. She was looking at him, eyes wide with terror. Could he leave her? If he continued by himself, Madam Blackwell would be suspicious. She'd ask questions about her granddaughter. He needed Marisee. He had to save her to get the Freedom... But... But... What was he thinking? Marisee Blackwell was his friend! That was the biggest and only reason to save her!

A young man in torn breeches and a pale, loose wig stepped clumsily over the butcher and picked up the meat hook. His lips moved.

"March lamb, walk lamb, follow my sheep,
Close eyes, never wake, sleep, lambkins, sleep."

The mob sang with him. This was no longer a lullaby. It was the chant of a crowd as they watched the condemned being led to the gallows.

"March lamb, walk lamb…"

More sleepwalkers came, a ragged line of them, chanting the words. The mob parted to reveal the elderly man, still dragging his sword. In the other hand, he carried a whip. It was made of plaited leather from the handle to the tip. It flicked up the mud behind him. Robert swallowed hard. It wasn't the manatee whip. It was just a whip. The elderly man jerked upright as if he was tied to a pulley. His tongue ran across his lips. Robert smelt the sickness in his tainted breath, decay and blood and age. He lifted the whip.

"Run!" Robert shouted to Marisee and pushed the old man away.

The sword dropped to the ground. The widow picked it up, but the butcher had already taken the elderly man's place. The sleepwalkers fanned out around them so Marisee and Robert had no place to go. The barrels were behind them, the sleeping army in front.

"Cheap cuts," the butcher whined. "Cheap cuts."

"There are too many of them," Marisee said. "We need help."

Help. Robert thought hard. Could he send Red Rum for someone? But who? There must be someone, something… Oh. There *was* someone, something he could call on. At least, he could try. *Please work! Please work!* He raised his head high and shouted.

"A favour for a favour! I freed you, now you free me!"

All was still, then the wind coursed through the street towards them, bringing coal smoke and the tang of hot malt. The darkness was alive with it. The air screeched with it. Spots of pink popped in the smoke as if the Fumi that Robert had freed from the tithe-master was shouting its name.

A barrel exploded as if an invisible fist had smashed down on it. Beer gushed on to the road, and shards of wood shot through the air towards the sleepers. The widow screamed and shielded her eyes. Another barrel was lifted in the air and hurled towards the mob. It caught the young man with the loose wig in the chest and he fell, knocking over many behind him. The Fumi closed like a shroud around the butcher. Robert heard the butcher coughing, still calling "cheap cuts" when he could barely breathe. His weapons clanged as they dropped from his hands.

"A favour for a favour," the Fumi shrieked. "Favour fulfilled. But hurry."

The sleepwalkers were already picking themselves up and scrabbling around for their weapons.

"Go, Red Rum, go!" Marisee shouted.

The horse trotted away, the chaise swinging from side to side behind him.

Robert and Marisee ran through the swampish beery mud and shattered barrels along Chick Lane. No one stopped them. The taverns behind the wall of barrels were dark and silent, the houses too. No window held a candle.

And then, there it was: the ruined house. The dark space in the wall above the window was still there, though it was barely a house now, just crumbling bricks and a flapping door. He could see little of the roof but imagined that there was little roof left to see.

"March lamb, walk lamb, follow my sheep…"

The young man in the crooked wig was stepping through the debris of the broken barrels towards them. A musician carrying a violin and a bow trailed behind him. His violin had been smashed so its neck ended in jagged wood, but he scraped the bow across it as if trying to play.

"Close eyes, never wake, sleep, lambkins, sleep."

"This way!" Robert shouted. He ran towards the ruin and through the open door into what once may have been a small parlour. A staircase in the corner led both upwards and down. There would be no up. The holes in the ceiling revealed that the floor above had rotted away. There was only down. Robert knew where they would take him. Just like in his dream, he did not want to go.

Marisee ran to the stairs. "Down here!"

He followed Marisee, treading carefully, guiding himself with one hand on the wall. The stench rising from the cellar made him want to retch, but he forced one step after the other. There was no light at all now. He heard Marisee stumble, stop, then carry on. There may have been less than twenty stairs, but it felt like a hundred. Finally, his foot jarred as he stepped on to a brick floor. He heard Marisee breathing next to him.

"I can't see anything," she said.

The floorboards above them creaked. A light flickered on the wall by the stairs. A footstep sounded.

"*Ten tears…*"

"It's in the middle of the floor," Robert said.

"What is?"

"The trapdoor."

"How do you…"

"We have to find it! Help me look!"

He dropped to his knees and swept his hand across the floor. Backwards and forwards, his hand brushing chunks of brick and nails, and things that he would rather not think about. He could hear Marisee doing the same. His fingers touched a wooden panel.

"It's here!" he said. "I've found it!"

As he fumbled for the catch, the cellar lit with a dim light. The musician was carrying a lantern in one hand, the shattered violin in the other, like a cudgel.

"Would you like to hear a tune?" His voice was weak and breathy. "*She* asked me to play it especially for you."

Robert yanked open the trapdoor. The room filled with the reek of decay. Below, there was a darkness that didn't move. The musician's torchlight flickered across Marisee. She was still on her hands and knees.

Robert shook his head. "I don't think I can…"

Marisee stood up, gave him a little smile. "Yes," she said. "We can. There's a ladder. I'll go first this time."

Marisee lowered herself down. Her head disappeared.

The musician's foot slapped down on to the brick floor. He shuffled towards Robert, bent towards him and whispered.

"*You* promised the Shepherdess. She trusts you." The musician handed Robert the lantern. "She's waiting."

Robert took the lantern and followed Marisee into the dark water below.

CHASE

Marisee waited. Her feet slipped in the mud and the cold water pressed against her ribs. The darkness, the water, the staleness in the air – she could barely breathe. Would Robert come? Why did she think that he might not? That perhaps the trapdoor would slam shut after her. There'd been a moment, just a tiny moment, when they were cornered against the barrels. She could have been sure that Robert was going to run off and leave her to the sleepwalkers. But he hadn't. He'd made sure they'd escaped.

She felt a movement above her, saw a flicker of light,

then Robert dropped from the ladder into the river next to her. He gasped with the cold. He held a lantern. That was good, though Marisee certainly couldn't remember seeing one in the basement. Robert's arms flailed as his feet slithered from beneath him. She grabbed his wrist to steady him, hoping he was holding the light tight. If he dropped it, they would be in total darkness. He regained his balance, and they looked around. She could see dark walls made from broken bricks. Wooden planks crisscrossed the roof. All of it was oozing with muck.

"There's no Turnmill to carry us this time," Marisee said.

She kept the words light, but she knew that the Shepherdess must have survived the fight in the chapel, or how else could she still control the sleepwalkers? Where was Turnmill? And the Fleet Ditch boar? Had they survived?

Please, she whispered to herself. *Please don't find us.*

She started wading forward.

Robert was splashing along behind her, the light flicking side to side. Her feet slid away, and her hand grasped a wooden strut poking through the mud. It must be the foundations of a house. She mustn't think about the press of all the buildings in the mud above her. She tried to take another step but couldn't. It was too much. The darkness. The shifting, sucking mud beneath her feet, oozing down into her boots and between her toes. Every single part of her ached. She couldn't go back. She had no idea what was ahead. She couldn't move another inch.

Robert touched her shoulder. "Marisee? We should carry on walking. I think I heard sounds from behind us."

Marisee didn't care. Her weariness engulfed her.

Robert touched her shoulder again. "Marisee?"

She wailed. She hadn't known that she could make a sound like that, but it was like her sadness had found its own voice. Then she was clinging to the strut, sobbing.

"Why?" The words found their way out between the sobs. "We can't win! We've found the Shepherdess, but it didn't make any difference. I don't know how to stop her and…" The sobs tumbled over each other. "I don't know if I'm ever going to see Grandma again."

"We can win," Robert said. "We must keep on going."

"Why?"

"Because … because when I was sleeping, I did dream about the Shepherdess. She brought me to this house in Chick Lane."

A sob sank back into Marisee's chest. "Why didn't

you tell me before, Robert?"

"I'm telling you now," he said. "And you were already coming here."

Did he really think that was a good enough answer? But he was still talking.

"Sally Blake was dropped through that hatch," Robert said. "Caroline Lamb came here trying to find her, but she found the Freedom instead. This place is the last part of our puzzle, Marisee. That's why we have to keep going."

"Did she tell you all of that in your dream?"

"Yes," he said. "She did."

"Is there anything else useful you would like to tell me now?"

"This isn't the time to…"

"Yes!" she yelled. "It is! How can I trust you if you keep secrets like that? What else have you and the Shepherdess talked about?"

"Can little lambs swim?" The woman's voice seemed to creep out from the walls. "Can their little feet paddle when the water grows deep?"

Marisee's anger shrank away. "It's her," she said. "The Shepherdess is in the tunnels."

But was she behind them or ahead of them?

"I told you," Marisee whispered. "I told you that

we can't win."

"We can." Robert took her hand. "We have to keep moving. The water's rising."

He was right. The iciness had crept upwards and soaked through her skirt. Every step felt like she was walking up a mountain. Below her feet, the tunnel floor changed from wet mud to stone. The only noise was the slosh of water as they moved and Robert's breathing ahead of her.

"Paddle, paddle, little lambs! The Shepherdess is coming for you!"

Was she closer or further away? Where *was* she?

The water rose again. It splashed the bottom of Marisee's chin. "Can you see anything, Robert?"

"Yes!" He lifted the lantern higher. "We're nearly there!"

Marisee peered ahead. The shadows seemed to taper away. The tunnel branched into two. The right tunnel seemed to dip downwards. Marisee could see the surface of the water inside it, as still as a stagnant pond. The other tunnel sloped upwards. They had no choice. She felt… She felt like a lamb being herded into a pen.

Robert let go of her hand. He seemed to grow taller, but she realized that he was climbing steps out of the water on to a brick path. She followed quickly, her sodden skirt tangling around her legs. The walls here were lined with wooden planks nailed between brick pillars. The pillars were decorated with stone circles. Marisee squinted at one. There was a face etched into the circles, the same face each time. She knew that face! It was Lady Fleet.

The tunnel turned a sharp corner ahead. Robert was already hurrying towards it, his lamp still held high. She stared at her feet trudging the uneven path after him. She bent down and stared at the ground. In spite of everything, she grinned.

"Robert!" she said. "I need the lamp."

"We have to hurry, Marisee!"

"Please!"

He came back. She took the lamp and rested it on the path.

"Do you see, Robert?" she asked. "Footprints."

"Of course there are footprints," Robert said. "I just walked along there."

"No." Even his impatience couldn't stop her smile. "Your feet are much smaller than that. I'd know these footprints anywhere. They're from Grandma's boots! She's alive and not long ago she came this way."

"That's good." Marisee heard the smile in Robert's

voice. "We're definitely going the right way."

He grabbed the lamp again and hurried on. This time he didn't wait. He turned the corner, and she was plunged into darkness. Marisee's smile disappeared. They *were* going the right way to find Grandma, but if the Shepherdess was in the tunnel, they'd be leading her straight to the Freedom. What had Grandma's note said? *Together we must stop the threat and keep London safe.* That's what Grandma had done. Now that's what Marisee must do – she must lead the Shepherdess away.

"Robert!"

The new tunnel was more roughly built and so low that Marisee had to bend her head. The light from Robert's lantern flashed across things scattered over the path. Was this a broken oar? And that part of a sail from a windmill? She jumped over them, catching up with him.

"Robert! Not this way! We're taking the Shepherdess straight to Grandma and the Freedom!"

He didn't stop walking. "We'll reach your grandma first. We can warn her." He spoke quickly and calmly, as if nothing could change his mind.

"Robert?"

"Yes?"

Could she say it? *Are you helping the Shepherdess?*

Am I the only lamb they're coming for?

Instead, she asked, "If the Shepherdess tries to hurt me, Robert, will you help me?"

He still didn't stop walking, or even turn to look at her. "Why do you think I won't?"

"Because you're taking her straight to the Freedom," she said.

He stopped then. She could see his face. He was looking straight at her.

"I will do everything I can to make sure you're not hurt," he said. He turned away again and carried on along the tunnel.

Marisee stayed where she was for a moment. She had wanted him to just say "yes". He was hiding behind words. She couldn't trust him. She wished that Red Rum hadn't stopped for Robert outside the Foundling Hospital, but here she was, deep in a tunnel with him. What was she going to do? No, she didn't want to lead the Shepherdess straight to Grandma, but Robert had the only light. Marisee would be no help to anyone stumbling through flooded tunnels by herself in darkness and – maybe – straight into the Shepherdess or her sleepwalkers.

Marisee caught up with Robert again, stepping into the path of his shadow. The way ahead was becoming more cluttered. Marisee stepped around the cracked hulk of a giant millstone and then the wooden ribs of a small boat. A tailor's mannequin lay on its side, the shreds of a cape still clinging to it. Next to this a small white bonnet was tucked into itself like a hedgehog. And next to that, folded so neatly that its soft edges looked sharp, was a brown drugget dress. The sleeves crossed in front ended in white cuffs and the collar flashed a band of red.

Marisee grabbed the lamp from Robert's hands and bent over the clothes.

"It's the Foundling Hospital uniform." Marisee moved the lamp so the light fell on to a patch of white fabric. She picked it up. It was a tippet that would have laid across the girl's shoulders and, underneath that, she found an apron. Marisee felt a hum of excitement and lifted the lantern higher.

"She would have worn boots," she said.

She pointed the lamp towards the wall. There was a pair of dark laced boots, carefully placed side by side as if arranged by a maid. She stood up. The hum of excitement was growing louder. Of course she couldn't be sure. These clothes could belong to any Foundling Hospital child who had … who had the misfortune to find their way into the river, though Marisee had never heard of this happening before. These clothes were so neatly arranged and surprisingly clean, as if something or someone had protected them on their journey.

But there was one way that Marisee could know for sure who these clothes had belonged to. She carefully untucked the bonnet. There it was. She held it up, the chain spooling through her hand to show the tag. The number glowed in the lamplight.

"Number 33," Marisee said.

"Sally Blake," Robert said. "That was the number given to her when she was admitted, wasn't it?"

"Yes." The excitement was so loud it could burst out of Marisee, but she had to remember – she could not trust Robert.

"So what does it mean?" he asked.

This is a place of lost things, Marisee wanted to say. *It catches what's cast into the river. But Sally Blake's clothes are here, so carefully tidied away.*

"I don't know what it means." Marisee kept her voice even.

For a moment, she and Robert looked at each other. Did Robert look a little sad? Did she? She wished they could share what they were both thinking. Marisee replaced the clothes as tidily as she had found them but slipped the number tag around her neck. Somehow it seemed important to have something of Sally's with her.

Then they walked on.

Marisee needed a plan. She took a few deep breaths to help clear her head. Luckily, the smell wasn't so strong here or perhaps she'd grown used to it, but the deep breaths worked and her excitement quietened down. The plan had been to find out everything she could about what – or who – was causing the sickness. She'd done that. She knew that the Shepherdess was a Chad who wanted revenge for the ill treatment of her human friend. Marisee touched the tag. What if something else had happened to Sally, something good? The Shepherdess didn't know that, but if Marisee told her... Sally could be in this very tunnel. Could it really be a coincidence that Grandma was here too?

"Why are you shaking your head?" Robert asked.

She hadn't realized that Robert was looking at her. As she tried to scramble together a reason, a light flickered behind Robert. It was another lantern. She saw the shadow first, an arm, a hand, the jagged end of a broken violin.

"I have a tune for you." The musician emerged from the tunnel behind Robert. "Sing with me, little lamb."

"*March lamb, walk lamb…*" came a thin, tuneless voice. It belonged to the young man with the badly fitting wig. He placed his hand on the musician's shoulder, the meat hook he held tapping a beat against the musician's chest.

Then weaving through it all a woman signing, "*Open eyes, close eyes…*"

Robert's eyes fluttered.

"*Ten years, ten tears, dripping from my eyes.*"

Marisee couldn't move. She wanted to touch the chain around her neck, but the sadness and the drowsiness and her own weariness made it impossible. There was something about the chain, something she should show the Shepherdess, something very important. But it didn't matter now. She had been running away all day, but now she could be still.

Perhaps Marisee's mother had sung lullabies like this to her when she was a baby. Marisee couldn't dream, but a little sleep would be good. She was so weary. As her eyelids drooped shut, the last thing she saw was Robert, mouth open like a choirboy, singing her to sleep.

RESCUE

"Oh no you don't!" Robert knew that voice! It was the rescue voice. Turnmill.

Then came a silver explosion. Robert did not just see it through his eyelids; he felt it through his whole body. It rose in a wave and washed out the drowsiness that had taken over his limbs. He opened his eyes. A sheet of silver shimmered in front of him, then shredded into threads.

"This way!" Turnmill yelled.

He heard a snort and a squeal behind him. Before he

could look back, he was being pulled along the tunnel. Silver dots danced in front of his eyes. He wasn't sure if they were from the explosion or if there were real silver dots in the air. They reminded him of fireflies and of someone ... of someone who used to sit beside him, counting the fireflies as the sky turned dark.

It was another blurred memory; he had to push it away because right now he had to make his body move. He felt like an automaton, his legs stiff little engines slapping his feet up and down. But as he ran, he began to feel more human, his knees jarring, feet aching, spine jolting.

Where was he? Where was Marisee? He was still in a tunnel, but had to hunch over to fit through it.

"Ready!" that voice yelled again.

Ready for what...?

The silver drops grew bigger, bouncing off each other until they surged towards him, knocking him off his feet. He opened his mouth to yell, but it filled with water. Not gritty water, but sweet water as a thousand watery hands bore him along.

"Turnmill?"

"Who else?" came the reply. "Brace yourself. We're reaching the end of the ride."

They shot through a stone archway. Robert slid across the floor and halted just before he hit a pillar. Two rows of long candles lit the space. At first Robert thought he was back in a cellar, but there were no barrels or jars. The ceiling was vaulted stone, the floor paved, though many slabs were cracked. He stared around. A mound of mud was piled against one wall and in the corner – he flinched. There were bones, piles of them. They looked human too.

"They won't hurt you," a woman said.

She crouched down next to him. She was older than his mother, perhaps the same age that his grandmother would have been if he had ever known her. She had the same wide face and arched brows as Marisee. Her head was bare; two thick plaits coiled round her head, though her hair was doing its best to escape them. She wore heavy soldiers' boots and a cloak with a lining that shimmered when she moved.

"It's a charnel house," the woman said. "It holds the bones of the dead." Then she laughed. "Some were even monks, but don't worry, none have become ghosts. Marisee told me that you met the Hyde Park dead."

Robert couldn't stop staring at her. "You are Madam Blackwell?" he asked.

"I am." She held out her hand as if to help him rise, then winced and rubbed her back. "And I feel so old."

"You're not old!" Marisee clutched her Grandma's arm.

"And you are old before your time, my darling!" Madam Blackwell wrapped her arms around Marisee, resting her head on Marisee's shoulder. Marisee grasped her grandmother's cloak tight as if to stop her ever leaving again. Robert knew that there was no one in England who would ever hold him like that.

"I am so proud of you!" Madam Blackwell's voice was a little muffled. "I promise that I'll never keep secrets from you again." She laughed. "Well, most secrets." She lifted her hand and touched the side of Marisee's head. "What happened to your hair?"

Marisee wriggled free. "We haven't got time to tell you now. We have to leave, Grandma. *She*'s going to find us here."

"And I've told you, honey. I can't leave. Turnmill?"

Turnmill strolled from the shadows. She rested one hand in her breeches pocket, the other on the Fleet Ditch boar's tusk. Her arm bent at a strange angle and she seemed to waver, as if keeping her human shape was costing too much strength. There was a rip along the boar's flank and one eye was squeezed closed.

"Take the children," Madam Blackwell said. "Keep them safe for as long as you can."

Turnmill shook her head. "I'm not leaving until we take all the children."

The boar's hooves sparked against the ground.

"Nor is he," Turnmill said.

"I am not a helpless child," Marisee said. "If I was, I wouldn't still be alive." She glanced over at Robert, but she kept his eye for a little too long. He looked away. "Nor would Robert. And what do you mean by 'all' the children?"

Robert let Marisee's voice fade away. This was Madam Blackwell! Here she was at last, the woman with the Freedom of London. Just a few inches away, perhaps hidden beneath her cloak, she held the power to change London. The Shepherdess would be here soon. He felt her song winding its way down the tunnel towards them. What was he going to do?

Madam Blackwell cocked her head towards the tunnel. "She's getting closer. Turnmill, you're not at your full strength. You must go. You can't match her."

"After ten years? No!" Turnmill stood straighter and became more solid. "I am not leaving now."

"March lamb, walk lamb, follow my sheep,
Close eyes, never wake, sleep, lambkins, sleep.
Ten years, ten tears, dripping from my eyes,
Freedom comes if Robert's brave, so cruel London dies."

Robert searched the others' faces. Could anyone else hear the words? Was it just him? He *had* promised the Shepherdess he would help her. Could he keep his promise? Surely London would be better if everyone was warm and had enough to eat. There would be no more injustice and no more cruelty. This was the London that the Shepherdess wanted. It was the London that Robert wanted too.

"Take it!" Madam Blackwell said. "And go!"

Robert almost missed the words and the flash of gold. Madam Blackwell was holding out a small golden box. Its surface was pitted and dull, its hinge plain iron. There was no lock, but the seal was so complete that Robert could not see where the lid joined the body. This was it. This was the Freedom. He had just to reach out and take it.

The box was snatched from Madam Blackwell's hand. Marisee clenched her own hand around it. She seemed to be purposefully not looking at Robert. *She must know*, he thought.

357

"Nobody has to leave," Marisee said. "I know what will stop the Shepherdess." She flipped the tag from beneath her collar. "I found this in the tunnel. It was Sally Blake's number. We found her clothes. I think she's down here somewhere, Grandma. Turnmill?" Marisee turned to the water spirit. "Do you know where she is? All we have to do is let the Shepherdess see her and—"

"Absolutely not!" Madam Blackwell said.

Marisee stepped back. She looked astonished, as if she'd never heard her grandmother sound so stern. Madam Blackwell sighed and stroked Marisee's cheek.

"I'm sorry, honey," she said. "My heart hurts to imagine the pain and suffering she endured. When that evil man threw her through the trapdoor, Fleet tried to protect her, then Turnmill hid her well."

Turnmill gave a little bow, her face serious. "And the Fleet Ditch guarded her."

The boar snorted.

"They used kind, gentle magic to keep her alive. She's only a child," Madam Blackwell said. "She must not be used as a weapon against the Shepherdess."

"How can she be a child?" Marisee asked. "She came here ten years ago! Let the Shepherdess know she's alive, because…"

Marisee's voice disappeared again. Robert could hear nothing but the lullaby. The song slid off the curved ceiling and rose from the floor and slipped through the walls to surround him. It filled his lungs so he wanted to sing the loudest he'd ever sung. His eyelids were heavy, but he was fully awake. And his breath was clear.

"Ten years, ten tears, dripping from my eyes,
Freedom comes if Robert's brave, so cruel London dies."

She was coming.

"Freedom comes if Robert's brave, so cruel London dies."

She was here.

The musician came through the archway first. He held the bone saw. He scraped it across the cracked wood of the ruined violin. Beside him was the young man, the meat hook dark and dripping with water. The Shepherdess strolled behind them and stood by the mud heaped against the wall. She banged her crook on the charnel house floor, so hard that the bones in the corner juddered. Her green eyes shone.

Silver threads swirled around Turnmill's hands and shot towards the Shepherdess. The Shepherdess swung her crook, swiping them away. The Fleet Ditch boar shrieked: the squeal of a pig, mixed with human rage. He charged. The crook swung again, catching his legs. He crumpled silently to the ground, his teeth bared in pain.

Immediately, the musician was crouched over the boar, the bone saw at its neck. "Don't move," he hissed. "*She*'s made this a special saw. It cuts through river flesh."

Robert caught the flicker of silver around Turnmill again. The Shepherdess turned to her and grinned. She pushed back the wide brim of her hat. The square, box-shaped bruise on her forehead seemed to shine gold.

"I raised the plague monster from the Serpentine," she said. "And you still think you can defeat me?"

She spun suddenly towards Madam Blackwell, crook lifted high. The ground cracked, and shards of ancient stone lifted in the air and skittered around the charnel house. Marisee shrieked as a spike from a slab caught her cheek. Water erupted through the cracks in thin, spitting columns, flickering like fire. One by one, they rose around Madam Blackwell until she was caught in their cage.

"You cannot hurt her!" Turnmill shouted. "She is the Keeper of Wells!"

The young man in the wig moved quickly, though his limbs seemed to jumble around him. Robert was reminded of his own legs, when for a while they hadn't felt like his own. Had the Shepherdess given *him*, Robert, extra strength to make sure he arrived here to fulfil his promise? The young man leaped towards Turnmill, and in one quick movement he had twisted Turnmill's arm behind her back, while his other hand held the meat hook at her throat. Turnmill's skin was smudged with sand where the metal touched it.

Marisee ran towards her grandmother, tugging at the chain with the baby's number around her neck.

"Please, Grandma! Let me show her!"

"No, Marisee." Madam Blackwell's face was still and angry. "You must not."

Marisee turned towards Robert. Tears streamed down her face. "Robert! We can't let her have the Freedom!"

"No." He shook his head. "We can't."

And they should not. Marisee didn't understand what it was like when people close to you were hurt. He had seen children whipped, men drop to the ground

361

because their bodies could take no more work. And his own … his own what? Someone he knew had… The memory blurred again.

The water cage closed around Madam Blackwell. It reminded Robert of the dead pirates that were displayed in gibbets at Execution Dock. Unlike the iron cages, the water moved, constantly spinning. It bound her ankles together, pressed against her cloak, making it ripple, until finally, it hung like a noose from the roof of the water cage.

Marisee grabbed Robert's shoulders.

"She did this to the nurse in the Hospital chapel," she said. "She hanged her with a rope made from water. The nurse would have died if Turnmill hadn't come. Help me stop her!"

"Your grandmother can stop me herself with ease," the Shepherdess said. "All she has to do is give me the Freedom."

"No," Madam Blackwell said. "I will not. It is not yours."

The watery noose lowered, slipping over Madam Blackwell's head. She gasped.

"Robert!" Marisee was shaking him.

"Robert?" A calmer voice. He had thought that the

Shepherdess had forgotten him, but now he felt her power turn on him. "Are you wavering?"

"Robert!" He wished she'd stop shouting at him. If you do what she wants, she will control London. She will turn everyone into sleepwalkers and—"

The Shepherdess slammed her crook into the ground. A jet of water burst out from between the stones next to Marisee. It twisted around her, sending her tumbling to the floor. She cried out in pain as silvery threads bound her wrists and ankles. Robert started towards her. The Shepherdess stepped in his way. His head filled with the smell of the damp earth at the back of the woodshed after a rainstorm, horses' hooves churning up the verges in Hyde Park. His thoughts were muddy. The real world seemed to be spinning around him and away.

"There was a boy," the Shepherdess said. Her words merged into the splash of flooding water. "He was a frightened boy who was treated badly."

Robert's eyelids drooped. He was standing beneath an orange tree laden with fruit. Why? Did he like oranges? He thought that he did, but he couldn't remember why. The thought of them filled him with sadness. It made him think of Mama and... The trees smudged into mist and he was back in the charnel house.

"You have many memories." The Shepherdess still stood between him and Marisee. "But the tithe-master was paid his fee. You have a brother called Zeke. He comforted you when you were frightened and then you lost him."

Robert had a brother? The Shepherdess was speaking the truth, Robert knew it. Zeke. Robert couldn't remember the name or the face, but there had been someone with him in Barbados, someone who had told him stories and counted fireflies with him and sometimes just held him close when the world was full of terror.

He looked at Madam Blackwell in her watery gibbet and Marisee lying on the floor.

"Help us, Robert," Marisee whispered. "Please."

Turnmill was watching him too, and the Boar.

"The girl doesn't understand," the Shepherdess said. "She has a home and her grandma and all of her memories. You have the Hibberts and their cruelty. Remember the painting in the chapel, Robert. The king."

The king who had looked just like Robert.

"You remember him, don't you?" the Shepherdess said. "Give me the Freedom and I will change the world so that you *can* be a king, Robert."

He wouldn't have to sleep in the corner of the kitchen. He wouldn't be beaten by Mrs Wandle or paraded in ridiculous clothes in front of Lady Hibbert's friends.

"What about Lizzie?" he said. "And Marisee and Madam Blackwell?"

"You have the power to choose what happens to them."

"They won't be hurt?"

"It's your choice."

It was Robert's choice. He could choose to keep them safe. And even the poor villagers who had been forced to attack them. There would be no more families sleeping below the hulks of shops or begging on the Strand for a few pennies for food. He would make the Hibberts leave that mansion and open its doors and many rooms to anyone who needed them.

He walked over to Marisee and kneeled down on the wet stone next to her.

"We can make London better," he said. "We can make sure that what happened to Sally Blake will never happen again."

Marisee tried to wriggle free from her binds. "You mustn't listen to her! Who can you trust? Her or me?"

Marisee still didn't understand. Hopefully she would.

"She has the Freedom." Robert pointed at Marisee. "It's in her hand."

The wrist binds pulled tighter. Marisee screamed and her hand flew open. The golden box fell at Robert's feet. He picked it up and walked towards the Shepherdess. Robert heard the swill of voices around him: Marisee's, Madam Blackwell's, Turnmill's, even the Fleet Ditch boar speaking in his human voice. All of them were shouting, "No!"

But who were they to tell him what he should do? They didn't know him. The Shepherdess knew more about him than they ever would. The pitted gold box was light, but he held it as if it was full of wild things.

"Here." Robert held out the Freedom.

The Shepherdess plucked it from his palm. She smiled and closed her eyes.

"Thank you, Robert." She opened her eyes again. The green was as sharp as blades. Suddenly, Robert knew it. He should have known all along. The Shepherdess dealt in dreams. What she had promised him was just a dream. She had never planned to give him power at all. She nodded, as if she had read his thoughts.

"No!" He lunged forward to grab back the Freedom.

She twisted away from him and banged her crook on the ground.

"Sleep well," she said.

He opened his mouth to shout, but his words were muffled in a thick cloud of yellow. He saw the musician drop to the floor, and then the young man, and he tried to fight it, but it was too strong.

The world fell away from him and there was just darkness.

THE CHILD

Marisee was shaking. She was cold and wet and frightened.

"Come." Grandma bent down to help her up. Her bindings were gone.

Marisee just wanted to crawl into a corner behind the pile of bones. She would stay there until she became bones too.

Grandma held Marisee's face between her hands and kissed her forehead.

"It isn't your fault, honey," she said.

"Yes, it is!" Marisee had never shouted at Grandma before. She hated doing it, but couldn't stop herself. "I let Robert take the Freedom! I brought him here even though I knew I couldn't trust him!"

She allowed herself a quick look at him, then looked away again. When the Shepherdess disappeared with the Freedom, he had flopped to the floor. He didn't move. The sick yellow mist wafted around him, but unlike the sleeping musician and the young man, Robert wasn't smiling. Who knew where he was in his dreams? It wasn't making him happy. *Good*. Tears prickled behind her eyes. She tried to swallow back her fury, took Grandma's hand and stood up.

"I suppose he'll never wake up again," Marisee said. "Not unless the Shepherdess wants him to destroy something for her." She shrugged. "That's what he deserves."

"No, honey," Grandma said, gently. "He doesn't deserve that. This boy made a mistake, but he did it because he truly believed he was doing the right thing."

"It doesn't matter what he believed," Marisee sniffed. "He still gave the Shepherdess the Freedom. Everyone we know will fall asleep and never wake up."

Grandma smiled. "Perhaps not."

Marisee stared at her grandmother. "Have you been keeping more secrets?" she asked.

"Madam Blackwell!" Turnmill was bowed over the mound of mud by the wall. "I think it's time!"

Grandma ran over to Turnmill. The edges of the mound were crumbling into the water left from the Shepherdess's attack. The boar was snuffling around it as if searching for something lost. Grandma kneeled by the mud and placed her ear against the dirt.

"You're right!" she said.

Why did Grandma sound so excited about a pile of dirt when any moment soon, the London they knew could be pulled apart? Grandma yanked Marisee down next to her.

"Listen!" Grandma said.

Marisee's tears were gone. Her fury was taking over. They did not have time to kneel around a pile of mud. "Grandma! We have to find the Shepherdess and…"

Grandma wasn't listening. Her eyes were closed and her smile widened. It was like she was a sleepwalker, but enchanted by her own spell. She opened her eyes again.

"This may never happen again in your lifetime," Grandma said. She curled an arm around Marisee's shoulders and drew her closer to the mound. "Listen."

Marisee would listen, just for moment, if it made Grandma happy. Then she would say what she had to say. She placed the side of her face against the mud. She had expected cold clay. It was warm and soft like skin.

"It is time," Grandma whispered. "You can come out now. You're ready."

Marisee's eyes widened. Who? "Grandma? What's in there?"

Grandma held her finger to her lips. Marisee nodded.

The girl uncurled from her sleep. The mud slid from her body and settled back around her. The water shifted, lapping against her eyes and into her nose.

It's time.

She rolled herself back into a ball and the heavy warmth reshaped itself. She knew what was supposed to happen next. She was supposed to open her eyes. She had been in darkness for a long time, but she had heard them when they'd whispered to her. You are safe, Sally. You are safe.

She could hear them talking.

You can come out now.

She knew what she must do. She must slowly stretch. Her fingers, her toes, her feet, her arms.

It's time.

She must break through the crust of gravel and clay that held her in. She would feel her skin grow dry again. She would feel cold then heat, but she would not be the same. Her eyelids flickered. The weight of the sand on her lashes sealed them closed. She was happy here.

You're ready.

Memories sometimes snaked through her sleep. They were jagged and cruel, but distant. She was already safe. She didn't need to wake. But they were calling for her.

It's time, Sally, it's time.

The earth hummed with it. The water whispered in her ears.

It **was** time.

She gathered up her strength and forced her eyes to open. It made no difference. She was still in darkness. She fluttered her eyelashes to try and shake them free from dirt, but her eyelids were too heavy and she let them close again. Her throat was blocked with grit. She flexed her hands, her fingertips scraping the earth shell surrounding her. She balled her hands back into a fist.

Time!

She punched. The earth shook then split into damp clods. Strong arms grabbed her and she was pulled free.

Marisee stared at the girl lying on the shattered mound of mud and gravel. She was about the same age as Marisee. She was wrapped in a thick blanket, her bare toes poking out from the edge. Her forehead was scabbed with mud. Her eyes were closed, but her chest moved as if she was breathing. How could she be breathing? There would have been no air in the mound.

"Sally Blake." Marisee shook her head in shock. "Has she been here all this time?"

"Fleet managed to carry her as far as the vault of lost things," Turnmill said, "but she was too sick to take her further. I found Sally there, hovering in that Solid place between living and dying. I didn't expect her to live. I tended her and dressed her and brought her here. It's a peaceful place." She sighed. "Well, it is peaceful when a furious water spirit isn't trying to blast it into matchwood. I planned to sit with her in her last moments. No one should die alone."

"But she didn't die." Madam Blackwell stroked Sally Blake's hand. "Something else happened."

Turnmill nodded. "When her skin grew grey, I thought that her time had come. But I was wrong. Very happily wrong. Fleet's magic had made a shell for her. It grew thicker and thicker every day until Sally was sealed inside. We had no idea what would happen next, but we were prepared to wait."

Marisee wondered if Sally Blake had known what was happening to her. Had she slept all that time, or had she been awake in the dark?

"How long have you known, Grandma?" Marisee asked.

"Only since yesterday," Grandma said. "After Turnmill knocked at our door, she brought me here to safety. There was no need for me to know before then."

"The fewer people the better," Turnmill agreed.

That was at least one secret that Grandma hadn't kept from Marisee.

"Perhaps I wouldn't even have noticed the mud piled against the wall," Grandma continued. "But when Turnmill touched it this morning, she felt the warmth. She told me about Sally. She was sure that whatever was going to happen, it would be soon."

"Does Lady Walbrook know about Sally?" Marisee asked.

Fleet Ditch snorted so hard a flake of mud fell from the mound.

"We felt it was best to keep this to ourselves," Turnmill said. "Lady Walbrook wouldn't have let Sally rest. She thinks anything she doesn't understand is a threat to the Chads."

"She was right about this threat, though." Grandma waved her arm around the shattered paving stones and puddles of water. "When I visited Walbrook on Friday morning, she told me that something bad was coming. I don't know if she suspected that it was another Chad. Walbrook would never speak ill of her own people, but she said that she'd posted a lookout to keep watch and warn me if danger was close."

"Poor Sadler," Marisee said. She would never forget the terrified pony dissolving into sand. "He didn't deserve what happened to him."

Grandma looked confused. Of course, she didn't know. Marisee and Turnmill swapped a look, a silent agreement that they would tell Grandma about that later.

"But you disappeared," Marisee said. "You sent me off to fetch marmalade and when I came back, you were gone. All I had was that note."

"That was my fault," Turnmill said. "That lullaby... I felt its dangerous magic ripple through the air. I peered out from the well on the village green and saw the sleepwalkers. I knew they were coming for Madam Blackwell and the Freedom."

Grandma hugged Marisee to her. "I'm sorry I left you so quickly, my darling."

Marisee sniffed. She *would not* cry.

"I had been worried for days," Grandma said. "I did nothing. There was the rag seller, and the rock doves, and then when I heard that lullaby and felt its power – I knew I had to leave. Turnmill brought me to the safest place she knows. She brought me here."

Marisee disentangled herself from Grandma's arms. "But now the Shepherdess has the Freedom anyway."

"No, honey," Grandma said. "Not yet. We still have some time."

"But the golden box," Marisee said.

"It's just an empty golden box... It used to hold the Freedom, but no longer does."

Marisee looked from Grandma to Turnmill. "But then ... where is it?"

Grandma smiled. "Sometimes it's best if you hide things in plain sight. The box was just the vessel. The real magic of the Freedom is in the mix of the four elements: Dragon fire, Chad water..."

"Magog clay and Fumi air," Marisee finished. She looked at Grandma, mouth open. "Is it—?"

"Sally's waking!" Turnmill said.

Grandma took Marisee's hand, and they crouched next to the mud-covered girl.

Sally Blake's skin glistened except where the mud stuck to her. Slowly, her eyes opened. They were deep brown with no white around them. Her mouth moved, but no sound came out. Turnmill reached a finger into Sally's mouth and pulled out a cake of mud.

Sally gurgled, then coughed.

"Thank you." It was a girl's voice, hoarse and unused.

Sally pushed herself into a sitting position. Her arms were so thin, her face too. Her hair was clumped with mud, her eyebrows, even her eyelashes. She drew the blanket tightly around her.

"I don't understand," Marisee said. "Is she ... is she like me? A human girl? Did she sleep for ten years?"

"No," Grandma said. "Well, yes. She was a girl and perhaps is still. But we think that Fleet's magic has made her something more."

Sally Blake was definitely more than a girl. As Marisee watched, Sally's face became plumper. She shook her head and the earth dropped from her hair. The mud shrank away from her skin and scattered like raindrops. She rubbed her fingers together and a spark of silver shot out from her palm.

Turnmill clapped her hand to her mouth. "She's one of us!" Then Turnmill laughed. "Well, almost one of us. London is changing. Our rivers are being covered over. Soon, we'll be flowing more beneath the surface than above it. We need new spirits to care for our underground rivers. Perhaps Sally is the first of many."

Sally Blake rose from the mud. She moved smoothly, almost flowed. There was no sign that she had been still for ten years. Sally walked over to Robert, her bare feet silent on the stones.

"Who is this?" Sally asked.

Marisee shrugged. Her wrists stung where the bindings had tightened and her hand had flown open. Could she ever forgive Robert for handing the gold box to the Shepherdess ? He had really believed that it was the Freedom.

"His name is Robert Strong," Grandma said.

Robert sighed, as if he had heard his name. "She won't win," he muttered. "I will stop her."

Then he cried out, as if in pain. Marisee winced. He *had* betrayed her. He had betrayed all of them, but… He'd saved her life at the pump room, and again when he solved the riddle. He'd only come on the adventure because he'd wanted to help his friend. Should she forgive him?

"Can we wake him, Grandma?" she asked.

Grandma shook her head. "I don't know how. Turnmill?"

"No," Turnmill said. "The Shepherdess is holding him in the Ether. He can only wake up when she allows it."

Robert's hands jerked up as if warding off a blow.

"Who is he fighting?" Sally asked.

"Someone bad," Marisee said. "She calls herself the Shepherdess, but her name was Caroline Lamb and—"

"Marisee!" Grandma said sharply. "No!"

Marisee clapped her hand over her mouth. There was silence. What had Marisee done? In those few words, had she brought back all the bad memories that Sally should be allowed to forget?

Then Sally smiled. "Caroline Lamb isn't bad. She's my friend. I want to see her."

"No, child," Turnmill said. "She's gone somewhere none of us can follow."

"But she'll want to see me!" A twist of silver threaded around Sally Blake's fingers. "She'll be worried about me!"

"We think the Shepherdess is hurting that boy," Grandma said. "She's not the same friend that you remember."

Sally Blake folded her arms. "I can stop her," she said.

"Caroline Lamb wanted to find you," Marisee said, ignoring Grandma glaring at her. She pulled out the chain from inside her dress and tugged it over her head. Sally watched with interest. Marisee handed the chain to her. "Do you remember this?" she asked.

Sally rubbed the tag between her fingers as if the shape of the numbers told a story.

"Baby 33," she said. "I was Baby 33." Her strange brown eyes were fixed on Marisee. "Caroline Lamb was my friend. I've missed her."

Sally Blake lifted Robert's head with one hand and slipped the tag over his head with the other. She lay down next to him, her fingertips touching his.

"Bring her to me, Robert."

TRICKED

The stone walls were gone. Robert stood alone in Leicester Fields. Then he was staring at the painted king in the chapel. As he reached out to the picture, he tumbled through a trapdoor into bottomless black water. A small engraved brooch floated past him. It bore an image of a lamb with a sprig of green in its mouth. Robert tried to snatch it, but a hummingbird swooped down and hooked it with its beak. Its bright wings fluttered faster than Robert could see.

The bird disappeared, and Robert fell into a narrow

gutter in a busy street. At least it *should* be busy. He could hear people and traffic, but could see no one. Across the road, though, there was a pie shop. A pie shop!

The door flew open. Robert stood up and breathed in. Mutton, potato, chicken, gravy … pies sitting in their dishes on the counter, steam wafting up from the slits in the pastry. They were waiting for him. He was so hungry. When was the last time he'd eaten? It was… It was…

He crossed the road towards the shop and went in. There was a shadow in the back room behind the counter. He heard them moving about, but they didn't show themself. Robert reached out to break off a piece of crust. It was tough, but it snapped and he crammed it into his mouth. It tasted like dust. He stared into the dish. The pie filling was putrid meat.

The song came from the back room.

"March lamb, walk lamb, you followed the sheep.
Smile, lambkin Robert, for you'll never leave this
sleep."

The pie shop disappeared. He was standing in the bright green meadow. There was nothing here except him and the Shepherdess. The rusty crook was hooked over one arm. The Freedom box nestled in the palm of her hand. The bruise on her forehead was red and angry.

"You tricked me," she said. She tipped her hand and the box dropped to the grass. The lid snapped open. It was empty. "Where is the real Freedom?"

"You told me that you couldn't bring it into the Ether," Robert said. "Perhaps it's just lost its power."

"Don't anger me, Robert." The Shepherdess kicked the golden box across the too-green grass. "When I held it in the charnel house, I felt the traces of its power. The four elements were in here, but they are gone." She stepped towards Robert. "I will ask you again. Where is the Freedom now?"

He stared at the empty, useless box. He'd been tricked too. And then the laughter bubbled up in him. He had trusted the Shepherdess, but she had trusted him too. She had been so sure of his help that she had never questioned whether it was the real Freedom.

"Madam Blackwell knew you were coming for her," Robert said. "She must have hidden it somewhere else."

The Shepherdess tapped her crook gently. Every blade of grass quivered, melting as it trembled. They collapsed into a pool of water that widened around Robert's feet.

"So, tell me where it is, Robert."

He shook his head. "I don't know."

"I don't believe you."

The water around him churned. A tentacle whipped out and wrapped around his legs. It was glossy and almost transparent apart from a faint silver sheen. He cried out in pain as the sharp tip dug through his shirt.

"I can keep you in the Ether," the Shepherdess. "But there will be no clothes fit for a king or tasty pies for you. Every dream you dream until you die will be filled with terror."

"No!" He pushed at the tentacle but his hands slid away. The smooth surface was bubbling as if it would burst apart. Robert's breath caught. His chest pumped, trying to get the air out. The rest of his body could not move. The tentacle skin was stretching into pustules. They rose one at a time, pulsing like tiny hearts. He did not need to look closely to see the creatures moving inside them.

"This is a dream!" he shouted. "It's not real!"

"It is real for you," the Shepherdess said. "Isn't that how the Ether works? Whatever happens to you here is real until you wake up."

A second tentacle rose from the water. His hands flew up to push it away. This wasn't real! The puddle

384

of water only came up to his ankles. There couldn't be monsters beneath it. The ground beneath his feet rumbled and the water rose higher, lapping at his knees. The tentacle swayed lazily in the air as if it had all the time it needed. It did. Robert would be here for the rest of his life. *The rest of his life.*

"You will never wake up," the Shepherdess said. "Unless you tell me where the real Freedom is."

"I don't know where it is."

Another rumble. A tentacle coiled around his waist, the pustules pressing through his wet shirt into his skin. But Robert knew that there were more than tentacles to the monster. There was the hideous beaked head, the head with no eyes. The water rippled. He could see the dome of its skull, the cracked leather skin…

"I don't know where the Freedom is!" His words were garbled. "It doesn't matter what you do to me, I can't help you!"

"That's a pity," the Shepherdess said. "Then I have no reason to send monsters to you other than the fact that I can. And Robert?" She tapped her crook gently on the ground. "I know *your* monsters."

The head rose from the water. The empty eyes, the bone of its nose, but the skull didn't taper into a beak.

There was a mouth. It opened. The teeth were human.

"You let me die, Robert." The voice – it was Lizzie's. "You let me die. You said you'd save me."

Lizzie! Oh, Lizzie! No, it wasn't real. She was asleep waiting for him, dreaming of her little sister. He would save her. He would.

The tentacle tightened around his legs. He staggered, batting at the water as he tried to keep from falling. His flailing hand caught something around his neck: it was a chain. There was a small metal tag at the end of it.

33.

It belonged to Baby 33. This was Sally Blake's tag. He was sure that he wasn't wearing it before.

"I was so hungry," the Lizzie-monster said. "But I couldn't wake up for food. You let me die, Robert."

He gripped the tag. It sparked silver against his palm. He took a deep breath.

"They found Sally Blake!" he shouted. "Stop! Please!"

The Lizzie-monster's jaws opened and snapped shut, human teeth grinding against each other.

"Don't ever think that you can trick me again!" the Shepherdess screamed. "I know your monsters, Robert! I can make your death the worst it could ever be!"

"I'm not tricking you!" He held up the tag. "Sally

Blake was Baby 33 at the Foundling Hospital. You know that. We found her clothes in the tunnel and then…"

Then what? The tag could be part of the dream, a tiny fragment of hope pushing through the horror. It sparked silver again, brighter and longer. And somehow he knew that this was real. Beyond the Ether, someone was trying to help him.

"She's safe," he said. "I promise you! Sally Blake is safe!"

The Shepherdess strode towards him. She held her crook high in both hands. Silver skimmed across the rust on the staff and congealed in the tip. The handle glowed. The tentacle squeezed tighter. Robert's ribs bowed inwards. He couldn't breathe. Everything was fading.

The crook slammed down.

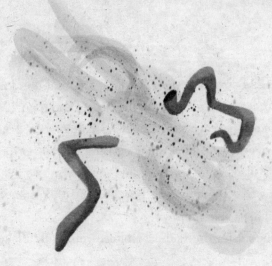

PARTING

"Robert? Robert?" Someone was squeezing Robert's hand. "Talk to us. Are you hurt?"

Cold, wet stone. Robert was sure that he was lying on the charnel house floor, but he would not open his eyes yet in case he was wrong.

He heard the clatter of footsteps running. Someone else shouted, "No, Ditch! Let them leave. They were enchanted. They didn't know what they were doing."

"Robert?" The voice sounded like Madam Blackwell.

He let his eyes open a little. He saw a broken violin

and a meat saw lying on the ground. Then soldiers' boots. The false Freedom box was lying in a puddle. A hand scooped it up. Footsteps came towards him and Madam Blackwell lifted him so he was sitting. Her hands were warm and safe.

"Don't worry. The sleepwalkers have gone." She helped him stand up. Every part of his body hurt. "Come," she said. "I need you to meet someone."

Madam Blackwell bore his weight as he shuffled towards a wall. Marisee was there. She looked at him and away. He wanted to say sorry. He wanted to explain. He wanted her to be his friend again.

"Look," Madam Blackwell said.

The Shepherdess was standing in the middle of the charnel house. Her silk dress and crook were gone. She wore the brown dress of the Foundling Hospital and clutched the useless gold box to her chest. She was staring at a girl. The girl stared back at the Shepherdess. This must be her, baby number 33. This was Sally Blake.

"Do you remember me, Sally?" The Shepherdess seemed so much smaller now. The sharp green of her eyes had faded; her face was almost as young as Sally Blake's. "I was Caroline, your friend."

"Yes." Sally Blake nodded slowly. "I know you. You were my only friend."

"I sang to you when you were lonely."

"I remember." Sally Blake smiled. "And we raced through the fields together, didn't we? The nurses were cross because I was supposed to be demure like all the other girls."

"We climbed the cobnut tree." The Shepherdess smiled back, although Robert felt the sadness beneath it. "We pelted the nurses with nuts. They were furious."

"And then..." Sally Blake shook her head. "I was sent away, and something bad happened."

The Shepherdess bent forward and placed her finger on Sally Blake's lips. "Don't ever think about it again."

She turned slowly and looked towards the archway above the tunnel. Robert followed her gaze. Lady Walbrook stood there, completely still, her eyes fixed on the Shepherdess.

"I have to go, Sally," the Shepherdess said.

"Please don't," Sally Blake said. "We can climb trees again. We can run across the fields and—"

The Shepherdess shook her head. "I looked for you everywhere, Sally. I searched for ten years. I thought I would never see you again, but somehow, you were saved."

"Fleet saved her," Turnmill said, moving closer to Sally Blake. She placed an arm around the girl's shoulders. "And we cared for her for all these years. There is kindness, Caroline."

"But so much more cruelty." The Shepherdess turned towards Lady Walbrook. "Who protects the lonely and the frightened, Walbrook? Who gives the tiny brooks as much care as the old, powerful rivers?" The brown foundling uniform dissolved. The Shepherdess was dressed once more in pale silk, the gleaming blue so bright it hurt Robert's eyes. She twirled the handle of the crook between her hands. "It certainly isn't you, Walbrook."

She tapped the crook against the floor. The silver sparks sprung from between the stones and twisted together.

"Caroline?" Sally Blake said. "What are you doing?"

She tried to take a step towards the Shepherdess, but Turnmill held her back.

"No, Sally," Turnmill said. "Wait."

"I thought that finding you would be enough, Sally." The Shepherdess tapped the floor again and again. Each time, the ball of slippery, shiny sparks grew bigger, twitching and squirming as if they were eager to be set free. "But it isn't enough. I have this power now. I *can* make the Solid world better. The rich have no need of the Ether so I cannot hold them there. But in this world, they are weak against my army of sleepers." She stuck her foot out from beneath her skirts. "I shall have the richest lord in London cleaning my boots."

Lady Walbrook struck then. A blast of threads fanned out in front of her, spreading like a net towards the Shepherdess. The Shepherdess smashed it aside with her crook. The threads caught like a spider's web around the crook's shaft, then dissolved into water.

"You are old and unpractised, Walbrook," the Shepherdess said.

She touched the ball of silver with the tip of her crook. It started whirring like a bobbin on a spinning wheel. A thread lashed out, so thin it was barely there. Lady Walbrook opened her mouth. Robert thought she intended to swallow it, or counter the attack with her own magic. While Lady Walbrook's eyes were on the whirring thread, the Shepherdess lunged forward with her crook and knocked Lady Walbrook off her feet.

Lady Walbrook fell backwards. There was no sound as she landed. The ball exploded into wriggling silver strands that stuck to Lady Walbrook's hands and face. Lady Walbrook clawed at her cheek. Sand crumbled from beneath the silver.

The Shepherdess walked towards her, lifting her crook high into the air.

"Perhaps it's time for the Chads to choose a new leader," she said. "A leader that cares about everybody."

"Caroline!" Sally Blake broke free from Turnmill and ran towards the Shepherdess. "You mustn't hurt her, Caroline! You mustn't hurt anyone!"

As the Shepherdess turned, Lady Walbrook moved quickly.

"No, Lady Walbrook!" Turnmill shouted. "You don't have to—"

Lady Walbrook opened her mouth. Silver threads spiralled out, looping and tightening into a shimmering cloak. It stretched wide and long, then snapped around the Shepherdess from neck to foot, trapping her inside. The Shepherdess screamed and tried to shake it off. Her crook fell to the ground, the handle snapping away from the twisted, rusty shaft.

"Don't hurt her," Madam Blackwell pleaded.

Lady Walbrook said nothing. Her eyes met those of the Shepherdess. There was a moment of silence, then the Shepherdess managed to twist around. Her face was streaked with sand. With a grunt, she pushed her arm through the cloak. She and Sally looked at each other, then the Shepherdess kissed the tips of her fingers and lifted her hand.

"Goodbye, Sally," she said.

Sally Blake reached out to her. "Caroline!"

The Shepherdess sighed. "Care for her, Turnmill."

Then the cloak crumpled. Soon, all that was left was a scattering of dark sand criss-crossed with fine, shiny trails.

"You didn't have to do that!" Turnmill's voice was low and angry.

"She was too strong," Lady Walbrook said. "And still full of fury. She would have returned to find the Freedom. You know that."

Robert stared at the broken crook. Lady Walbrook was right. The Shepherdess would have come back again and again. But was it such a bad thing to want the world to be a fairer place?

"Did you come here just to kill her?" Marisee said. Tears were running down her face.

"No," Lady Walbrook said. "I came to accompany my sister."

Lady Fleet was standing behind Lady Walbrook. She

was small, almost the same height as Robert himself. Her thin hair was now thick and dark. Her face smooth and unlined, like a child's.

Madam Blackwell wiped her eyes. "She's returning to her source."

Lady Fleet nodded. "I've been sick for so long. I welcome it." Her voice too was like a young girl's.

She beckoned Sally Blake towards her.

"Come," Turnmill said, guiding Sally forward.

Lady Fleet took Sally's hands and clasped them in her own. "I found you for a reason. Now I understand. I am going, but I am also becoming something new. The Fleet may be covered over, but it is still a London river. It still needs love."

Sally nodded.

"She's yours now, Sally Blake," Fleet said.

Sally nodded again. "I'll care for her."

"Thank you." Fleet sighed, then turned away and walked back through the archway and out of sight.

Robert bowed his head. He wished he could find the right words to say. He should know how to answer death by now.

LAST

The streets of London clamoured. It was a clamour of confusion. If Robert could listen to the inside of his own head, this was how it would sound.

All the sleepers had woken, many far from their homes. Madam Blackwell laughed and said that the ballad singers were most likely already composing songs about the Great Sleepwalking Plague of London. Robert thought that there would be sadder poems too, about people who were loved and lost again. He tried to calm the noise in his own head. He'd had a brother called

Zeke. There must be one tiny memory in there, just a little tuft that he could pull at. But there was nothing.

They were standing by the gateway to St Bartholomew's church. Marisee and Madam Blackwell would head north to Clerkenwell and Robert west to Bloomsbury.

"You can come with us," Madam Blackwell said. "You don't have to go back to the Hibberts."

"They own me," Robert said.

They were just three words, but he hated them with all his might. Mama said that the plantation owners may think they own his body, but his spirit was still free. He wanted all of him to be free.

"I can't leave unless they liberate me. The Hibberts are rich and powerful. They'd say you stole me and make you pay them."

"They bought you?" Marisee said. "And they can sell you like ... like shoes?"

He nodded, though Lord Hibbert treated his shoes much better than Robert's friends and family on the plantation.

"That's even more reason why you should come and live with us!" Marisee said.

Marisee was looking at him properly again. She

seemed to have forgotten that she was angry. But had she forgotten that he had betrayed her? He was sure it would take her longer to forget *that*.

"I'm sorry," he said, "for giving the Freedom to the Shepherdess." He frowned. "Or what I thought was the Freedom. I didn't want anyone to be hurt. I just thought I could make things better."

Madam Blackwell bent forward and kissed him on the forehead. "I understand," she said. She looked at Marisee. "Sweetheart?"

Marisee gave a little nod. "So do I." She sighed. "And I wish you didn't have to live with those terrible people."

"We will find a way to get you away from there," Madam Blackwell muttered. "We will definitely find a way."

The three of them stood there together. It was still dark, but dawn was close. Robert knew that Marisee and Madam Blackwell didn't want to leave him. He would have to be the one to walk away.

"May I just ask, Madam Blackwell," he said, "is the real Freedom safe?"

Madam Blackwell drew the gold box from the folds of her cloak. "This *was* the Freedom box." She held it high. "This is what a thief would look for if they came to take it from me. But it was what was inside that was more important. So, yes, Robert, don't worry. It is still safe." She handed the gold box to him. "Take it," she said. "Gold is always useful in this city. Sell it if you must." She took Marisee's hand. "Turnmill has offered to carry us home the quick way, but I've had enough of being underground. Perhaps a hackney carriage will take us."

Marisee touched her grandma's arm. "I think we should tell Robert where the real Freedom is."

Madam Blackwell raised her eyebrows.

"Can we trust you?" Marisee asked.

"Yes." He nodded as hard as his weary head would let him. "You can."

Madam Blackwell laughed. "I'll show you when you come to our cottage. I will light the fire from my red jar and boil water in my never-empty kettle and stand on the ladder that the air pushes upwards and spread butter from the clay dish that keeps it just the right temperature no matter how cold or hot the room. Oh, look! A free hackney carriage, I think!"

Madam Blackwell ran towards the carriage that was just slowing to a trot.

"Come and visit us," Marisee said, "and I promise I'll show you!"

She ran after her grandmother. They climbed into the carriage and waved as it trotted away.

For a moment, Robert stood there. He felt the loneliest that he had ever been. A rock dove flopped down and pecked at something by his feet. It moved sluggishly as if it had little strength left to eat. Robert wondered if the birds he had moved to the verge in Hyde Park on Tuesday had woken or died of starvation in their sleep. He watched it for a while as it grew stronger. Another joined it, and another. London had been saved. He should be happy.

He started the long trudge back to Bloomsbury. Perhaps Lady Hibbert was resting and he could slip into the kitchen unnoticed. Or, knowing her, she would be stomping around the mansion yelling for her servants to attend her. They would be awake now too. In the confusion, maybe no one would notice his return. If Lizzie saw him first, she would certainly help him. He smiled to himself. He had promised Lizzie he would help her and he had. He would have to change from the Foundling Hospital uniform quickly, though. That would cause more questions. And Lady Hibbert would be furious that he had lost his silk finery, especially as he could never explain how.

As he finally approached Bloomsbury Square, he looked up at the steeple of St George's church. The unicorn and lion were hugging the steeple and the statue of the king in his toga did not move. Had it ever? Was it the dream fog playing tricks on his mind? Robert touched his forehead. There was still a dull ache from where the horn had pierced him. It hadn't been a dream. They could be watching him now. He hurried on.

He heard the din from the stables before he reached them. The yard was filled with movement. Grooms and stablehands ran backwards and forwards with buckets and bales of hay and blankets. No one did notice him. He slipped around the woodpile and into the kitchen where a fire was already burning.

"Robert! You're alive!" Lizzie ran towards him.

"And you!" he said. That monster with the tentacles and her face would stalk his nightmares, but he'd known for certain that it wasn't real. Lizzie was alive and he had helped save her.

"But there's something you should know," she said.

He stared past her at the long table in the kitchen. She didn't have to tell him. A whip lay on it, its red leather handle worn bare with use. He had last seen it flicking through the air in Barbados.

"Lord Hibbert has returned, hasn't he?" he whispered.

She nodded.

"Robert!" Lord Hibbert strode into the kitchen. "I am glad to see you looking so well. Perhaps London air has been strangely good for you."

Robert realized that he was backing towards the door.

"My cousin has a new business in Jamaica," Lord Hibbert said. "A healthy, hardworking boy like you will be perfect for him."

Robert looked at the big-boned man with the sunburnt face. He looked at the whip on the table.

"No," Robert said, "I will not."

He gathered every last shred of strength and ran long and fast into the London dawn. He heard a roar of anger behind him, but this was it. This was Robert's chance.

He raced back through the stables, weaving through the confused grooms and out into the street. The cold air seemed to shake him awake. He ran and ran, past the new museum, then down into the dark winding alleyways of St Giles. His heart was beating hard, but he was grinning. This was his freedom and he was going to hold on to it for as long as he possibly could.

And maybe it would lead to another adventure…

TEN STRANGE
FACTS THAT INSPIRED
THE ELEMENTAL DETECTIVES

1. There is an old map of London from the 1740s. I looked at it all the time when I was writing this book. There's a place marked Black Mary's Hole or Black Mary's Well on the banks of the Fleet river, north of the city that was London then. No one knows for sure why it was called that, but there is a reference to a Black woman called Mary living on the site in the 1760s. When I read that, she immediately became Madam Mary–Ay Blackwell, Keeper of London's Wells!

2. On the same map there is a spot by the northern wall of Hyde Park marked Where Soldiers Are

Shot. I decided that there would be soldier ghosts there.

3. On the other side of the wall, there was the Tyburn gallows. Henry VIII ordered the gruesome execution of some monks who refused to change their faith. So why wouldn't there be an extremely cross monk ghost with stomach problems?

4. In February and March 1750, there really were earth tremors in London. Londoners thought there was going to be another one in April and many fled their homes. (There wasn't.) Could it be the silent Magogs flexing their power?

5. There is a story that in 1736, a live boar went missing from a butcher's yard. It climbed out of the Fleet Ditch five months later, looking very well fed. He had to be in my story.

6. My dragon is inspired by tardigrades. They are strange looking eight-legged microbeasts that can live almost anywhere and withstand all sorts of

extremes of temperature. Imagine if a dragon could take itself apart and put itself together again?

7.   The steeple on the roof of St George's of Bloomsbury Church is really topped by a giant statue. (You can see it in the famous painting, *Gin Lane*, by William Hogarth.) It's meant to be King George I dressed as a Roman. Stone lions and unicorns look like they're chasing each other around the base of the steeple. What if they came alive?

8.   The London Stone is a real stone and was once part of something bigger. It has probably been on display in parts of the City of London for at least a thousand years. It's even mentioned in a Shakespeare play! You can still see it set into the wall of a shop.

9. The tithe-master and his coat of live swans was inspired by a story from 1811 about swans missing from the Serpentine. A man had stolen them and sent their skins and feathers to be made into Christmas decorations. I wanted my swans to be very alive!

10. The ruins of the Mithraeum or Temple of Mithras were discovered in 1954 during building works on a London bomb site. Everyone wanted to see it! There were queues of thirty thousand people for two weeks. The Romans built it on the banks of the Walbrook river.

AND:

11. Did you know that the composer Amadeus Mozart visited England when he was eight as part of a European tour? What if... Well, you'll have to read the next book to see.

KNOW YOUR ELEMENTALS!

THE WATER ELEMENTALS –
AKA THE CHADS

WHO ARE THEY? Shape–shifting water spirits. They usually take a solid(ish) shape that matches their location and its history.

REALM The overground and underground springs and rivers of London. (Or waiting at the bottom of a well for Madam Blackwell or Marisee to drop in.) Also found guarding the plague monster of the Serpentine.

HEADQUARTERS The Court Beneath the Wells, though Lady Walbrook may let chosen Chads into the Mithraeum, her personal domain.

LANGUAGES Official language name translates as Fluenta in human script, although it's a series of splashes and surges in Chad language. They also speak Cockney River, London Horse and contemporary and historic human.

POWERS Have you seen the size of those stone watermill grinding wheels? Turnmill was pushing them for centuries. Chads can manipulate

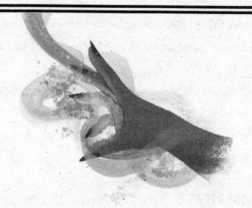

river water and also have a rather unnerving ability to trap their enemies in gloopy silver binding.

WEAK SPOT They presumed they were immortal, but pollution is defeating them. Can they survive being the city's waste disposal unit?

GRUDGES The humans of Solid London for the nastiness being thrown into the rivers. The Magogs for losing the Freedom of London. The Dragons for guarding the merchants that build over the rivers to create new halls and mansions. The Fumis, just because they're airheads.

THE FIRE ELEMENTALS –
AKA THE DRAGONS

WHO ARE THEY? Minute indestructible creatures that form the shape of dragons who guard the wealth of the City. They also eat humans.

REALM The City of London, the walled financial quarter inside London. The cellar in the Lord Mayor of London's Mansion House. In the cracks in the walls of coffee houses and banks. Sometimes on top of church steeples overseeing their domain.

HEADQUARTERS On top of The Monument to the Great Fire of London. It's lucky that they can make themselves small so that they can fit in.

LANGUAGES Official language name translates as Click in human script, although it's a series of scuttles and smoulders in Dragon language. They are also fluent in the language of trade-dealing and money-making in any human tongue.

POWERS Sheer quantity. It takes over a million to make one full-size Dragon. They are telepathic so know how to fall apart and reform. Like bees, they all have all roles, which is especially important when they need to talk as a few thousand need to say the same thing at the same time to be heard. They presume they are indestructible. Oh — and not bad at riddling.

WEAK SPOT Smugness. They presume they're indestructible, so might not see their destruction coming... They will not, if they can ever help it, leave the City of London.

GRUDGES A massive grudge against the Fumis for the incident of 1666. The Fumis blew the flames towards the flammable cargo by the river but never took the blame for the Great Fire of London. An enduring dislike of Richard Whittington for creating the Elemental Truce. Dragons should not have to follow Solid human rules. Everyone else is too inferior to have a grudge against.

THE AIR ELEMENTALS –
AKA THE FUMIS

WHO ARE THEY? Air spirits who are increasingly more smoke than air. They waft away the pollution – or are supposed to.

REALM Across London, below the clouds. (Though a rogue Fumi is rumoured to live in a feral windmill on the Isle of Dogs.)

HEADQUARTERS The Whispering Gallery in St Paul's Cathedral.

LANGUAGES Official language name has no accurate translation. The closest is Spots-Of-Colour-Carried-On-A-Gust. Weathervane is most Fumis' second language. Also speak London Sparrow, Traditional Chimney and Human English.

POWERS They can work up a hurricane and probably a tornado too, if forced. They move clouds and musical sound. They can boost a fire and put a fire out.

WEAK SPOT Being made from air, they absorb everything around them, including the stinking smoke billowing from London's chimneys.

GRUDGES The Solid humans who insist on polluting London's air. The Dragons because ... well, let's just say that 1666 was revenge for something earlier. Fumis like to swap favours — and they will claim back their favour, or else!

THE EARTH ELEMENTALS –
AKA THE MAGOGS

WHO ARE THEY? Gog and Magog, the giants that slumber at the bottom of the River Thames – or do they? No one knows for sure. They have a spy network all over London that keeps an eye on things.

REALM The clay, gravel and mud foundations of London itself.
HEADQUARTERS The spies are rumoured to meet in an old Roman amphitheatre beneath the Guildhall.

LANGUAGES The language of the earth, a growling, rumbling, squirming noise that only Gog and Magog remember and speak. The spies are mostly fluent in London English and the other human languages of London.

POWERS Extreme patience. The power to move the earth and make London crumble into the ground.

WEAK SPOT Absence. Will the other elementals make secret plans against them?

GRUDGES The rivers cut into the earth. The fires scorch it. The air drops soot across it. The humans push the foundations of their buildings deep into it and score their roads through it. Perhaps it's better to ask – against whom don't they hold a grudge?

WHO IS THE REAL
ROBERT
STRONG?

I've been thinking about *The Elemental Detectives* for a long time. A few years ago, I was asked to research and deliver a Black History Month walk in Hackney, east London. I came across the story of Jonathan Strong, an enslaved teenager who was baptized in 1765 in St Leonard's Church in Shoreditch.

Like all enslaved people, his life was shaped by violence and exploitation. He was brought to England and was so violently beaten by David Lisle, his "master", that he was considered useless and thrown out to survive on the London streets. He was helped by William and Granville Sharp who paid for Jonathan to be treated in hospital and found him employment when he was discharged.

Lisle spotted Jonathan in the street and sold him to James Kerr, a plantation owner, who kidnapped Jonathan and organized for him to be shipped to Jamaica. Granville Sharp found out, mounted a legal challenge and eventually

Jonathan was freed. He died when he was twenty-five, possibly as a result of his injuries.

Granville Sharp became very prominent in the movement to abolish slavery. He is remembered in history and his tomb can be found in All Saints Churchyard, Fulham, West London. Jonathan's name was mostly forgotten. No one knows where he is buried. I wanted to find a way to remember him.

Enslaved children were part of English society and can often be seen in the portraits of nobility painted in the eighteenth century. I wanted to find a way of giving stolen young children like Jonathan a voice. I've taken elements of Jonathan's story and given them to Robert.

I HOPE YOU ENJOY IT – but please find out about Jonathan Strong too!

A RIDDLE

The Dragons enjoy a good riddle, but the stakes can be high if you don't solve it. Can you answer this tough riddle? You can have as many goes as you like without being eaten.

MY FIRST IS IN FOLLOW BUT NOT IN CHASE.

MY SECOND'S IN FLOWING BUT NOT IN RACE.

MY NEXT TWO ARE DOUBLE, IN TEEMING ABOVE GROUND,

MY LAST IS IN LOST, NOW HARD TO BE FOUND.

WHO AM I?

You can check your answer on the copyright page at the beginning of the book.

ACKNOWLEDGEMENTS

Firstly, this book would never have been written without writers such as Catherine Johnson and S. I. Martin who have carved a place in children's publishing for British historical stories with Black lead characters.

A massive "thank you" to my agent, Caroline Sheldon, for persuading me to hold on to my desire to write about Jonathan Strong until I had a story worthy of him.

Thank you to the Society of Authors for the grant that gave me time to research this book and buy copious second-hand books.

To Lauren Fortune at Scholastic for seeing the book's potential and performing elemental editorial therapist magic to help me make it the best it possibly can be.

I absolutely love Paul Kellam's stunning cover, Luke Ashforth's map and Amanda Quartey's chapter art. Thank you also to Aimee Stewart for her design vision; Gen Herr, Julia Sanderson and Sarah Dutton in Editorial; Tracey Cunnell in Design; Harriet Dunlea, Hannah Griffiths, Ella Probert, Ellen Thomson, Michelle Herlihy, Penelope Daukes and Rachel Partridge in Marketing and Publicity; and Georgina Russell in Production.

A special mention to Julia, the guide for the Mansion House tours, who answered my queries about the Lord Mayor of London's kitchens and the best place to put a dragon with thoroughness and wonderful good will. It was really appreciated.

Also – the fact that so many of London's museums remain free to enter is a joy.

And finally, thanks to my mum for making me a history nerd. Those endless visits to stately homes and castles did their work.